Mr. Right or Mr. Thong?

"Just cut to the nitty-gritty," Pilar said.

"I asked him to hand over the thong, and he looked at me like I was Glenn Close from *Fatal Attraction*. Can you blame him? I mean, it was a pretty far-fetched idea," Kitty said, raising a brow at Shea.

"It was the most logical conclusion based on the facts I was given," Shea said. "Besides, I only suggested he took it. *You're* the one who ran with it and had to confront him. We told you it was a bad idea."

Pilar cradled her chin in the palm of her hand. "Let's get this straight. Your thong was folded on top of the dryer along with the towels?"

"I guess somehow it ended up on the floor in the bathroom. He must have scooped it up with the wet towels."

Shea readjusted her sunglasses. "Why would he do your laundry?"

"Maybe because he didn't want me to wake up and not have a clean towel?" Kitty suggested.

"Did he use fabric softener?" Shea asked.

"He doesn't wake you up to say good-bye and he doesn't leave a note, but he leaves you an apple and does your laundry," Pilar mused. "What does it mean?"

Bunco Babes Tell All

MARIA GERACI

BERKLEY BOOKS, NEW YORK

THE BERKLEY PUBLISHING GROUP
Published by the Penguin Group
Penguin Group (USA) Inc.
375 Hudson Street, New York, New York 10014, USA
Penguin Group (Canada), 90 Eglinton Avenue East, Suite 700, Toronto, Ontario M4P 2Y3, Canada
(a division of Pearson Penguin Canada Inc.)
Penguin Books Ltd., 80 Strand, London WC2R 0RL, England
Penguin Group Ireland, 25 St. Stephen's Green, Dublin 2, Ireland (a division of Penguin Books Ltd.)
Penguin Group (Australia), 250 Camberwell Road, Camberwell, Victoria 3124, Australia
(a division of Pearson Australia Group Pty. Ltd.)
Penguin Books India Pvt. Ltd., 11 Community Centre, Panchsheel Park, New Delhi—110 017, India
Penguin Group (NZ), 67 Apollo Drive, Rosedale, North Shore 0632, New Zealand
(a division of Pearson New Zealand Ltd.)
Penguin Books (South Africa) (Pty.) Ltd., 24 Sturdee Avenue, Rosebank, Johannesburg 2196,
South Africa

Penguin Books Ltd., Registered Offices: 80 Strand, London WC2R 0RL, England

This book is an original publication of The Berkley Publishing Group.

This is a work of fiction. Names, characters, places, and incidents either are the product of the author's imagination or are used fictitiously, and any resemblance to actual persons, living or dead, business establishments, events, or locales is entirely coincidental. The publisher does not have any control over and does not assume any responsibility for author or third-party websites or their content.

PUBLISHER'S NOTE: The recipes contained in this book are to be followed exactly as written. The publisher is not responsible for your specific health or allergy needs that may require medical supervision. The publisher is not responsible for any adverse reactions to the recipes contained in this book.

PRINTING HISTORY
Berkley trade paperback edition / May 2009

Library of Congress Cataloging-in-Publication Data

Geraci, Maria.
  Bunco babes tell all / Maria Geraci.—Berkley trade paperback ed.
      p. cm.
  ISBN 978-0-425-22758-9
1. Female friendship—Fiction.   2. Dice games—Fiction.   3. Florida—Fiction.   I Title.
PS3607.E7256B86   2009
813'6—dc22   2008054336

PRINTED IN THE UNITED STATES OF AMERICA

10   9   8   7   6   5   4   3   2   1

For Mike. Thanks for letting me be me.

Acknowledgments

I wanted to write a story that celebrated the way women need other women in their lives. So it's only fitting that I thank the women in my life who've helped make my dream of publication come true.

First, thank you to my mother, Carmen Palacios, one of the smartest, most down-to-earth women you'll ever meet; and to my sisters; and ultimately to my first friends, Carmen and Aileen.

A huge hug of thanks goes out to Rhoda, who first put the writing bug in me, and to the best nursing crew in the world—Pari and the rest of the Labor and Delivery nurses at Tallahassee Memorial Hospital. Your encouragement has meant more to me than I can ever express.

Thank you to my wonderful editor, Wendy McCurdy, and her assistant, Allison Brandau. To my friend and agent, the ever supportive Deidre Knight. Without your belief in me, none of this would have been possible.

A special shout-out goes to my own Bunco group—the ever fabulous, never-aging Bunco Broads of Tallahassee. You all make me laugh more than should be legally allowed. If a couple of our antics show up in my books, well, I know I'll be forgiven.

And last but not least, to my critique partners and super friends extraordinaire, Melissa Francis and Louisa Edwards. Louisa, you're the whipped cream on my latte. And Mel, well, I think you know no one rocks my world the way you do.

1

It was all Kevin Costner's fault. If he hadn't been so sexy in *Bull Durham*, Kitty Burke wouldn't still be single on the eve of her thirty-fifth birthday.

For her grandmother, it had been Clark Gable in *Gone with the Wind*. For her mother, it had been *both* Paul Newman and Robert Redford in *Butch Cassidy and the Sundance Kid*. At some point, almost every woman fell in love, or at least in lust, with a character from the big screen. But most other women got over it and went on to marry normal men.

Not Kitty.

Eighteen years ago, she fell in love with Crash Davis, the character Kevin had played so brilliantly in the film. Which wouldn't have been that big a deal. Except that no flesh-and-blood, real, live man had ever come close to giving her the spine-tingling, mind-melting, heart-stopping sensation she got from watching Crash.

It's not that she hadn't tried to find a guy who made her feel all that. But after half a lifetime of dating the Ebby Calvin "Nuke" LaLooshes of the world, it was time to face facts. As her best friend Pilar had said, time and time again, "Crash Davis is a fahottie. He doesn't exist." Despite Pilar's irritating habit of making up words you couldn't find in Webster's Dictionary, Kitty had come to the depressing conclusion that, as usual, Pilar was right. Crash Davis was nothing more than a fantasy hottie.

But that was okay. Because as of today, Kitty was officially over it.

So what if she was the only one of her friends not married? The rest of her life was perfect. She had a great job selling real estate, a fantastic income (well, maybe not so fantastic in the last couple of years, but things had to start picking up soon), and she had recently moved into her grandmother's old place just two blocks from the beach. In north Florida, life didn't get much better than that.

But what made Kitty's life really special was her Bunco group. The Bunco Babes of Whispering Bay had been established ten years ago by what Pilar referred to as "the nucleus." The nucleus consisted of the three founding members: Kitty Burke, Pilar Diaz-Rothman, and their other best friend, Shea Masterson. Exactly who the protons or the neutrons were, Kitty wasn't sure, although she was fairly certain Pilar did. But whoever was what, one thing was indisputable. Admission into the Bunco Babes was exclusive. No one got in without the unanimous consent of the nucleus. There were nine other members (the electrons, so to speak), for a total of twelve Babes. For the past ten years they had been there for each other through boyfriends, marriages, babies, spreading hips, and sagging boobs.

With friends like the Babes, who needed a man?

If Susan Sarandon could worship at the Church of Baseball, then Kitty could worship at the Church of Bunco. It was every Thursday night while rolling the dice and chugging frozen margaritas that Kitty found her true salvation. It was the friendship of those eleven other women that provided the balance in her life. The yin to her yang. The cherry on top of her hot fudge sundae.

Tonight, however, a perfectly nasty imbalance was taking shape in the form of an overflowing toilet.

"Damn it!" Kitty reached behind the porcelain base to find the rusty water valve. "Righty tighty, lefty loosey," she chanted, shutting off the water.

But it was too late. Her bathroom floor was flooded.

Great.

In exactly twenty minutes her house was going to be overrun by the Babes. Not that she wasn't thrilled to be hosting Bunco tonight. But twelve women, lots of alcohol, and no toilet was a recipe for sure disaster.

She slipped out of her leather flip-flops and tiptoed through the water to her hall closet to grab a handful of towels. This was a job for Henry.

Henry was a super-duper industrial-strength plunger that was fast becoming Kitty's new best friend. When you lived in a house that was nearly seventy years old, friends like Henry came in handy.

And so did chocolate. But Kitty refused to feel guilty about the two Snickers bars she had gobbled down after last night's rain uncovered yet another leak in the roof.

She tossed the towels onto the floor to mop up the water, ignoring her ringing doorbell. It was probably Shea and Pilar.

They had promised to come over early to set up for tonight's Bunco party. They were also used to walking into Kitty's house if Kitty didn't answer the doorbell right away.

"Hey!" Shea cried. "Where are you?"

"In the bathroom," Kitty yelled. She wrapped her hands around Henry and plunged downward, but instead of unclogging the toilet, more water spilled onto the floor. After several attempts, she took a second to catch her breath. You'd think three days a week with a personal trainer would have her biceps in primo shape, but this clog wasn't a-budging.

Shea appeared in the bathroom doorway, her hands on her hips, Jolly Green Giant style. Shea was tall, with glorious red hair that cost her three figures at a Panama City hairdresser she visited religiously the first week of each month. She also had the longest legs and best boobs of anyone Kitty knew. The legs were all hers, but the boobs had been a gift from her husband, Moose, after she had given birth to their second daughter three years ago. Kitty was tall too. But not model-thin tall like Shea. Kitty was more like slump-your-shoulders-so-you-won't-be-taller-than-your-date tall.

Shea's forehead scrunched in disgust, which meant she must be really grossed out because Shea avoided any facial movements that might lead to premature wrinkling. "Please tell me there's another toilet in the house."

"The other toilet was falling apart, so I had it ripped out. Remember?"

"Moose said your mom was going to sell this place. Why isn't there a For Sale sign out front?" Shea demanded.

Moose was a stockbroker, and Kitty's self-proclaimed financial advisor. His real name was Andrew Harville Masterson Jr., but only his mother called him Andrew. Back when they were all in fifth grade at Whispering Bay Elementary, he had chased Shea through the playground and spit in her hair on picture day. Shea had vowed to one day get even. Their senior year in high school, Shea gave Moose her virginity after he scored the winning touchdown in the state double-A football playoffs. Moose had gone on to play football for Florida State, but he hadn't been good enough for the pros. He was, however, damn good at making money. Which was excellent, because Shea was damn good at spending it. Kitty sometimes wondered if that wasn't Shea's passive-aggressive way of getting even with Moose after all these years.

"I'll get around to putting out the sign . . . eventually. But not until the house looks perfect." Kitty blotted the sweat from her forehead with the back of her arm. "Are you going to stand there and watch, or are you going to help?"

Between the two of them they scooped up the wet towels and tossed them into the bathtub.

"It's like an oven in here," Shea said.

"That's because I'm making you work." Although Kitty had to secretly agree. It felt like ninety degrees in the house. Could the air conditioner be on the fritz too?

No. She refused to go there. She was sweating because of her exertion with the toilet. And the fact that tomorrow was July 1 didn't help either. The meteorologists were predicting one of the hottest summers in history.

Damn that global warming.

Pilar popped her head in the bathroom doorway. "Does this mean we have to play Girl Scout and pee in the backyard?"

"Sorry, no peeing allowed on my hibiscus," Kitty replied.

Pilar still wore her work clothes—Ann Taylor suit, size nothing (petite size nothing, that is), flesh-colored hose, and brown pumps. Her chin-length dark hair was straight and neatly flipped under. She wore her standard pearl earrings and silver watch. Pilar worked as a contract attorney at Hillaman, Soloman, and Kaufman, a fancy law firm in Panama City. It was no coincidence Pilar's last name also ended in "man." According to her, it was a sure sign she was on the partner track. Pilar was Cuban-American, worked too much, and was married to Nick, the most understanding man on the planet.

Kitty frowned. "You haven't been home yet?"

"I had to help Shea get the food, remember?"

Kitty washed her hands in the antique marble sink and pinned up her rapidly frizzing hair. Her bathroom reeked of wet towel, but the rest of the house smelled like warm cheese and hot pepperoni. She followed the trail into the kitchen. "This is your idea of food? Pizza?"

"It's not just pizza. It's Tiny's pizza," Shea said. She opened a box and pulled off a slice. Shea not only had the longest legs and the best boobs, she also had the metabolism of a sixteen-year-old boy. And other than the nine months Pilar had carried her son, Anthony, she never wavered from her perfect 110 pounds.

It was so unfair. Kitty had the metabolism of a snail. She could gain a pound just smelling Tiny's. "You know at least half the Babes are on a diet."

"Tough," said Pilar. "Besides, no one sticks to their diet on Bunco night."

"That's right," said Shea. "It's pizza and my secret frozen margaritas for your birthday."

Each week the Babes did a different signature drink. Last week it had been mojitos and the week before that, cosmopolitans. But there was nothing better than Shea's secret margaritas. Shea refused to disclose the recipe, even to Kitty and Pilar.

"Tomorrow's your birthday," Pilar said. "Live a little." She eyed Kitty up and down. "Besides, you have nothing to worry about. You look great. I'd kill for boobs that still point north. Only you could get away without wearing a bra in that sundress."

"I guess that's one advantage to being flat-chested." Kitty flipped through the Whispering Bay yellow pages till she found the P's. Why hadn't she kept Gus's card next to the phone?

"No woman likes her own boobs," Shea said, her mouth full of pizza. "Except me. And that's because I picked them out of a lineup."

"You're not flat-chested," Pilar said to Kitty. "Not really. And you're *not* fat. You're athletic."

"Staying *athletic* means not eating pizza."

"I could call Moose," Shea offered. "He's great with household disasters."

It was tempting. But if Moose came over to unclog her toilet, Kitty would have to listen to another lecture on how moving into Gram's place was driving her into the poorhouse. For a man nicknamed after a big, hairy animal with horns, Moose could be a real drama queen.

"Thanks, but I'm sure Moose has his hands full babysitting the girls," Kitty said, skimming her index finger down the short list of plumbers.

"You'd better get the toilet fixed, and fast. Everyone's going to be here soon," Shea said. She threw Pilar a sideways glance that made Kitty's finger freeze halfway down the page.

Kitty stared hard at Pilar. "You didn't."

"Didn't what?" Pilar asked, her brown eyes going wide.

Which was an immediate tip-off. Innocent wasn't a natural look for Pilar. Shrewd and lawyerlike, definitely. But innocent, never.

"Tell me you didn't get a stripper for tonight."

"I didn't," Pilar said, helping herself to some pizza. "I got you an exotic dancer."

Kitty tried to ignore the way the cheese stretched out into long glorious gooey strings. "You're so unoriginal. You got Shea a *stripper* for her last birthday too. It was horrible." The stripper had been cute, but he couldn't have been older than nineteen and he had kept sticking his wanker in Shea's face. It had been funny for about five seconds. "Cancel him," Kitty said.

"We can't cancel," Shea said. "Everyone's expecting him."

"Plus, we've already paid him," Pilar added. "He's nonrefundable."

Fighting off some pimple-faced college kid wasn't Kitty's idea of a good time. But Pilar and Shea were right. If they canceled him now, the Babes would be disappointed.

Kitty sighed. "Is he hot?"

Pilar looked offended. "Of course he's hot. I picked him out myself. Look, we're not doing this for us. We're doing it for you. It's the only way to get over your stripperphobia."

"My *what*?"

"Stripperphobia," Pilar said. "It's an unnatural fear of men who take off their clothes."

Shea nodded, a serious look on her face. "Really, Kit. Do you think *we* want to see some hot young guy get naked?"

Kitty shook her head. It was easier just to give in. "Okay, but *no* handcuffs. Got it?"

Pilar smiled. "I knew you'd come around. You always do."

Wasn't that the truth?

Kitty gave Pilar a snarky smile and concentrated her energy on what was really important—her plumbing. She punched Gus's number into the phone. It was almost seven p.m. *Please, God*, she prayed, *don't let me get his voice mail.*

A gruff voice on the other end answered on the fifth ring. "Pappas and Son Plumbing."

Crap. Not the plumber she was hoping for. "Joey?"

"Yeah. Who's this?"

Across the kitchen, Pilar locked eyes with her and giggled. Kitty gave Pilar her best eat-shit-and-die look. In eighth grade, for about three weeks, Joey Pappas had been Kitty's first boyfriend.

"It's Kitty Burke. Is Gus in?"

"Hey, Kit Kat. Whatcha up to?"

"About an inch of water," she said, inwardly cringing at the old nickname. "Can Gus come over for an emergency after-hours call?"

"What kind of emergency?"

"Overflowing toilet."

"Did you turn off the water?"

Her right eyelid began to twitch. "Yeah, Joey, I shut off the water."

"You got a plunger?"

"I already tried that," she said, keeping her voice as pleasant as possible.

"Humph," he grumbled. Then after a long, drawn-out pause, as if he had to think hard about it, he said, "I'll tell you what. Just use another toilet for tonight. Dad or I will be out first thing in the morning."

"I only have one toilet in the house."

"I thought you just moved into your grandma's old place. The one on Seville Street. Only one toilet?"

Kitty could almost see Joey now, pulling up his pants to cover his exposed ass crack. "Gus had to yank out the other toilet. Really, Joey, I wouldn't be calling unless I needed help. Bunco's at my house tonight."

"Oh."

Everyone in Whispering Bay knew about the Babes. Joey's wife Christy subbed for them occasionally and was number one on the waiting list to join as a permanent member. None of the women on the sub list were holding their breath, though. There were only two reasons anyone would quit the Babes. Death or moving away from Whispering Bay. Neither had ever happened.

"We were just heading out to Panama City Beach. There's a big bowling thing going on tonight." Joey paused. "I'll tell you what, my cousin Steve is here visiting. I'll send him over. He doesn't bowl."

"That would be wonderful. Thanks, Joey," Kitty said in a falsely sweet voice. She hung up just as Pilar and Shea burst out laughing.

"I don't know how you can keep a straight face when you talk to him," Shea said.

"This is Kitty Burke," Pilar said, imitating Joey's deep voice. "She's the reason I'm such a damn good kisser."

"I still can't believe that's how he first introduced you to Christy in the middle of the grocery-store line," Shea said, giggling.

"Welcome to my life," Kitty said, eyeing the Tiny's pizza box.

Pilar took a blue plastic bag from the countertop and emptied the contents onto the kitchen table. "Check this out." She held up a large, fluffy pink feather boa and a glittery silver tiara. "For the birthday girl." She plopped the tiara on top of Kitty's head while Shea placed the feather boa around Kitty's neck.

Kitty stifled a sneeze. "Do I have to wear this? You know how feathers make me itch."

Pilar frowned. "This way the strip—the exotic dancer will be able to recognize you right away."

Kitty stared at the stubborn look in their eyes. It was no use. Gram's house was falling apart, a man-boy was on his way over to shake his groove thing in her face, and she was going to have to pay overtime to Joey Pappas's cousin to fix the toilet.

She rearranged the boa higher around her neck and pulled free the largest slice of pizza she could sink her teeth into.

Snail metabolism be damned.

2

||||||

In less than an hour, the place was full of women. Loud women rolling dice. Women consuming large quantities of pizza and margaritas. It wouldn't be long before one of the Babes needed to pee. Kitty's own bladder felt like Krakatoa ready to blow.

Lorraine Wilson sat across from her at the card table, jiggling the dice in her hand. "What number are we on?" she asked. Lorraine sucked as a partner. She always talked too much while playing and never kept score.

"I think we had fourteen," Kitty said, crossing her legs tightly. Why did she have that second margarita? She glanced at her watch. When was this Steve character going to show up?

"You had thirteen," said Brenda Middlemas, frowning. If anyone would know the score, it was Brenda. She was their resident Bunco Nazi.

Lorraine shrugged. "Whatever."

"But if you think you had fourteen, then I'll give it to you," Brenda said. "I don't want to cheat you out of your score."

"Oh, for Christ's sake, don't do me any favors," Lorraine grumbled, throwing the dice. "I'll take the thirteen."

Last week, Brenda and Lorraine had gotten into an argument over who had thrown the most Buncos during a game. Brenda had eventually backed down and the situation had been defused, but Kitty didn't want a repeat.

"When is the stripper supposed to show up?" Kitty asked in a voice loud enough to carry over all three tables.

The dice stopped rolling and the Babes let out a collective moan of disappointment.

"Exotic dancer," Pilar clarified.

Tina Navarone threw her dice on the table in disgust. "I thought it was supposed to be a surprise."

"I guessed," Kitty said, giving them what she hoped was a bright smile.

"Do you think he'll be in costume?" Brenda asked, her near-miss brouhaha with Lorraine seemingly forgotten.

"For what we're paying him, he'd better be," Pilar said. "Maybe he'll be dressed as a cop. Or a fireman. I *love* firemen."

Kitty liked firemen too. But they reminded her of water. And water made her think of . . .

She gave up trying to hold it in. "I'm going next door to throw myself on Mrs. Pantini's mercy and beg to use her toilet. Anyone else in?"

The Babes shook their heads and the chatter resumed. Kitty went to pull off her tiara.

"Oh no, you don't!" Shea said. "The tiara and the boa stay."

"Whatever, just so long as I get to pee."

"Go ahead," Pilar said, waving her away. "I'll warm up your seat if the exotic dancer comes while you're gone."

Kitty ran next door and rang the bell. After a minute of painfully shuffling from leg to leg, she pressed the bell again. "Mrs. Pantini?" she cried. "It's Kitty!" Her grandmother had been at least a decade older than Mrs. Pantini, but the two women had been best friends. Together, they had founded the Gray Flamingos, Whispering Bay's answer to the Gray Panthers. The Flamingos were always protesting or passing around a petition for something or other.

Still no answer at the door.

Kitty cupped her hands around her eyes and tried to peek through the side window, but the drapes were pulled too tightly. She ran to the back patio and looked through the French doors into the darkened kitchen. Armand, Mrs. Pantini's old yellow cat, stared back and meowed. With a sinking sensation, Kitty remembered it was bridge night at the senior center.

No longer able to run, she hobbled through the backyard and wedged herself between the tall azaleas that formed a natural fence between the two properties. The hibiscus plants she had warned Pilar off were now looking like a pretty good option. She'd never peed outdoors before—she didn't count that time in college when she'd had too much to drink, because, quite frankly, she didn't remember it. She only had Pilar's word on that and Pilar had been piss-ass drunk herself.

She searched out a secluded spot near an overgrown shrub. Thank God she was wearing a sundress. It made the whole process a lot easier. She bunched the skirt above her waist, then shimmied her way out of the new hot-pink-and-black-polka-dot silk thong she had purchased through the Victoria's Secret catalogue. She'd never been much of a thong girl, but it made her feel sexy and took some of the sting out of knowing that tomorrow she would be edging her way to the dark side of her thirties. Besides, it matched the pink boa. Not that anyone else would know that.

"Yes!" she half shouted, half moaned, finally relieving herself. She straightened her tiara and was about to slip the thong back on when she noticed the shiny red pickup truck parked on the side of her garage. Where had that come from?

She whirled around and locked gazes with a tall, dark-haired man standing less than a dozen feet away.

In the immortal words of Hugh Grant, *Fuck-a-doodle-doo.*

The man's right cheek twitched, like he was trying not to laugh. "Sorry to interrupt." His voice was deep and laced with humor. Not a native north Floridian, she thought, failing to detect any trace of the southern twang common to the area. He wore a white T-shirt, tan work boots, and a pair of faded, snug-fitting jeans. As exotic dancers went, the construction costume seemed pretty lame. But she couldn't see this guy dressed as a fireman either. Something about him exuded an Old World sort of danger. Like pinstripe suits, fedora hats, and tommy guns.

The gangster image suited him perfectly.

Pilar was right. This guy was hot. Maybe the stripper idea wasn't so bad after all.

She took a deep breath and relaxed. He didn't act as if he'd just witnessed anything weird. If the guy took his clothes off for a living, he'd probably seen a lot stranger things than a woman with a tiara and a pink feather boa peeing in the bushes.

He walked up to her and glanced at the slip of paper in his hand. "Kitty Burke?" he asked. He was close enough now that she could see a few isolated strands of gray along his temples.

Her heart began to thump wildly.

Something here wasn't right. For one thing, he seemed oddly familiar. And he was no man-boy. He looked to be in his mid to late thirties. Maybe just a tad too old to be a stripper . . .

"You're Joey's cousin?" she heard herself squeak.

"Steve Pappas," he said with a smile, extending his hand.

Kitty froze. The pink-and-black-polka-dot thong burned a hole through her palm. Instinctively, she fisted the tiny scrap of silk in her hand and thrust it behind her back.

He immediately dropped his hand. But the smile was still there.

Oh God. She could hear Joey now. "This is Kitty Burke. Back in eighth grade we played tonsil hockey together, and according to my cousin Steve, she likes to pee in her backyard."

3
||||||

"If you'll show me where the toilet is, I can fix it and get out of your way," said Steve the Plumber. He nodded toward the parked cars along the street. "Looks like you got a party going on."

"It's my Bunco group," Kitty blurted.

"Bunco?"

"It's a dice game. You know, lots of rowdy women, frozen alcoholic beverages. That sort of thing," she babbled.

He smiled, like he knew exactly what she was talking about, but he was probably just humoring her. "So, can you show me the bathroom?"

Kitty jumped into action. "Sure, follow me." She led him through the empty kitchen. He walked directly behind her, and although Kitty couldn't see him, she had the horrible sensation he was staring straight at her ass. Her now thong-less ass, that is.

Picking up speed, she purposely left him trailing behind to have a few seconds alone in the bathroom. She flung open the medicine chest above the sink and jammed the thong in the space next to her disposable razors, then slammed the door shut.

There! Now she was in control again.

She turned to find him standing in the doorway, a blank expression on his face.

"Thanks for coming out here after hours. I know Joey probably told you I sounded like some pathetic loser woman who can't function without a man on the phone, but I'm renovating, and up until an hour ago, this was my only working toilet. And I really *did* try to unclog it myself," she said, spilling the words out so fast she had to catch her breath.

He grinned. "Joey never used the word 'loser.'" Steve the Plumber had a beautiful smile. Lots of even white teeth set against a day's worth of dark stubble.

She laughed nervously, suddenly aware of how tiny her bathroom was. The fact she wasn't wearing anything beneath the thin sundress didn't help either.

His gaze traveled over the bathroom, taking in the antique marble sink and the crown molding. "This is a great house. You don't see much Spanish Revival around here. Looks a lot like an Addison Mizner. When was it built? Early thirties?"

"Exactly," she said, surprised by his architectural knowledge. "It's a complete Mizner rip-off. The house belonged to my grandmother and I—"

A wave of laughter erupted from the living room. "Oh, Ki-i-i-tty!" she heard Pilar shout. "There's someone here to see you!"

The stripper. She had forgotten about him.

"I'll be right there!" she yelled back. "You think you can fix this?" she asked Steve.

He crouched down to inspect the toilet. "I have a closet auger in the truck that should do the job."

"A what?"

"It's like a mini-snake."

She nodded, way too familiar with the term. Two weeks ago the only snakes she knew about were the kind that slithered on the ground. Or a couple of her ex-boyfriends. She really needed to get this plumbing situation under control. And the leaky roof, and the air conditioner . . .

"If you need anything, just let me know," she said, wishing she could stay in the bathroom instead of facing whatever was out there.

Pilar and Shea were waiting for her in the kitchen. "I was about to send out a search party," Shea said, straining her neck to gaze down the hallway. "Who was the guy you brought in through the back?"

"Joey Pappas's cousin."

Pilar blinked. "You're kidding."

"Nope."

"Wow," said Shea.

"That's exactly what I thought," said Kitty.

She was about to tell them how Steve the Plumber had caught her whizzing in the bushes when Pilar grabbed her by the arm and shoved her toward the door. "C'mon. Everyone's waiting for you."

Kitty stood firm, refusing to budge until she made her point. "Remember, *no* handcuffs. And no letting this guy grind his thing in my face. You know how much I hate that shit."

"His *thing*?" Pilar laughed. "But that's the best part!"

A discreet cough from behind made Kitty whirl around. Naturally, it was Steve the Plumber. Maybe the earth would open up and swallow her whole. After all, tomorrow was her birthday. Something had to start going her way.

"I need to get the snake out of my truck," he said, by way of explanation.

"Oh sure. Um, this is Pilar and Shea," Kitty said, feeling her face go hot. "This is Steve Pappas."

"So *you're* Kitty's knight in shining armor," Pilar said, turning on the charm. "I went to school with your cousin."

"Along with half the town," he said in a friendly tone, shaking both their hands.

They waited till he was out the door, then Shea and Pilar burst out laughing.

"That is so *not* funny," Kitty said, peeking out the kitchen window to watch Steve go to his truck. The view from the back was just as good as the view from the front. She could almost feel the drool drip off her chin. He fished something out of the back of the truck and glanced toward the kitchen door. Kitty quickly ducked her head down.

Oh God. He hadn't caught her staring, had he?

What was wrong with her? It's not like she'd never seen a man with a great ass before.

Okay, so men with great asses weren't exactly a dime a dozen in Whispering Bay.

"Do you think he heard me?" Kitty asked. "About the 'thing' part?"

"Oh yeah," Pilar said. "He heard all right."

Kitty groaned. Would there be no end to tonight's humiliation? Apparently not, she thought, walking into the living room to face a man dressed as a cop.

"Are you Kitty Burke?" the "cop" asked. His serious tone implied she was in big trouble.

"Oh no, Mr. Policeman, what has Kitty done now?" Pilar asked dramatically.

A couple of the Babes started to twitter.

The man took off his hat. His wavy blond locks were pulled back in a ponytail. He was good-looking, Kitty supposed, in that obvious Fabio sort of way. Still, she couldn't help but feel disappointed as the image of a gangster in a fedora hat flashed in front of her.

Maybe she could sneak off and no one would notice.

"Yup," Shea said, pointing to her. "That's Kitty."

So much for sneaking off.

The man pulled a set of handcuffs from what appeared to be a belt, but in reality was a black shiny plastic strip glued over his dark blue pants. The sides of the pants had an obvious seam. No doubt, that seam was nothing more than a strip of Velcro designed for a fast takeoff.

"I'm Officer Bob, and I've been receiving reports you've been a bad girl, Kitty."

Someone pushed her into a chair, and before she knew it, "Officer Bob" had her hands cuffed behind the seat.

Just keep smiling, Kit. "Um, Officer Bob? Do you think we could lose the cuffs?"

"Sorry. But the interrogation is done best if the suspect can't escape."

Shouts and raucous laughter flew around her. The Jack Johnson CD playing in the background was replaced by something she didn't recognize. Something loud with a fast techno beat. She was going to kill Shea and Pilar.

No, first she would torture them. Then she would kill them.

Off came Officer Bob's shirt. Lorraine grabbed it and started swirling it over her head in time to the music. Shea and Pilar stood at her side, clapping and laughing. Even Liz Shultz, the shyest member of the Babes, was dancing behind Officer Bob's back, a frozen margarita in her hand.

"Take it all off!" Liz shouted.

Everyone appeared to be having a great time, including Officer Bob, who was pulling off clothes faster than Kitty could blink. But all she could think about was her clogged-up toilet. And the man who was fixing it.

Out of the corner of her eye, she spotted him. Steve the Plumber was carrying a thin silver apparatus, which must be the mini-snake. He gave her a curt, sympathetic smile before disappearing down the hall.

Please, God, don't let it be a tampon stopping up my toilet.

With that hideous thought, she turned her attention back to the stripper, who was now down to nothing but a G-string and a pair of black ankle boots. Officer Bob obviously waxed, because there wasn't a speck of hair on him anywhere she could see.

Ouch.

"Kitty, you bad puss, Officer Bob needs to teach you a lesson." He turned around, placed his hands behind his head, and began to frantically pump his hips back and forth for the crowd. "What say, ladies, should Kitty be punished?"

"I've been bad too!" Pilar cried. "Are you going to punish me?"

"Sorry, but Officer Bob can only handle one bad girl at a time. I'm afraid you'll have to wait your turn."

The Babes moaned in disappointment.

Officer Bob shook his very firm butt in front of Kitty. "You can look, but you can't touch."

Well, obviously, wankerhead, since you've got my hands cuffed. "Oh please, uncuff me so I can touch," Kitty wailed with as much drama as she could produce to satisfy her screaming friends.

This must have been the encouragement Officer Bob had been waiting for. He smiled and tried to wedge himself between her legs.

Kitty felt a sudden rush of air between her thighs. *Shit.* She'd forgotten she wasn't wearing underwear. This was definitely no time to be going alfresco.

She clamped her knees together, making Officer Bob frown. "C'mon, darlin, don't make this any harder than it has to be." He leaned over, braced his hands on the back of the chair, and pushed her knees apart, bringing his well-oiled, hairless body next to her. He then began to gyrate his groin inches from her face.

4

‎‖ ‖ ‖‖

"I don't want to break up the fun, but I need Ms. Burke's signature on my work form."

Thirteen heads swung in the direction of the kitchen where
Steve the Plumber stood in the doorway.

"Can we make this quick?" he asked. "I'm on overtime."

"I'll sign it," Pilar said, already halfway across the living
room.

"Sorry, but only Ms. Burke's signature will do."

Officer Bob shot Steve a dirty look as he slithered around
the chair to unlock the handcuffs. "Hurry back, Kitty. Officer
Bob isn't letting you off the hook this easily," he purred in his
bad-boy-stripper voice.

Kitty jumped from the chair and ran to the kitchen. Her
hand shook as she signed the bottom of the work invoice. "You
don't happen to have a cigarette, do you?"

"Sorry, I don't smoke," Steve said.

"Neither do I," she muttered.

One side of his mouth twitched up. She met his gaze and they both laughed.

"So, how much do I owe you?"

"Forget it. It's on the house."

"But I thought—"

The shouting in the living room reached an all-time high. Kitty turned and stuck her head through the doorway. Pilar was handcuffed in the chair while Officer Bob danced in front of her. The Babes had resumed their good-natured ribbing, and from the expression on Bob's face, one strip recipient was as good as another.

"Guess Officer Bob's found a new civilian to harass," a deep male voice said from behind.

Kitty spun around to find Steve standing only inches away. She raised her eyes to meet his gaze, only this time there was no amusement. Instead he looked at her curiously as if trying to figure something out. "Guess so," she said, feeling her newly regained composure start to slip. She hadn't been this attracted to a man in ages. She stole a glance at his left hand in what she hoped was a discreet wedding-ring checkout.

No ring.

Of course, that didn't mean he wasn't married. Some men didn't wear wedding bands. Especially if they did manual labor. Still, it was a good sign.

Steve stepped back, widening the space between them. *Damn.* He was moving in the wrong direction.

"Tomorrow's my birthday. That's the reason for the stripper. My friends got him as a present. In case you were wondering or anything," she added quickly.

He nodded, as if making house calls where a woman was

handcuffed to a chair while a nearly naked man danced in front of her was an everyday occurrence. "If you have any more problems, call Gus."

"Wait." She opened a kitchen drawer. "Let me find my checkbook."

"I told you, there's no charge." He made a motion to leave.

Without thinking, she reached out and grabbed his wrist. "You're not going anywhere until I pay you."

He glanced down at her hand over his skin, his voice suddenly husky. "What are you going to do? Handcuff me?"

Now there was an idea.

For a few seconds, neither of them moved. Then he tipped his head in the direction of the living room. "That was a joke." But there was nothing funny about the smoky look in his eyes.

She'd never found the whole bondage thing particularly appealing, but she wouldn't mind being handcuffed by Steve the Plumber. She reluctantly let go of his arm.

"Gus told me to tell you there's no charge. He says you're one of his best customers."

"You lied about the signature on the work order?"

"Not exactly."

"But it didn't have to be my signature, did it? Pilar could have been the one to sign it. Right?" she asked, holding her breath. Not that it meant anything really. Except that he was a nice guy. Or that he wanted to talk to her again before he left. That last thought made her heart speed up a bit.

He shrugged. "I figured you could use a break in the interrogation," he admitted.

She couldn't help but smile. "So you discovered my ultimate secret. I have . . . stripperphobia."

He laughed again, making her insides go mushy. One of Pilar's made-up words had finally come in handy.

"I'm in your debt. First for the toilet fix and then for saving me from Officer Bob. Pilar was right. You really are my knight in shining armor."

Instead of smiling or flirting back like she expected, he picked up the work order and tucked it into his shirt pocket. The smoky look in his eyes was gone.

Had she said something wrong?

She cleared her throat. "Joey says you're here visiting?"

"Yeah, I plan to be in town for a couple of weeks. I'm sort of in between jobs right now." With one hand on the back door, he turned, hesitating only briefly before saying, "Make sure your friends give Officer Bob a good tip. My first wife was a stripper. It's not as glamorous as it looks."

5

||||||

"Well, that was fun," Pilar said, flopping down on the living room sofa. She kicked off her pumps and propped her stockinged feet onto the walnut coffee table. "Was it as good for you as it was for me?"

"Why am I sensing sarcasm here?" Kitty moved the throw pillows off to the side so she could sit next to her. "Does it feel hot? I swear, if my air conditioner is going—"

"Don't do that," Pilar warned.

"Do what?"

"Don't change the subject."

"Yeah," Shea said on her way to the kitchen with the last of the glasses. The rest of the Babes had left, but Shea and Pilar had stayed to help clean. Or rather, Shea was cleaning. Housework wasn't one of Pilar's strengths. "We got the stripper for you, not us."

"Exotic dancer!" Pilar shouted. "Get it straight." She flipped her dark hair off her neck and laid her head on the top of the sofa. "You spent more time in the kitchen with the plumber than you did in the living room with Robert. Not that I blame you," she said, wagging her brows up and down.

"Robert?"

"The exotic dancer. He only goes by Officer Bob when he's working."

Shea reappeared in the kitchen doorway. "Guess what I found in the trash?" she asked, holding up a *Bull Durham* DVD in her hand. "It must have fallen in when you were straightening up the kitchen."

Kitty sniffed. "I tossed it on purpose."

Pilar's head shot off the sofa. "What?"

Shea sat next to Kitty, a stunned expression on her face. "On purpose?"

"In about one hour, I'm going to turn thirty-five. Don't you think it's time I outgrew that little obsession?"

"But you love Crash!" Shea said, clutching the DVD to her chest.

"Crash has a receding hairline now," Kitty said.

"Kevin Costner has a receding hairline. Not Crash. Crash is immortal," Shea added.

"Crash is a fahottie," Kitty said, warming up to the word. She looked to Pilar, who nodded in approval. "He was great when we were in college, but I'm not a kid anymore. I'm totally over him."

"I'm glad to see you've come to your senses. But Crash isn't the reason you're still single," Pilar said.

She shouldn't encourage her, but Kitty couldn't help wanting to find out Pilar's latest theory on Kitty's marital status. Or rather, lack of. "So tell me, Great One, why am I still single?"

"You say you want a guy like Crash, but you never go after him. You always go for the nice, safe guy. And when he doesn't live up to your expectations, you drop him."

"Are you saying I'm overly picky?"

"What about Jeff?" Pilar said. "He was a nice guy. Good-looking, great job—"

"Wasn't he the one who liked to spank you?" Shea asked Kitty. "Or did he like being spanked? I can't remember which way it was."

"Oh yeah, I forgot about that," Pilar said, frowning. "Well, he seemed normal in the office."

"Jeff was a perfectly nice guy. And he did *not* like to be spanked," Kitty said, glaring at Shea. "There was just that one time he tapped me on the butt. Maybe he did tap a little too hard, but after I told him I didn't like it, he never did it again. In the end it didn't work out because—"

"Because there wasn't any excitement," finished Pilar.

"Because I wasn't in love with him," Kitty said.

"Because he wasn't Crash. Plus, there was that weird butt-tapping thing," Shea added.

"Remind me never to fix Jeff up with anyone again," Pilar said.

"Face it, Kit. The only exciting guy you've ever dated was Joey Pappas," Shea said, humor etched in her light blue eyes. "I wonder why it didn't work out?"

Pilar giggled.

Kitty giggled too. She didn't mind going along with their little game. Sometimes. "I broke up with Joey Pappas when he told everyone we had French-kissed behind the cafeteria. Remember? You said I had to, or everyone would think I was a ho."

"I never said that," Shea protested. "I never even heard the word 'ho' till we got to high school."

"What about his cousin? Now there's excitement. At least he looks exciting," Pilar said.

Shea narrowed her eyes. "What was going on between you two in the kitchen?"

"Nothing. Much," she said, trying to sound casual. Should she tell them about her humiliation by the azalea bushes? No. She'd keep that little tidbit to herself. At least for tonight. But she definitely wanted to know what Shea and Pilar thought of Steve the Plumber.

"Is he going to start working with Gus and Joey?" Pilar asked.

"Plumbers make great money," Shea said.

"He told me he's in between jobs." Kitty hesitated a second. "And he's only planning to be in town for a couple of weeks. Plus, he might be married."

"Did you check out his ring finger?" Pilar asked.

"Of course I did. He wasn't wearing one. But that doesn't mean he's not married." She thought about Steve's parting remark and frowned. "I think he's been married and divorced at least twice."

"He told you that?" Shea asked.

"He told me his first wife was a stripper."

Pilar swung her legs off the coffee table to sit straight up. "What kind of man marries a stripper?"

"The kind who likes big boobs and easy sex," Kitty said. "The first one I don't have, and the second one I don't do."

"You're such a stereotyper," Pilar said. "Just because a woman is a stripper doesn't mean she's easy."

"It doesn't make her Mother Teresa either."

"What about the second wife?" Shea asked.

"That was a deduction on my part. He used the term 'first wife' when he talked about the stripper. That means he's given them a number. If she had been his only divorce, he would have said 'ex-wife.' Which probably means he's been married and divorced at least twice."

"Wow. Very sleuthful of you," Pilar said, looking impressed.

Kitty smiled. "Isn't it?"

Shea sighed. "So, he's out of work and he's been married at least twice."

"I bet he's got a truckload of kids and child-support payments out the ass," Pilar said.

Kitty's smile evaporated. "I thought he was interested, so I tried to flirt a little, but I think I scared him away because he took off pretty fast."

Shea rolled her eyes in disgust. "Loser."

"Yeah," added Pilar. "Any guy who's not interested in you needs his head examined."

Kitty was about to protest, but what did it matter? She was probably never going to see Steve again anyway. Time to redirect the conversation. She got up to inspect the wall thermostat. "Something's not right with my air conditioner."

"You're changing the subject again," Pilar said.

"I think she's right," Shea said, following Kitty to peer over her shoulder. "It *is* hot. What does the thermostat say?"

"Shit! It's eighty degrees in here. But I have the setting at seventy-four."

"Maybe it's not totally broken," Pilar offered. "Maybe the unit is just working too hard. Mine's on practically all the time these days. But what can you expect? It's global warming."

Shea glared at Pilar. "Global warming is a myth."

"No. Santa Claus living at the North Pole is a myth. I can't believe how duped you are by the right-wing media."

Kitty silently moaned.

"Al Gore is an alarmist," Shea said.

"Al Gore is a genius," Pilar retorted.

"Don't let your mother hear you say that," Kitty said to Pilar. "She thinks Al Gore's a communist. She told me so last Christmas at your house."

"My mother thinks everyone who's not a Republican is a communist. And getting *back* to the subject," she said, glaring at Kitty, "the reason you haven't found Mr. Right is because we live in the middle of Bumfuck, Egypt. Half the men in this town are retirees, and the other half are either already married or still wearing braces. You need to go somewhere big. Somewhere there's a lot of eligible men. Like Atlanta or Miami."

"Now you sound like my mother," Kitty said.

"Miami?" Shea echoed in horror.

"What's wrong with Miami?" Pilar asked.

"Your own parents left Miami because it was too crowded," Shea said. "All that traffic and crime, and—"

"And the theater and all that great shopping, not to mention all the jobs and all the hot guys," Pilar said. "You can't compare Isabel and Antonio leaving Miami to come here. They were already married and had four kids. Besides, they both came from small towns in Cuba. They weren't used to that big-city stuff. You and I are stuck here," she said to Shea. "But Kitty can go anywhere."

"Are you serious?" asked Shea.

"Okay," Pilar said, turning to Kitty, "when was the last time you had a date?"

"Her last date was with Jeff," Shea said, her shoulders slumping.

"When was that, a year ago? Please tell us you've gotten laid since then," Pilar said.

Kitty put her hand up in the air. "We've had this conversation before. I'm not moving just in hopes of meeting a guy. If Mr. Right comes along, fine. But if he doesn't, I'm not going to curl up and die. I have a great job and a great life right here. And I have you guys. What more do I need?"

"Woman cannot live by Bunco alone," Pilar said.

"Speaking of great jobs," Shea said, "I saw you got the listing for that house on the corner of Ocean Avenue. Moose was really impressed."

"Then Moose is easily impressed," Kitty said, grateful for the change in topic. "It's a good property, but the owners want too much. It'll be a hard sale."

"You can do it. After all, you are the Jerry Maguire of north Florida real estate," Shea said cheerfully. She pulled a business card from her shorts pocket and handed it to Kitty. "I keep one on me all the time, in case I run into a potential client for you."

Kitty moaned. "I love your loyalty, but I really have to find something better than 'Help me help you find the house of your dreams,'" she said, quoting the tagline on the bottom of the card.

"Yeah, you do. That really sucks, Kit," Pilar said, standing up. She stretched her arms above her head and yawned. "I have to go."

"It's not even midnight yet. And you're the one who came up with that line," she reminded Pilar.

"Isabel is babysitting tonight and she gets nasty if I stay out too late."

"You're lucky your mom will babysit," Shea said. "Do you know what a good sitter charges these days?"

"Isabel charges in guilt. And she gets overtime for every second after eleven."

"Where's Nick?" Kitty asked.

"At a teaching conference," Pilar said. "I hate his job."

"He hates your job."

"Yeah, well, he can kiss my Cuban ass. He knew what he was getting when he married me."

"A workaholic attorney who doesn't cook, doesn't clean, and doesn't do laundry?"

"But I give great head. That's all guys care about anyway. Since you don't like their 'things' in your face, you wouldn't know that."

Kitty stiffened. "I've had bad experiences. Which you know all about since you know everything about my sex life."

"Well, get over them, because guys definitely like to stick their thing in your face," Pilar said. "It's no wonder you're not married."

"Okay, that's enough. I'm officially kicking you guys out."

"I need to get home anyway," Shea said. "I'm pretty sure I'm ovulating right now and I want to catch Moose before he falls asleep."

Kitty and Pilar turned to stare at her.

"Moose and I want another baby," Shea announced.

"You're kidding," Pilar said.

"He wants a boy. We *both* want a boy," Shea clarified. "Besides, it's not like we can't afford it. Moose is doing great. People always need financial advice."

Pilar shook her head. "You're a better woman than I am. I'm done."

"You're not going to have another baby?" Shea asked. "But that will make Anthony an only child."

"So what? Kitty's an only child and she turned out perfect." Pilar kissed Kitty on the cheek. "Bye, doll. We're still meeting for lunch tomorrow, right?"

"I guess so," Kitty said, feeling a little deflated even if she was the one kicking them out. But it was late, and Pilar had to relieve Isabel and Shea had to go home and have sex with Moose.

"Of course we're meeting for lunch," Shea said. "Tomorrow's your official birthday, and we haven't missed a birthday lunch since . . . well, never."

"I'm meeting with a potential client at ten," Kitty said, "so I should be finished by noon."

"Noon is perfect. How about the Italian place next to my office?" Pilar asked.

"Pasta? But we just had pizza tonight. Are you guys trying to—" At the look on Pilar's face, Kitty faked a smile and added, "Sounds yummy."

"Who's the new client?" Shea asked Kitty. "Maybe it's someone Moose recommended you to."

"His name's Ted Ferguson. Ever heard of him?"

Shea shook her head.

"From what I gathered on the phone, he's from out of town and wants to invest in a beach house."

"Maybe he'll want to look at that listing on Ocean Avenue," Pilar suggested.

"I could only be so lucky," Kitty said wistfully. "I got the impression on the phone that he's still in the process of interviewing Realtors. After meeting me, he might decide I'm not right for him."

"Ha!" scoffed Pilar. "He'll love you. Everyone does."

Shea nodded vehemently.

"And I love you both for thinking that." Kitty waved them good-bye as she watched them get in their cars.

Shea had cleaned up, which left her nothing to do, but she was too restless to sleep so she flipped on the TV. As if mocking her, Kevin Costner and Susan Sarandon were going at it in living color.

What were the odds that *Bull Durham* would be playing on cable tonight?

She should turn it off. It was exactly this sort of Hollywood malarkey that had given her unrealistic expectations about men.

On the other hand, what could it hurt to watch just one more time?

She upped the volume.

The doorbell rang. Kitty peeled herself off the sofa. Shea was always leaving something behind.

"What did you forget?" she asked, throwing open the door.

But it wasn't Shea at her doorstep.

"My snake," said Steve the Plumber.

6

"Your *what*?"

"You know, the thing I unclogged your toilet with?" Steve said.

After a few moments of staring at him like an idiot, Kitty stepped back to let him inside the house. "Oh yeah."

Of course. *That* snake.

He wiped his feet on the mat, his gaze taking in the empty living room and her blaring TV. It was Kitty's favorite scene in the movie. The part where Susan Sarandon was tied to the bed and Kevin Costner was painting her toenails. Kitty felt her face go hot. She dove across the couch to find the remote and turned off the set.

"Sorry to bother you so late, but I was driving by and saw your light was still on, and I wasn't sure if I'd catch you before you left for work in the morning."

"No problem."

"Do you mind?" he asked, motioning toward the back of the house. "It'll just take a minute and then I'll get out of your way."

"Sure," she said, feeling her pulse speed up as she watched him disappear down the hallway.

Talk about kismet. Why else had he landed on her doorstep twice in one night?

A bead of sweat trickled down her forehead, snapping her back into the moment. Shit. This was no global warming. She knelt on the wooden floor and placed her palm over the air-conditioning vent. The air swooshing out was definitely not cold.

"Something the matter?" Steve asked, walking back into the room.

"I think my air conditioner's broken."

He set the snake on the floor and crouched next to her, placing his hand alongside hers. A tingle of energy shot straight up her arm. His hand was big and calloused, his nails neat and clean. "I think you're right," he said.

Neither of them made a move to stand. Or move their hands away from the vent. "I can't believe this." She laughed nervously. "First my toilet, now my air conditioner."

"A house this old needs a lot of updating. But you must have known that when you bought it."

"I didn't buy it. The house belongs to my mother. My grandmother left it to her after she passed away last year. I'm just living here temporarily while I fix it up to put on the market."

"It's a pretty big place for just one person," he said, giving her a hand up.

Was that his way of asking her if she lived alone?

"It's over two thousand square feet. I'd love to buy it, but I really can't afford it."

"Your mother won't cut you a break on the price?"

She couldn't tell if he was really interested in the house or if he was just making small talk to keep from leaving. As much as she identified with his appreciation of the house, she definitely liked option number two better.

"My mother thinks I should leave Whispering Bay, marry a banker, and have babies."

He grinned. "What do you think?"

I think I'd like to get you naked. Definitely no stripperphobia for her. At least not where Steve Pappas was concerned. She tried to shake the image out of her head. "Um, I think I'd like to gut the kitchen and update the bathrooms."

"That would work. But there's a lot more you could do to bring this place up to speed."

"Like what?"

He pointed to the small den sitting off the living room. "If you knocked that wall out it would expand your living area and bring in more light."

"Oh, I couldn't do that," Kitty said, frowning.

He glanced at her.

"I mean, that's where Shea and Pilar and I always had our slumber parties. When we were kids, of course."

"You grew up in this house?"

She nodded. "From the time I was ten. That's when my parents divorced and my mom and I came here to live with my grandmother. My mom remarried when I was fourteen and we moved in with my stepfather, but I still spent a lot of time here."

He leaned his head back to look at the ceiling. "Your

mother could just sell it as is and save you the headache of renovating. Let someone else worry about it."

"That's what everyone keeps telling me. But I hate the thought of her selling it like this and not knowing what the new owners would do. This place was really something twenty years ago, but my grandmother didn't have the resources to keep it up. I want to see this house done right again."

The way he was visually measuring the walls made her wonder if he really knew what he was talking about, or if he was just feeding her a load of bull. "How do you know so much about architecture? I mean, the average person doesn't know who Addison Mizner is."

"I lived in Boca Raton for a few months. They love this kind of stuff down there."

"Do you have construction experience?"

"Some."

"Maybe you could recommend a contractor. I know a couple from my line of work, but I'm having a hard time finding one who's willing to renovate an old house on a shoestring budget. They all want to do new construction."

"What do you do for a living?"

"I'm a real estate broker," she said, spying her business card on the coffee table. She picked it up and handed it to him, pleased with herself for thinking of it. It seemed like a clever, not-too-obvious way to give him her phone number.

"'Help me help you find the house of your dreams'?" he read.

Shit. She'd forgotten about that.

"It's a line from *Jerry Maguire*," she said, feeling like a moron. "I've been meaning to change it."

He pocketed her card. "I'm afraid I don't know any contractors in the area. You should ask Gus." He picked up the snake as if to leave.

She didn't want him to go. No yet. She thought she'd detected some interest earlier tonight. The more she thought about it, the more she wondered if he hadn't left the snake on purpose so he would have to come back.

And Pilar was right. She hadn't had sex in over a year. It was depressing.

No, it was more than depressing. Her shelf life was dwindling, and fast.

She'd never had a one-night stand before. But she wasn't a kid. Who cared if Steve the Plumber wasn't husband material? He was definitely have-a-roll-in-the-hay material. And he wasn't a complete stranger. He was Gus's nephew. Gus wouldn't have a serial killer for a nephew. Would he?

"Are you hungry?" she asked. "There's tons of leftover pizza. Or maybe you want a drink? Some wine? A soda? Watered-down leftover secret margarita mix?"

Me?

"I just ate, but some water would be great."

He set down the snake and followed her into the kitchen, where he quickly tossed back a glass of ice water in one long, smooth swallow. Steve the Plumber had a great neck.

Think, Kit. Make some small talk. "Wow, you were thirsty." *Ugh.*

"It's pretty hot outside."

It was pretty hot in here too. And it wasn't just because the air conditioner was broken.

"So you're helping Gus out?"

"Just for a few weeks."

"Where are you staying?"

He looked at her strangely. Oh God. She was being too personal. "I'm staying with Gus."

"Gus is a great guy."

"The best."

Could he not make a little more conversation? But then, she didn't want him for his conversation.

He placed the glass on the counter.

Quick, say something witty!

"Wait, don't go." She inwardly moaned. Not exactly razor sharp. Maybe she had only imagined he was interested. Maybe she was desperate and clutching at straws.

"Is there something else you need me to fix? I'm afraid I don't know much about air conditioners."

She shook her head. "No, nothing."

It was official. She sucked at one-night-stand seduction. Either he wasn't interested or she wasn't giving out the right signals. But other than throw herself at him, there wasn't much else she could do.

She was certain he was on the verge of leaving, so it surprised her when he asked, "Is that glass of wine still available?"

"Sure."

All right. So maybe he *was* interested. But this was as far as she'd go. She'd invited him to stay for a drink. The rest was going to have to be up to him. She found a bottle of Merlot in the pantry and handed him a corkscrew.

But instead of opening the bottle, he placed it on the kitchen counter, leaned in, and softly brushed his mouth over hers. "Is this what you want me to stay for? Because if it isn't, just say so and I'll leave."

Oh my God. When Steve the Plumber made his move, he didn't mess around.

"Yes!" she nearly shouted in relief.

He frowned. "Are you drunk?"

"Why? Would it make a difference?"

"Maybe." Then he added more firmly, "Yes."

"I'm not drunk." At the uncertainty on his face, she said, "Honestly. I'm not. If I were drunk, I'd be crying."

"I'll have to remember that." He kissed her again. This time, the kiss was deeper, more urgent. He slipped his hand beneath the hem of her sundress and slowly slid his palm around to the back of her thigh and up to her bare bottom. "I've wanted to do that since the moment I met you."

"Kiss me?" she asked breathlessly.

"No. Check out if you were wearing panties or not."

Her breath hitched. "Oh. Um, I'm not wearing a bra either."

"You're right," he murmured, palming her breast as he trailed kisses down her neck.

"I normally do, of course," Kitty said, unable to stop babbling. "Wear a bra, that is. But this was a casual thing, my Bunco party, and the sundress really covers everything up and it's not like I really need a bra. I mean, my boobs aren't much, you know."

They locked gazes, but he didn't say anything. He started to lift the hem of her dress again.

"Wait," she said, wiggling out of his reach. It occurred to her they needed to clear up a few things. He might not be a serial killer, but maybe he was something worse . . . "You're not married. Are you?"

What if he said yes? What if he said no and it was a lie? What if—

"You wait till *now* to ask that?" Before she could respond

he added, "I'm not married. At least, not at the moment. Are you?" He glanced at the kitchen door as if expecting an irate husband to come barging through.

"What kind of question is that? Of course not!"

His dark eyes narrowed. "Maybe this is happening too fast. You seem nervous or something."

"I'm not nervous!" she squeaked. "This is the way I normally act. Look, I know what this is. I just want to have sex. I'm not like . . . planning on falling in love with you or anything." She smiled and rolled her eyes to emphasize her point.

"Good. Because I'm not planning on falling in love with you either."

He bent his head to kiss her, but she placed her hand on his chest to hold him off. "I feel sticky. Let me shower first." She motioned to the refrigerator. "Help yourself to whatever you want. I won't be long."

She scurried down the hallway and into the bathroom. Her reflection in the mirror above the sink looked like someone else, her face pale, her brown eyes huge. She was about to have sex with a man she'd only met a few hours ago.

What the hell was she doing?

Now wasn't the time to think about that. She'd do a Scarlett O'Hara and think about it tomorrow.

Kitty pulled back the shower curtain to find the tub filled with the water-soaked towels she had thrown in earlier. She quickly wrung them out one by one and tossed them onto the floor. She turned on the water, letting it warm up, then flipped the shower knob and pulled off her sundress. Her hair was already twisted out of the way, so she got in the tub and lathered up.

She usually knew a guy more than a few hours before she

let him see her naked. What would he think of her? Her stomach was good. It was tight and flat from years of crunches. And her former boyfriends had always liked her legs. But no matter how Pilar tried to spin it, her boobs were still too small, and no matter how many squats her trainer made her do, her ass was still too big.

The bathroom door clicked open.

"I hope you don't mind," she heard Steve say from the other side of the shower curtain, "but I'm a little grimy too. I think I'll join you."

7

░░ ░ ░ ░ ░ ░

The bar of soap fell from her hands. *Join her?*

"Um, sure." What else could she say? *No, I don't want to shower with you. I just want to have sex with you. Preferably in the dark.* Somehow, she didn't think Steve would find that too sexy.

He must have undressed in record time, because the next thing she knew, he was holding her in his arms. "Relax," he whispered.

She tried to take his advice and let out a pent-up breath. He bent down and kissed her. It was a gentler kiss than the ones in the kitchen, and after a few seconds, she began to respond. She'd been so nervous earlier she hadn't taken in any of the details. He was big and hard and tasted good. She broke off the kiss and let her gaze travel over his broad shoulders, his thick arms. His chest was nicely muscled with a light scattering of dark hair that narrowed into a thin line all the way down to his . . .

Yup, definitely big and hard.

Hap-py Birth-day, Kitty.

She couldn't help grinning like a sex-starved idiot. He grinned back as if he could read her mind, which wouldn't have been too great a feat at this point.

He scooped up the soap and lathered it, running his slippery hands over her breasts, down her belly, and in between her legs. He touched her clit, lightly pressing it with his finger. "Was Officer Bob right? Are you a bad girl, Kitty?"

A giggle bubbled up in the back of her throat. That line had sounded ridiculous coming from Officer Bob. But when Steve said it, his voice dark and rough, his hard body pressed up against hers, it was something altogether different.

"I . . . not usually," she stammered.

She immediately sensed it wasn't the response he was hoping for. But "Yeah, I'm a bad girl, all right" just wasn't something that came naturally out of her mouth. She wasn't a prude, but he had been right. This was all happening a little too fast for her.

She closed her eyes and concentrated on the warm water and Steve's fingers. Unable to help herself, she let out a laugh.

"You sure you're not drunk?"

Why did he keep asking her that? "I'm positive. Please, don't stop."

He kissed her again, his hands working their way down to cup her bottom as he pressed his erection against her belly. "You have a great ass," he murmured against her lips.

She broke off the kiss to stare at him.

Did he mean great as in fantastic? Or great as in big? No

one had ever told her she had a great ass before. Surely he couldn't be telling her that her butt was too big. Not at such a crucial moment. "So do you," she said lamely.

He laughed as if he thought her comment strange. "Um, thanks." Maybe no one had ever told him he had a great ass before either. But somehow, she doubted that.

She picked up the bar of soap. "Your turn." She lathered it over his arms, over his tight stomach. "I thought all plumbers had beer bellies," she said, feeling the need to lighten things up.

"I'm not a plumber," he rasped.

"Oh."

Before she could think of a response, he guided her hand over his erection. After less than a minute of stroking, he broke away and slipped out of the shower without saying anything.

Her heart flopped to her knees. Where was he going?

He came back a few minutes later. This time, he was gloved up.

Dear God. She hadn't even thought about a condom. She *really* sucked at this one-night-stand thing. "Good idea." Her heart began to pick up speed again. She had assumed they would mess around in the shower and leave the big finale for the bedroom. Apparently, Steve the Non-Plumber had other ideas.

He pressed her against the tile wall and slid his hands under her bottom, lifting her off her feet. The motion took her by surprise.

"This is the part where you wrap your legs around my waist," he said, sounding a little exasperated.

"You . . . you won't drop me, will you?"

"Not unless you plan on making some wild crazy-ass gyrations. Then I can't guarantee anything."

"I was just planning on the usual gyrations," she said.

The corner of his mouth twitched up slightly. "Then I think I can handle it."

He braced his legs apart and adjusted her hips to slowly lower her over him. She closed her eyes and held on tight as he began rocking her up and down.

Suddenly nothing else mattered.

Not the feel of the cold tile against her back or the apprehension of being semi-suspended in midair by a man she'd only just met tonight. A delicious heat swiftly rose, causing a tight laugh to form in the back of her throat.

How had she gotten to this point so fast? Of course, she hadn't gotten laid in over a year. Her G-spot was probably set on some type of split trigger detonation. Either that, or Steve the Non-Plumber was just really good.

She tucked her head in the crook of his neck to muffle her giggles as the wildfire died down.

A few seconds later, he let out a low groan, pumping into her one last time. "Shit," he muttered, lowering her feet to the floor. "Sorry. I'll do better next time."

He held her by the waist until her rubbery legs could adjust to support her weight. The warm water fell over them as he rubbed his hands over her back causing a languid drowsiness to wash through her.

Did he say "next time"? And what exactly had he apologized for?

The water suddenly stopped.

She opened her eyes and squinted at the harsh bathroom light above them.

"No towels?" he asked, glancing at the empty towel rack.

"They're all on the floor," she said, still feeling dazed. She pointed to the heap of wet towels in the bathroom corner. "I used them all to soak up the water from the toilet."

"I'll be right back." He trekked out of the bathroom, naked and dripping water. By the time he returned, the dreamy afterglow had worn off and goose bumps had spread over her arms and legs. He used a sheet, the one she'd ordered from the Pottery Barn catalogue with the little red sailboats, to dry her off, then blotted the water off his own body.

She was just starting to feel warm again when he opened the medicine cabinet, pulled out the crumpled-up thong, and tossed it at her.

Kitty caught it with one hand. He'd known it was there all along!

"Put it on."

"But—"

"I've waited all night to see you in that. And where's that pink thing with the feathers?" he asked, glancing around the bathroom floor.

"My boa?"

"Yeah, put that on too."

Okay. That sounded a little weird. But the man had just given her an orgasm. With stand-up shower sex, no less. The least she could do was humor him.

She slipped on the thong and had barely gotten the boa around her neck when he bent over and wrapped one arm around the back of her knees, swinging her over his shoulder like he was Tarzan and she was Jane.

"Oh my God!"

With one smooth movement he deposited her directly in the center of the bed.

The lamp on the nightstand cast a soft glow over the room.

Steve gazed down at her with a pensive look on his face. She felt kind of silly, lying there with the pink feather boa wrapped around her neck. Was he going to use it to tie her hands to the bedpost? She suddenly felt all warm and languid again. He'd caught her watching the toenail-painting scene in *Bull Durham*. Was he going to—

Before she could think too much, he came down onto the bed and kissed her, and then his mouth found her breasts. And she could only think a little bit as he inched his way down, his tongue trailing over her ribs, to her belly button and then finally to the top of her panties. She lifted her hips to take off the thong, but he placed his palm over her tummy to gently press her back into the mattress. "Keep it on," he said, right before he flicked his warm tongue over the cool silk.

A tiny snicker escaped her throat.

His mouth stilled. She raised her head to find him staring at her.

"I'm not drunk," she said, for the third time that night.

He smiled. "I know. I get it now."

Then he placed his mouth back between her legs and began to eat her through the pink-and-black-polka-dot thong until she forgot all about her breasts being too small or her ass being too big, and all she could do was laugh.

Later that night, Kitty's last coherent thought as she drifted to sleep was the sound of Joey Pappas's voice saying, "This is Kitty Burke. Back in eighth grade, she let me stick my tongue down her throat. And according to my cousin Steve, she laughs when she comes."

8

The shrill ringing next to Kitty's ear forced her to crack her eyes open. The obnoxious bright light leaking through the blinds was the final insult. She pulled the pillow over her head and hit the snooze button, but the ringing continued. She was about to bitchslap the alarm clock when she realized it was her phone making the noise.

"Hello?" she whispered, wincing at the squeaky roughness coming from her throat. She sounded like a Chihuahua on crack.

"Katherine, is that you?" her mother asked.

Kitty bolted upright. She quickly scanned the room. There was no sign of Steve the Plumber.

No, she thought, he wasn't Steve the Plumber.

He was Steve of the clever hands and the magical mouth and the rock-hard—"Hey, Mom," she said, clearing both her throat and the image that last thought produced in her head.

No matter how old you were, talking to your mother while thinking about sex was just gross.

"Happy birthday!"

"Thanks," Kitty said. She froze when she spotted a large red apple propped on the pillow from what had been Steve's side of the bed. Weird. It was exactly what Kevin Costner had left Susan Sarandon after sleeping with her in *Bull Durham*.

Kitty cradled the receiver under her chin and felt around the sheets for a note.

But there was nothing.

No slip of paper with *I had a great time* or *Can I call you?* scribbled on it.

At least Kevin had had the decency to leave a note along with his apple.

For a second, she felt like she'd been kicked in the teeth. And then she quickly analyzed the events of last night. The sex had been spectacular, no doubt about that. But there was no future with an out-of-work non-plumber who was only going to be in town temporarily. So what was the point of seeing him again?

Last night had been a one-time deal. It was definitely better to wake up to an empty bed. Much less awkward this way.

"Katherine, are you still there?"

"Yeah, I'm here," Kitty said, biting into the apple. It was crisp and juicy and her stomach rumbled in appreciation. Steve's version of breakfast in bed wasn't too shabby. Of course, neither was his version of anything else in bed.

"I was worried about you," continued her mother. "I called the office, but I got your voice mail. Then I tried your cell, but you didn't pick up on that either."

The office consisted of Kitty and her assistant, Becky. But

Becky was taking the day off. She and her boyfriend, Brad, were going to Disney World for the Fourth of July holiday weekend.

Kitty squinted at the clock.

It was five minutes to eleven. *Fuck!*

She tossed the apple onto the bed and jumped to her feet. "I . . . I must have overslept." How the hell she was going to explain that to her ten a.m. appointment?

"On a workday? Are you sick?"

"I'm fine. Mom, I'm sorry, I really have to go."

But Dana Hanahan Burke Lewis Cartwright wasn't a woman easily cut off. "When are you coming to visit me?" There was a pause. "I take it your father hasn't called to wish you a happy birthday yet?"

"You know Dad never remembers the actual day. Besides, he's in Greece right now and the time thing is all messed up."

"Greece? How nice for him."

"He's a pilot, Mom. It's his job."

"Whatever. You know, sweetie, St. Augustine is just a five-hour drive. I'm dying to show you what I've done to the condo."

"Look, Mom, I really have to go. Give Larry a hug for me." Larry Cartwright was her mother's third husband. He was a retired Oneida flatware salesman and had made a good enough living that he could spend his retirement golfing and taking frequent vacations to the Caribbean. Kitty liked Larry. He was a nice guy and he made her mother happy. He also kept her mother out of Whispering Bay—which made Kitty happy. Not that she didn't love her mother. But Whispering Bay just wasn't big enough for the both of them.

"Larry would be thrilled to see you, you know. You're like a daughter to him."

"How's Pam?" Pam was Larry's daughter by his first marriage. She was around Kitty's age, married, and pregnant with her fourth child.

"Big as a house and due any day now. It's a shame she never lost the weight she put on carrying Henry two years ago. They're going to have to roll her into the hospital to have this one."

"Well, that's great, Mom. Call me when the baby's here. I have to go."

"All right, darling. Have a wonderful day. Oh, and, Katherine, by the way, did you put the house on the market yet?"

"Mom, I'm almost out the door. Bye!"

She would deal with her mother and the house situation later.

Still feeling a little disoriented, she looked around the room. Something was wrong. Despite the fact that the ceiling fan was at full blast, it was hot as Hades.

The air conditioner.

How could she have forgotten it was broken? But there was no time to worry about that now.

She grabbed the cell phone from her purse and hit her search list. Her heart steadied a bit when she discovered she had Ted Ferguson's number. Thank God for Becky. She must have programmed the number into Kitty's phone.

He picked up on the second ring. "Ferguson."

"Mr. Ferguson, this is Katherine Burke. I can't tell you how incredibly embarrassed I am, but—"

"Miss Burke, when I say ten, that's what I mean."

Kitty gulped. "I have no excuse other than the fact I overslept." At his silence, Kitty felt emboldened to go on. "Please, let me make it up to you at lunch. Can you meet me at the Harbor House in an hour?"

"That place is a zoo. We'll never get a table."

"I'll have a table. Overlooking the water. I promise."

"Make it thirty minutes," he said and hung up.

Thirty minutes!

She ran to her closet and flipped through all the brightly colored clothes until she found the right outfit. A somber just-above-the-knee black skirt and a sleeveless cream-colored shell. It seemed a little stark for summer, but she had started off on the wrong foot with Ted Ferguson and this outfit screamed "serious businesswoman."

The next step was the bathroom. There was no time to shower. Of course, technically, she had showered last night. A warm flush crept up her spine. *Focus, Kit.*

She caught a glimpse of her first morning self in the bathroom mirror and moaned. The humidity in the house had caused her hair to frizz, making her look like a cross between Medusa and Roseanne Roseannadanna. She threw on some deodorant, brushed her teeth, splashed water on her face and some Chanel No. 5 on her neck (a little boring, but it was her standard professional smell). Minimal makeup could be done in the car. She fished around the sink area for her hair clip, but there was no sign of it.

Then she remembered she had gone to bed wearing the hair clip and the pink-and-black-polka-dot thong. And the boa, of course.

She ran back into the bedroom. The pink feather boa was looped around the bedpost. She looked around the sheets and on the floor for the hair clip. It was under the bed next to one of the designer pillows that matched her duvet comforter. How it ended up there, Kitty could only imagine. She took an extra minute to search for the thong, but it was nowhere to be found, so she gave up, picked up her briefcase, and made one last dash to the closet for shoes.

She usually wore the black skirt with a pair of low-heeled, open-backed slings that were practical in the Florida heat. But the shoes made her feel frumpy, and for some reason, she didn't feel like wearing those today. She rummaged in the back of the closet to find the four-inch black stilettos she reserved for a hot date night and dusted them off.

She was almost to her car when Mrs. Pantini appeared in the driveway. "Happy birthday!" the older woman cried cheerfully. Mrs. Pantini wore a pair of loose exercise pants and her standard New Balance walking shoes. Her chin-length salt-and-pepper hair was pulled back with a headband and her skin glowed with perspiration.

Kitty frowned. "You haven't been walking, have you?" Mrs. Pantini made a trek to the beach every morning, but never this late. The heat was just too stifling. "I really wish you'd consider joining my gym in Destin. They have an awesome indoor walking track," said Kitty.

Mrs. Pantini made a face. "Who wants to drive all the way to Destin just to walk? Besides, it's only now getting hot," she said, handing Kitty a small wrapped box. "I was going to wait till this evening to bring it over, but I saw your car in the driveway and I was hoping you'd have a chance to open it before heading into work."

"You didn't have to buy me anything!" Kitty gave her a quick hug, then tossed the gift alongside her briefcase in the passenger seat of her silver BMW convertible. "I'm sorry, but I really don't have time to open it now. I overslept and missed an appointment this morning."

Mrs. Pantini's blue eyes widened. "Overslept? You?" Her face split into a knowing grin. "That wouldn't have anything to do with the red pickup truck parked in front of your house this morning, would it?"

So, Steve had stayed the night. Then why hadn't he woken her before leaving?

"That was a . . . repair man," Kitty blurted. "My air conditioner's broken, and he was giving me an estimate. I must have fallen back asleep after he left." She made a mental note to call a real repairman as soon as her meeting with Ted Ferguson was over.

"I didn't know repairmen made house calls at six a.m. You'll have to give me his name."

"Um, I don't remember it off the top of my head, but I'm sure I wrote it down somewhere," Kitty said, feeling like the world's biggest shit for lying to her grandmother's best friend. But what was the alternative? "*Oh, the red pickup truck? It belongs to a man I barely know that I invited in for a booty call.*"

"I can't believe you're thirty-five now! Of course, you don't look it, not that thirty-five is old, but I'll always think of you as little Kitty. I still remember the day you and your mother came here to live. When was that, twenty-five years ago? Do you remember Sebastian? You used to love to play with him." Mrs. Pantini leaned in to whisper conspiratorially. "Don't tell Armand, but Sebastian will always be my favorite cat."

Kitty couldn't help but grin. Mrs. Pantini was just so damn cute. She thought back to that first day in Whispering Bay. Her parents had just divorced and she and her mother had moved in with Gram. Her mother had spent the morning crying, forcing Gram to oversee the movers. Afterward, Gram took Kitty next door to meet Mrs. Pantini, who in turn introduced her to Sebastian and the best sugar cookies in the world. Kitty spent the next four years as a regular visitor in the Pantini household. Then her mother married Jim Lewis and they had moved into Jim's house on the other side of Whispering Bay.

Kitty pulled the gift out of her car. "I'm already running late," she said, ripping into the blue-and-yellow-striped paper. "A couple more minutes won't hurt."

Inside the box was a silver flamingo pin with two tiny rubies for eyes. Kitty recognized it immediately. It had been a gift from her grandmother to Mrs. Pantini after the two of them had founded their senior citizen watch group. Kitty had always loved it. "Mrs. Pantini, I can't accept this!"

"Call me Viola. Mrs. Pantini was my mother-in-law." She smiled. "I always knew I would give it to you one day. It might as well be now when I'm around to enjoy seeing you wear it."

Kitty fastened the pin onto the cream-colored shell and stood back so Mrs. Pantini, or rather, Viola (she would have to get used to that) could admire it.

"It looks perfect with your outfit. Gives it just a hint of color."

Kitty fingered the pin, unable to keep from staring at it. "It does, doesn't it?"

"You know, all this hectic running around can't be good for you. You need to learn to de-stress. You should come to my Saturday-morning yoga class."

"I thought you took that at the senior center."

"Normally, you do have to be a member of the center to take a class there," Viola conceded, her blue eyes twinkling.

"But in your case we can make an exception. We're not that far apart in age. Seventy is the new fifty, you know."

Kitty laughed. "I might have to give that yoga class a try." She hugged Viola one more time, then jumped in her car. It was eleven twenty. If she booked it, she should make it to the Harbor House in time.

Now all she had to worry about was getting an ocean-view table. She put the car in reverse and prayed that Ricky, the assistant manager, was working today.

9

|||||

Ten minutes later and fifty dollars poorer (desperate times called for desperate measures), she was sitting at the Harbor House's best ocean-view table. Thank God Ricky could be bought. The crowd waiting in the small bar area of the restaurant had practically hissed at her as she had breezed by.

At exactly eleven thirty, Ricky ushered a tall, sandy-haired man to the table. Kitty had only talked to Ted a few times on the phone. She'd pictured him older, but he looked like he was in his late thirties, maybe forty. He wore a white knit polo shirt and khaki pants, which, despite the humidity, retained their perfect straight-from-the-dry-cleaner crease down the legs. He was good-looking, in a country-club sort of way.

Kitty squelched the urge to pull out her compact and make sure her lipstick was on straight. She stood and shook his hand. "Mr. Ferguson, thank you for agreeing to meet me."

"I thought this place didn't do reservations," he said, taking the seat across from her.

"They don't."

His gaze sharpened in approval. "Let's get right to it. I'm looking for someone who can help pull together a big land deal."

"I see." *There went fifty bucks down the drain.* She tried not to show her disappointment. "I think there's been a mistake. I specialize in single-family residential property." She leaned back in her seat to allow the waiter to set their menus on the table.

Ted smiled. "I never make mistakes." He put aside the menu without opening it and ordered a glass of Glenfiddich, neat, and the house special. Kitty wasn't hungry, but she ordered the special too, along with a glass of white wine.

Ted pulled a business card from his wallet. "'Help me help you find the house of your dreams,'" he read with a chuckle.

Dear God, not that again. She took a sip of her water. "I've been meaning to change that."

"Why? It's a great tagline."

She crossed her legs and began wiggling her right foot up and down in the air. It was a nervous habit, but she couldn't help herself.

"Let me tell you what I'm after," Ted said. "I need someone with strong ties in the community. Someone who grew up here, knows the locals, that sort of thing. You come highly recommended." His gaze drifted south. Kitty stilled her foot. Maybe the black stilettos had been a mistake. She hoped her face wasn't turning red.

"Who recommended me?"

"Practically everyone in town. It appears you're the local golden girl."

"That's flattering, but . . ." She cleared her throat. "Exactly how much land are you interested in?"

"Eventually, as much as I can buy, preferably all beachside. But for now, I want to start with ten acres."

She hesitated. "I have to warn you, this community isn't too keen on what I think you're after. Maybe you should try a little farther west, or maybe south? Where are you from, Mr. Ferguson, if you don't mind my asking?"

"Call me Ted. Originally, I'm from Miami, but I make my home wherever I set my hat. And I've decided to set my hat here." He said it like he was the new sheriff that had come to town.

"What do you intend to do with the land?" Not that she needed to ask. There was only one thing he could want with beachfront property.

"Condos, Katherine. But then, you've proven yourself a smart girl. You already figured that out, so let's cut the crap. If it's not me, it'll be someone else. And if it's not you, it'll be someone else again. Condos bring in tourists, who bring in money and boost the economy. It's as simple as that. There's an entire market here just waiting to be tapped."

The server brought them their drinks. Ted pushed his to the side. "Take this place," he said, waving his hand in the air. "Don't tell me all those saps waiting for a table out there are locals. Those are vacationers from the nearby beaches here to taste a little bit of panhandle cuisine. This place was cited in *Florida's Best Spots to Dine*, that's why they're out there. Do you think the owner gives a damn where his customers come from? It's just a matter of time before Whispering Bay joins the rest of the world. Hell, there isn't even a McDonald's in town."

"There are zoning laws, Mr. Ferg—uh, Ted, that we can't ignore."

"The land I'm looking at is already zoned for condos. And I'm not planning on building high-rises. Just a tasteful string of moderately priced units. The kind of place the little man can afford. Everyone wants to own a vacation home, Katherine. It's part of the American Dream."

Except he forgot to mention that very few "little men" could afford the American Dream without renting it out fifty weeks of the year. Which meant more traffic, more beachside erosion. But he was also right about condos boosting the economy. The Harbor House was the area's most popular tourist attraction. People drove from the larger neighboring towns of Destin and Panama City Beach to have some of their famous fried grouper and cheese grits. Ricky made a good living here. He had bought his first home from Kitty last year.

"I happen to know the owner might be interested in selling," Ted said. "To the right person, that is."

He had to be referring to Earl Handy. The Handys were Whispering Bay's founding family. Cyrus Handy, Earl's grandfather, had settled in north Florida in the early 1900s and opened a lumber mill that at one time had employed hundreds of workers. The mill had gone out of business in the seventies and Earl had sold off all the forested land, but as far as Kitty knew Earl hadn't sold anything in years. He still owned most of the land in town and almost all the good beachfront property. He was in his eighties now and lived in seclusion in a house near Mexico Beach. The last time Kitty had seen Earl in town was at her grandmother's funeral last year.

"This isn't exactly my area," she said cautiously, feeling the need to remind him. "I'm afraid I don't have any experience with this sort of deal."

"Don't sweat the small stuff," Ted said. "My partner's a broker, as well as a real estate attorney. Teresa handles all the fine print and she's a real sharpshooter. What I need is a local connection. Someone who knows the area. Like I said, if it's not you, then it'll be another broker. And I don't think I'll have any problem getting someone. The commission and incentive bonus I plan to offer on this is going to be sweet." He pulled another business card from his wallet and held it out to her. "But after meeting you, I've made up my mind. You're the one I want."

Incentive bonus? Kitty had no doubt Ted Ferguson could find another broker. And there was also no doubt she could use the money he was alluding to. Up to now, she hadn't been very smart with her finances. With the commission off this sale, she might even be able to afford Gram's house.

The thumping in her chest rose to her ears.

Ted was right. New construction meant jobs, more money for the local economy. If not her, then someone else was going to profit from this. Maybe she shouldn't turn him down right away.

She took his card. "Can I have a few days to think about it?"

"I'm going out of town for the holiday weekend, but I'll be back on Tuesday. Let's meet at nine a.m. sharp. Your office." He paused. "We aren't going to have any repeats of this morning, are we?"

"Oh no," Kitty said quickly. "I'm not trying to make excuses, but last night both my toilet and my air conditioner broke down, and—"

"Your air conditioner broke down?" He shook his head in sympathy. "God almighty." He glanced around the restaurant and whistled under his breath. "It's barely noon and this place is packed. I tell you, Katherine, this town is a gold mine."

Noon?

Shit! She had forgotten all about lunch with Shea and Pilar. They were probably already waiting at the restaurant. They would be furious with her, or worse, they would worry that something had happened to her.

Ted picked up his scotch. "Of course, I don't have to tell you that for now, at least, we need to keep this deal under wraps." He held his glass up in the air. It took a few seconds too long for Kitty to catch on. She clinked her wineglass a little too forcefully against his tumbler, but Ted didn't seem to notice. "Here's to making a truckload of money. If you should decide to come on board, that is," he said, winking at her.

Kitty smiled, feeling an awkward mixture of elation and unease. Ted Ferguson wasn't so bad. A bit hard-edged on first meet, maybe, but so were a lot of successful businessmen.

She would wait a few minutes, then politely excuse herself to the ladies' room where she would call the girls and explain what had happened. Pilar and Shea would understand if she was a little late.

10

"I can't believe you dissed us for a client," Pilar said. "I rearranged my whole day so we could do lunch together."

"And my sitter can't stay past two, so that only gives us time for this." Shea held up a spoonful of ice-cream-smothered brownie.

The second Kitty had walked into the restaurant, four servers carrying a gigantic chocolate brownie complete with lit candles had met her at the door. The entire place had joined in singing "Happy Birthday," making her feel silly, but at the same time, it had been fun too.

She winced at the stony looks on their faces. "I'm sorry, okay? How many times can I say that?"

"So did you get this Ferguson guy to nibble on that listing on Ocean Avenue?" Shea asked.

"Not exactly," Kitty said, hesitating. "Apparently, he's some big-time developer from Miami." She glanced around the restaurant and lowered her voice. "He's planning on building condos on the beach." Keeping the deal under wraps didn't include not telling Shea and Pilar.

"Condos?" Pilar said, frowning. "In Whispering Bay?"

"I thought there were zoning laws against that sort of thing," said Shea.

"Not if you don't build them higher than three stories," Kitty said. "But don't go spreading it around. I mean, you can tell Moose and Nick, of course, but not anyone else. It's kind of a secret for now."

"So, what's this got to do with you?" Shea asked.

"Ted wants me to rep him."

"But you sell houses," Shea said.

"I've sold lots before," Kitty said, trying not to sound irritated. So maybe this was a little different, but not that much. Not really. "Nothing's set in stone. I haven't agreed to anything yet."

Pilar looked thoughtful. "Would this be a good thing for you?"

"It would be friggin' great for me. Money-wise, that is." Kitty took her first bite of the gooey fudge brownie. There were probably a zillion calories in each spoonful, but she didn't care. Today was her birthday. Last night, she'd had the best sex of her life. And less than an hour ago, she'd been offered the business opportunity of a lifetime. Whether she took it or not wasn't the point. The point was that an outsider considered her the premier Realtor in the area. That had to be good. Despite the overflowing toilet and the broken air-conditioning, it had been a pretty fantastic twenty-four hours. A little celebratory chocolate couldn't hurt.

"So what's this Ted Ferguson like?" Pilar asked.

"Around forty, rich, and used to getting his way."

"Is he cute?"

"Is that all you think about?"

"Someone has to think about it. Is he potential husband material or what?"

"Pilar! He's probably married. Besides," Kitty said, trying not to think of the way Steve's eyes looked when they got all smoky, "I don't think Ted Ferguson's my type."

"If he's rich and single, then he's every woman's type," said Shea.

"If Ted Ferguson isn't such hot shit, how come he took up your whole morning, and why are you wearing your date pumps?" Pilar asked. "You know your legs look awesome in those."

"The shoes were a mistake," Kitty said, concentrating on piling equal portions of brownie, ice cream, and whipped topping onto her spoon. "And he didn't take up my whole morning. I missed our appointment and had to make it up to him with lunch."

Pilar blinked. "You missed an appointment?"

"I overslept."

"Are you sick?" Shea asked.

"No, Mommy, I'm not sick," Kitty said, careful to avoid Pilar's gaze. It was easy to fool Shea, but Pilar could always tell when she was hiding something. Face Reading 101 was probably a requisite class in law school.

"I didn't realize we had kicked your butt so hard at Bunco. You must be getting old," Pilar joked. She leaned back in the booth and studied her. "You're glowing. And it's not a money glow. What else happened?"

"Nothing," Kitty said, taking another spoonful of brownie.

Shea folded her arms over her six-thousand-dollar chest. "Pilar's right. You're grinning like an idiot."

Kitty tried to wipe the smile from her face. But it was no use. Kick-ass sex must produce some sort of lingering endorphins. She was going to tell them eventually, so why not now?

"Remember last night, when we were talking about my dismal sex life? Well, I fixed it. I got me some right after you guys left."

Shea's blue eyes went wide. "With Ted Ferguson?"

"No, idiot. With Steve the Plumber. I didn't even know Ted Ferguson last night."

Pilar gasped. "You slut!"

Kitty giggled. "I know."

"How did it happen?" Shea asked.

"He forgot his snake and came back for it. Although, the more I think about it, I'm positive he left it on purpose. Oh, and he's not a plumber either."

"Wow," Shea said, snapping her fingers. "Just like that?"

Pilar leaned forward. "How was it?"

"It was . . . great."

"Great? That's all we get?"

"What more do you want?"

"For starters, did he make you laugh?"

"Oh yeah," Kitty said, unable to keep the enthusiasm from her voice. "*Multiple* times."

Pilar pushed away the rest of her brownie. "I've just lost my appetite."

Kitty stared at her a moment, trying to figure out what that meant.

"When are you going to see him again?" Shea asked.

Kitty ran her spoon along the edge of the plate to scoop up as much ice cream as she could. "I'm not."

"What do you mean you're not?" Pilar said. "I thought you just said it was great."

"It *was* great. But it was just for last night."

"You told him not to call?" Shea said.

She must be eating the ice cream too fast because she suddenly got a brain freeze. She set down her spoon. "There was never any talk of calling. He came back to the house. We flirted a little, we had sex, and when I woke up this morning, he was gone. No big deal."

"No note?" Pilar asked.

"He left me an apple on the pillow," Kitty said.

Shea and Pilar exchanged a look. They knew *Bull Durham* almost as well as Kitty did.

"Strange coincidence, huh?" said Kitty.

"What do you mean he's not a plumber?" Shea asked.

Kitty shrugged. "He told me he's not a plumber."

"So what does he do?" persisted Pilar.

Shea dipped her spoon in Kitty's plate, taking away a healthy portion of brownie. "How old is he? Did you find out how many times he's been married?"

"What is this, twenty questions? And eat your own brownie," Kitty said, pointing to Shea's plate.

"We're your best friends, and between the two of us we've been married a total of over twenty years. To wonderful, fabulous men, of course," Shea said, "but if we have to put up with hearing about the woes of single life, then we deserve to hear the good stuff too."

Pilar nodded enthusiastically.

Kitty was beginning to feel sorry she had brought the whole

thing up. "There's not much to tell. Like I said, he came back and after some small talk, I asked him if he wanted to stay for a glass of wine. Then he kissed me, and before I knew it we were doing it in the shower. Honestly, we didn't talk a lot."

"*In the shower?*" Shea repeated.

"It was hot as hell in the house, which reminds me, my air conditioner is broken and I still haven't called a repairman."

Kitty flipped open her cell phone to call information, but Pilar snatched the phone away before she could punch in the number. "Your air conditioner can wait. Finish the rest of the story."

Kitty sighed. "Then we had some more incredible sex, and that's it. Satisfied?"

"Wow," said Shea. "Moose and I didn't do shower sex until we were engaged."

"So why aren't you going to see him for more incredible sex?" Pilar persisted. "Isn't he going to be in town for a few weeks?"

She wasn't going to see him again because he hadn't said he wanted to see *her* again. But it was too humiliating to admit. Even to her two best friends. Of course, there was no rule that said she couldn't call him. But she'd already decided there was no point.

"Maybe I'll see him again or maybe I won't," Kitty said, trying to sound nonchalant. "Who knows? But that's enough about me."

They both looked ready to protest, so Kitty intercepted them by turning to Shea. "Your turn. Tell us about last night. Is baby number three on the way?"

Shea flipped her red hair off her shoulders. "It's not that easy, you know. These things can take a while. Besides," she added with a sigh, "we never got to do it. Briana was in bed with Moose when I got home. She's afraid of the dark."

Pilar shook her head. "I still think you're crazy wanting another one."

Shea scowled. "What does Nick think of your 'one child only' proclamation? He told Moose last month he was hoping you'd get pregnant by the end of the year."

"He did? Well, considering we haven't had sex in over two months it would be a damn miracle."

Kitty felt her breath catch. She put down her spoon and laid her hand over Pilar's arm. "Are you and Nick having problems?"

"Not any a vasectomy won't take care of."

"I thought Catholics weren't supposed to practice birth control," Shea said.

"Nick's not Catholic."

"But you are," Shea said.

"Exactly. And the guilt of being on the pill is eating away at me."

Kitty shook her head and resumed eating. "You're so full of it."

"High blood pressure runs in my family," said Pilar. "Why should I be on the pill? I've already had a C-section. It's Nick's turn to go under the knife."

"But a vasectomy is permanent," Shea said.

"Exactly. I already told you I'm perfectly happy with just Anthony. If Nick Rothman ever wants to have sex again, he's going to have to get snipped."

"That's so mercenary." Shea narrowed her eyes. "So . . . well, so you."

Pilar tossed down her napkin on the table. "What the hell is that supposed to mean?"

"If you feel comfortable blackmailing your husband into a vasectomy, then—"

"I think Steve the Non-Plumber is a little kinky," Kitty blurted.

Where the hell had that come from? But it did the trick. They stopped their arguing and turned to stare at her.

"Really?" Pilar said, her voice rising a notch.

"Spill," Shea demanded.

They both leaned forward. The anticipation on their faces made Kitty laugh. "You guys are so high school. Okay, so maybe he's not exactly kinky . . ." She felt stupid now for bringing it up, but she also knew they would never let it go unless she gave them *something*. And it wasn't like she was betraying some sacred memory.

"He did get a big kick out of this pink-and-black-polka-dot thong I had—"

"Victoria's Secret catalogue? Summer issue?" Shea interrupted.

Kitty nodded.

"I ordered the baby blue one," Shea said. "Go on."

"He asked me to wear it while he . . . you know, went down on me."

They flopped back in their seats. "That's it?" Shea said. "That's not kinky."

"Well, he also asked me to wear the feather boa."

"Did he tie you up with it?" Shea asked eagerly.

"No. But for a few seconds there, I thought he was going to." Pilar giggled. "A pink-and-black-polka-dot thong?"

"Yeah, when I find it, I'm going to get that sucker bronzed."

Shea snapped to attention. "What do you mean, when you find it?"

"I looked, but I couldn't find it this morning."

Pilar wrinkled her forehead thoughtfully. "Maybe it fell under the bed."

"I checked there and under the sheets. I found my hair clip, but, I don't know, maybe—"

"Do you think he took it?" Shea asked.

"Who?"

"Steve the Non-Plumber, of course," Shea said.

"Why would he take my thong?"

"You said he had this thing for it, and he made you put it on, and now it's gone. The guy probably collects little souvenirs from all his conquests."

The chocolate brownie suddenly felt wedged in her chest. Kitty swallowed hard and glanced around the restaurant again. Thankfully, none of the nearby diners seemed to be listening in.

"Let's not jump to conclusions here," Pilar said carefully.

"What a perv," Shea muttered.

Pilar kicked Shea under the table with enough force that Kitty would have had to be totally clueless to miss it. *Shit*. Pilar thought Steve had taken the thong too.

"Don't listen to her," said Pilar. "You don't have any evidence to back that up."

"No, Shea's right." Why had she eaten so much of the brownie after her big lunch with Ted? She felt like throwing up. "If Steve didn't take my thong, then where is it?"

Pilar sighed. "So what if he did take it? You had a great night, which you totally deserve. You're never going to see him again, so I say forget it."

"*Forget it?*" How dare he take her thong? How dare he have sex with her and not stick around to say good-bye?

"The man probably has my underwear hanging off the rearview mirror of his pickup truck. I can't just forget it. I need to get my thong back."

"Bad idea," said Pilar.

"Pilar's right," said Shea. "He's probably just going to deny taking it anyway."

Pilar looked at Shea and nodded, the two of them back in sync. "And then what? You'll end up with egg on your face. Remember freshman year in college, when you had a crush on that guy from Pike house? What was his name . . ."

"Phil Fembarti," Shea supplied.

"Yeah, Phil," Pilar said. "And after a couple of weeks of giving you the rush, he dropped you for that slut Jenny Moorhouse? You insisted on going to see him, even though Shea and I told you it was a bad idea."

"I had a right to know why he stopped calling."

"Agreed. But we all know how that turned out. You stuck your nose in a book and didn't look at another guy for the rest of the year."

"Phil Fembarti was a dipshit and I was eighteen and stupid. What does that have to do with getting my thong back?"

"I had a bad feeling then, and I have a bad feeling now. Call it my Cuban intuition, but you need to let this go."

Kitty stood with as much dignity as her shaking legs would allow. "Thank you for the birthday song and the ice cream and brownie." She leaned down and gave them both a quick peck on the cheek, then picked up her bag and looped it around her shoulder.

"Where are you going?" Shea asked. "We're not finished."

"I'm going to get my underwear back."

Pilar placed her head in her hands. "*Ay, caramba.*"

11

If she wanted her thong back, she was going to have to go to Pappas and Son Plumbing to get it. She didn't have Steve's cell number—if he even had a cell phone, that is. And it didn't feel right to confront him at Gus's house. She would swing by the plumbing office and let Gus know she needed to talk to Steve. It would be awkward. Gus would wonder what she wanted to talk to his nephew about. But there was no other option. Kitty could only hope Joey was off somewhere waist-deep in the middle of a septic tank accident.

She pulled her convertible into the gravel lot. Steve's truck was parked in front of the office. Her stomach bungee jumped straight to her knees. Even though his being here made it a lot easier, she had thought she'd have a little more time before confronting him.

She threw back her shoulders and stepped out of the car.

This was no time to be having second thoughts. She was on a thong retrieval mission, damn it.

Her four-inch stiletto heels weren't meant for walking across rocks. Kitty stumbled twice before she reached the door to Pappas and Son Plumbing. She stepped inside the cool air-conditioned building and came face-to-face with Joey.

So much for septic tank fantasies.

His eyes widened. "Hey, Kitty. What's up?" His gaze nervously shot to the back door.

A warning bell rang in her head. Joey had never called her Kitty before. Not even when they were in school. She was always Kit Kat or some other cutesy-obnoxious version of her name.

"Hey, Joey," she said cautiously. "I came by to talk to Gus about installing that toilet for me. Is he around?" It wasn't actually a lie. She really did need that new toilet.

"I thought I heard someone," Gus said, stepping into the office from the back room. Gus was in his mid-sixties, tall, with a head still full of dark hair. Three years ago after his wife died, Kitty had helped him sell the large four-bedroom home where they had raised their family. "Too many memories here," he had said. He was now living in a two-bedroom, two-bath bungalow on the beach that Kitty had found for him. He opened his arms and gave her a bear hug. "What brings you here?"

From the corner of her eye, Kitty could see Steve lingering near the back door. "I . . . I want to schedule that toilet installation," she said, feeling her face go warm.

Steve wore a baseball cap, shorts, and a raggedy T-shirt. He looked like he'd just come in from a day of fishing. All sweaty and male and 100 percent gorgeous. Her mind went blank. What happened to the scathing speech she had rehearsed all the way from the restaurant?

She shuffled her weight from foot to foot.

"I was going to call you when the new toilet came in," Gus said. "Remember?"

"Oh, that's right. I guess I forgot. Well, that's great. I'll just wait for you to call then."

Why had she let Shea rile her up? Pilar was right. There was no actual evidence Steve had taken her thong. This was a mistake. Maybe if she slipped off the heels she could run all the way back to her car.

"How did my nephew do last night?" Gus asked, slapping Steve on the back.

Joey snickered.

Kitty glanced at Joey. He quickly wiped his expression clean. "He . . . he did fine."

Gus nodded. "Normally, I would have come myself, but I really didn't want to miss the bowling tournament."

"It was no problem," Kitty said.

"He's a good-looking guy, huh?" Gus asked.

Kitty couldn't be sure since his face was already a little sunburned, but she thought Steve's cheeks pinked up. She met his gaze head-on for the first time. He looked uncomfortable. *And guilty*.

Her knees began to wobble.

"He's had a string of bad luck," Gus continued. "What he needs is a nice Greek girl to straighten him out."

"He's already had one of those," Joey piped in. "More than one, actually."

"Hey!" Gus glared at his son. "There's a lady present."

Steve's mouth settled into a grim line.

Kitty swallowed past the knot in her throat and tried for a warm smile. "He's handsome enough, but he can't hold a candle to his uncle."

Gus beamed. "You sure you're not Greek?"

"I'm positive."

"We might have to make an exception, then," Gus said, still smiling.

"I don't think Steve cares if Kitty's Greek," Joey said smoothly. "Do you, big guy?" He winked at his cousin.

Oh my God.

It was her worst nightmare come true. No amount of kick-ass sex was worth this.

Steve took her by the elbow. "Let me walk you to your car." She barely had time to turn and say good-bye to Gus before he hustled her out the front door.

She yanked her arm from his grasp, almost losing her balance in the process. "Sorry," he said, backing away to lean against the side of his pickup truck. "I must smell like fish guts." He gave her a lazy smile. "Nice shoes."

"Yeah? Well, you can't have them."

"Huh?"

A low burst of music filled the air. The tune was "Free Bird." Steve pulled his cell from his shorts pocket. "I need to make sure this isn't important." He glanced at the screen. "Can you hold on a minute? I should take this call."

"Go ahead." He'd find out soon enough she wasn't going anywhere until they settled up.

"What do you want?" Steve asked into the phone. After an occasional "uh-huh," he finished the conversation with, "Look, Terrie, I'm busy. If I hear anything, I promise I'll call."

"Who's Terrie?" Kitty asked, before she could stop herself. She sounded like some jealous shrew. Which she most certainly wasn't. Jealousy implied she cared. Which she didn't. "Forget it. It's none of my business."

"Terrie's my ex-wife."

"The stripper?"

"No," he said in a cautious tone. "Terrie's my third ex-wife."

She gasped. "How many ex-wives do you have?"

"Just three."

Just three? "I want my underwear back," she blurted.

He pushed up the lid to his Tampa Bay Buccaneers cap. "Your what?"

"You heard me. I want my underwear back." She stooped down to peer inside the front seat of his truck. "At least it's not hanging off your rearview mirror."

He frowned. "Sweetheart, you're turning weird on me. What the hell are you talking about?"

"*I'm* weird? I'm not the one who collects women's under-wear."

He blinked.

"Last night, when you . . . you know, did that thing with my thong," she said, motioning with her hands to indicate the bedpost. He looked at her like she was losing it, which of course, was probably exactly what he wanted her to think. "Anyway, it doesn't matter. When I woke up this morning, it was gone."

"And you think I took it? Like some sort of memento?"

The expression on his face made her pause. But then, she remembered the way Joey had looked at her. Dear God, had he shown Joey her thong? "I looked for it everywhere. If you didn't take it, who did?"

"Wow." He laughed incredulously. "I must have some invisible crazy-chick magnet tattooed on my ass."

Her spine stiffened. How dare he try to turn this around on her? She had checked every inch of that floor. Shea was right. Her thong hadn't just walked off by itself. "Do you deny you told Joey we slept together?" She was shrieking, but she didn't care.

"Yeah, as a matter of fact, I do."

"Bullshit."

A muscle on the side of his jaw twitched. "Are you calling me a liar?"

"You can toss in pervert too."

His dark eyes narrowed. "I think we both know what this is really about. This is about your ego being bruised because I didn't declare some kind of undying devotion to you after last night. You're pissed because you woke up alone this morning."

"I am *not*! For your information, that happens to me all the time."

His brows shot up.

"I . . . I didn't mean it like that. Look," she said, trying to stay calm, "just give me back the thong and we'll forget we ever knew one another."

"Believe me, I'd love nothing better. You want your thong back?"

Her shoulders slumped. "So you have it?" It wasn't until that instant she realized just how much she had hoped she was wrong.

"Not on me."

"Then—"

"Go check your laundry room. You'll find your thong on top of the dryer." His voice turned low and hard. "For one thing, I didn't tell my cousin jack shit. Apparently, he cuts through your neighborhood on the way to work and saw my truck in your driveway. And I sure as hell don't need to collect trophies. But if I did, it wouldn't have been from last night. It was nice, but you didn't exactly rock my world."

She opened her mouth to speak, but nothing came out.

"Now, if you'll excuse me, I don't think you and I have anything left to talk about." He then calmly walked back inside the building.

Kitty stood there a minute, unable to speak, unable to move. She tried to walk to her car with as much dignity as she could, but her heel got stuck in the gravel and she fell, landing flat on her ass in the Pappas and Son Plumbing parking lot.

12

The Margaret Handy Senior Center was a rambling one-story brick building located directly on the beach. It was originally built as a family home by Earl Handy in the early fifties. Twenty years ago, after Earl's wife died, he graciously leased the building to the city of Whispering Bay for the sum of one dollar a year. To show their gratitude, the city turned it into a center for its retired citizens, naming the building after Earl's deceased mother. The roof leaked, and the kitchen needed new appliances, but the view from the main room was to die for. The city council had tried for years to get Earl to renovate. Earl's stance was that if the city wanted improvements, then they could pay for them. After all, what did they want for a buck a year?

Kitty didn't blame Earl one bit. She had signed the Gray Flamingos petition last year demanding the city council put some money into the building, but the referendum had been defeated. The council claimed there wasn't enough money in the budget. Viola and her coalition had vowed to keep fighting.

Besides being a place for Whispering Bay's senior citizens to socialize, the center offered arts and crafts classes, as well as yoga and music appreciation. When Gram was alive, Kitty would drop her off at the center and occasionally join her for a game of cards. But she hadn't stepped foot in the place since last year. It felt a little strange coming back.

A small group of seniors was huddled around Viola in the middle of the main room. By the looks on their faces, something serious was up.

Viola's hair was pulled back in a low ponytail. Her cheeks were flushed and her eyes were bright. "You came! Are you here to take the yoga class?" she asked Kitty.

"Yep," Kitty said, dropping her exercise mat onto the floor. Yesterday, she'd made a fool of herself in front of Steve Pappas only to find out later that afternoon that her new air conditioner was going to cost eight thousand dollars. As if things weren't bad enough, she must have slept with her head twisted, because she'd woken up with a crick in her neck. She needed to de-stress, and an hour of yoga seemed like a good way to do just that. She greeted the rest of the group, all of whom she knew pretty well since most of them had been friends with her Gram.

Eleanor Stenhope wagged her finger at the clock on the wall. "The instructor is supposed to be here fifteen minutes before class starts."

"I hope she shows up this time," said Mr. Milhouse, whose first name Kitty could never remember. Two long white hairs poked straight up from his left eyebrow. Kitty fought the urge to reach over and pluck them out. "Don't know why people can't keep their appointments. This wouldn't be happening if we lived in one of those retirement centers, like that Sun City place they have over in Arizona."

"Arizona is too hot," Eleanor Stenhope said.

"It's just as hot here," said Mr. Milhouse. "'Cept it's more humid. I don't remember it ever being this humid before."

"It's global warming," Viola said.

Mr. Milhouse's white brows came together to form a shaggy line. "Global what?"

The front door opened and the conversation stopped. But instead of the yoga instructor, it was Gus.

Great.

Not that she didn't adore Gus. But now, seeing him would always make her think of Steve, which of course, would make her think of the Thong Incident (which is what she'd named it last night in her head). Next time—not that she was planning on a next time, but if there ever were to be a next time—she would only have one-night stands with men she wouldn't be reminded of every five seconds.

"I must need glasses," Viola teased. "Is that Gus Pappas I see in front of me?"

"You win, Vi. I'm gonna try out this mumbo-jumbo yoga thing. Doc Lambert says I could use some de-stressing in my life." Gus wore a spotless white T-shirt and navy running shorts. Kitty had to admit, his legs were in awesome shape. Compared to the other men in the room, he was practically a stud.

"All my favorite people have come to class," Viola said, smiling at the two of them.

"You got roped into this as well, eh?" he asked Kitty, his brown eyes twinkling, his expression warm and friendly.

Kitty nodded, relieved that Gus seemed his usual self around her. What had she expected, though? That Steve would brag to his uncle about their sex romp? Or worse, tell him how she had turned into a raging maniac the next day? "Maybe I should go to the office and see if the instructor has called to say she's running late," she volunteered.

"Good idea," Viola said. "Meanwhile, we'll start to stretch." She guided Gus to a spot next to her. The rest of the seniors followed her lead, spreading their mats out across the room.

Kitty wandered down the long hallway until she reached the office. A man sat at the desk, his sneakered feet propped up on the window ledge. He was talking on the phone with the receiver cradled around his neck while frantically punching buttons on a handheld video game.

Kitty knocked on the open door.

The man turned around, and he wasn't a man at all. It was Josh Bailey, who couldn't have been older than seventeen. Josh's dad, Bruce Bailey, was vice president of the local bank. Bruce also served on the city council and consistently voiced the most vocal opposition to whatever petition the Gray Flamingos were touting. Kitty found it ironic that his son was working at the senior center of all places.

"Oh, hey, Ms. Burke. What can I do for you?"

"I didn't know you worked here, Josh."

"My dad got me this job." Josh didn't excuse himself from the call, but instead, continued to look at her expectantly.

"The yoga instructor hasn't shown up for the noon class yet. You know anything about that?"

He sighed heavily. "I gotta go," he said into the receiver. "The geezers have their Depends in a wad again." He laughed.

"Cool. I'll be there." He hung up and rummaged through a mess of papers on the desk until he found a small yellow Post-it note stuck behind a folder. "She's got a cold so she won't be here today."

"When were you going to let the class know?"

"No worries, Ms. B. I was just about to do that."

"Josh, are you getting paid to work here or is this a volunteer position?"

"*Volunteer?*" he croaked.

"So, you're getting paid. Isn't it in your job description to keep up with what's going on?"

His brown eyes looked wary. "I guess so."

Kitty bit her tongue. It wasn't Josh's fault the instructor was sick, but something had to be done about his attitude.

"You're not going to make a big deal out of this, are you? My dad is making me pay for my own car insurance. He'll ground me if I get fired. And if I don't have a car, I might as well be dead. There's nothing to do in this town."

"Maybe you should talk to your dad about that," Kitty said. "It's the city council that voted against the new community pool and basketball courts."

"He's always bitch—uh, complaining there's not enough money for that kind of stuff."

Kitty nodded. That sounded just like Bruce. "Look, I'm not trying to get anyone in trouble, but you need to stay on top of things."

"Will do," Josh promised, plunking his feet back on the ledge. He picked up his video game and resumed playing.

Kitty was trying to think of a way to tell the class the instructor was a no-show when she heard Viola's soothing voice drift through the hall. The group was settled around the floor on their exercise mats. Viola's arms were above her head, urging the class to expand their lungs and take a deep breath. It wasn't a bona fide yoga class, but over the next forty-five minutes, Viola led them through a series of gentle stretches and deep breathing exercises that left Kitty feeling rejuvenated.

"You should be teaching this class," Kitty told Viola as she rolled up her exercise mat. "You taught high school PE for years and you're in great shape."

"Maybe I'll think about it. But I'd have to get certified first," Viola said, looking pleased by the compliment.

"Kitty's right. You're a natural," Gus said.

Viola smiled.

"Hey," said Gus, "I have an idea. There's a refrigerator full of fish at my house just waiting to hit the grill. Why don't you ladies join me and my nephew for dinner tonight?"

Join them for dinner tonight?

Kitty tripped over a loose tile on the floor. She caught herself seconds before landing flat on her face.

Gus scowled. "Someone needs to fix that."

Viola eyed him with interest. "That's exactly the sort of thing the Gray Flamingos are trying to accomplish. We need you on our committee, Gus."

"I'm not retired yet, Vi. And I don't plan to quit working for a long time either."

"You don't have to be retired to join the Flamingos," Viola said, looping her arm through his. "What do you think, Kitty? Should we join them for dinner?"

She'd love to see the expression on Steve's face for that one. "Sorry, I've got other plans," Kitty lied.

"Can't you break them?" Gus asked. "I know my nephew would love it if you'd come."

I wouldn't bet on that.

"Is your nephew that dark-haired hunk I saw driving your truck the other day?" Viola asked.

"I'm the only one who drives my truck, Vi. Steve drives a fancy red pickup. The kind with all those slick gizmos on it."

Shit. Kitty hoped Viola didn't make the connection to the pickup truck parked in her driveway the other morning. If she did, she didn't let on. "Then it must have been you I saw," Viola said sweetly.

Gus actually blushed, which was adorable. Kitty couldn't help smiling at the two of them. "I have to go," she said. "But invite me again." *Like when your nephew leaves town,* she thought.

Kitty left the senior center and made a right on Ocean Avenue to Corbits Supermarket where she bought a sack of groceries—mainly salad stuff and low-fat ice cream. Even nuking something in this heat was out the question until she got her new air conditioner. Monday was the Fourth of July, and since she didn't want to pay overtime, she had to wait till Tuesday to get the unit installed.

Instead of taking her usual route home, she slipped over a couple of blocks to Dolphin Isles to check out the real estate competition. Dolphin Isles was a new subdivision catering to first-time buyers and retirees looking to downsize. It was owned by TNT Properties, an out-of-town corporation Kitty had never heard of before it appeared on the scene in Whispering Bay. The subdivision consisted of three-bedroom, two-bath tract homes with tiny manicured lawns and fenced-in backyards. There were five floor plans, each only a slight variation of the others. The show homes were decorated in different motifs and part of the sales pitch was a free three-hour session with an interior decorator, whom Shea had proclaimed incompetent. Shea had a degree in interior design but she hadn't worked since Casey was born. Of course, that didn't stop her from giving her unsolicited opinion whenever the opportunity arose.

Not that Kitty didn't agree 100 percent with Shea's views on Dolphin Isles. Ever since the subdivision opened two years ago it had put a big kink in Kitty's business. Dolphin Isles's rock-bottom prices made it hard to convince buyers that a slightly more expensive older home with character and more land might be a better deal for them.

The main street to the subdivision was crowded. Saturdays were a big day at Dolphin Isles. Kitty slowed her car as she drove by one of the model homes. Through the open door she could see the head salesman, Walt Walters, shaking hands with a young couple.

Walt liked to sell hard and never took no for an answer. He was in his early forties and divorced, and last year after the Jeff debacle, Kitty had made the mistake of going out with him. Walt was medium height, medium weight, medium good looks. But it wasn't Walt's blandness that had turned Kitty off. Apparently, Walt didn't take no for an answer in his personal life either. Their one and only date had ended in a wrestling match on her living room sofa. But even if Walt hadn't turned out to be a schmuck, Kitty didn't think she'd ever be able to get past the name thing.

Who gave their kid the same first name as their last? Kitty wondered if Walt hadn't changed his name on purpose. The tagline on his business card read: *There's only one name you need to remember in real estate, Walt Walters*. Bleh. It made her *Help me help you* spiel sound almost poetic.

She turned right on Flipper Court to head back to the main street, when she slammed her foot on the brakes. Shea's white Lincoln Navigator sat parked in front of one of the model homes. Kitty put her car in reverse and went back a few feet to get a look at the plates. It was Shea's car, all right. The custom FSU license tag was unique.

What was Shea doing here? She and Moose couldn't be looking for a new home. *Not* in Dolphin Isles. They already owned a custom-built, three-thousand-square-foot home a block from the beach. And if they were interested in a real estate investment, they would have come to her first.

A horn blasted, jolting Kitty from her thoughts. A man in a green sedan waved his hand impatiently, urging her on. Kitty put on her "oops sorry" face and placed her car in drive.

Maybe Moose had a client here. Or maybe they were checking out the market. It would be just like Moose to keep on top of local real estate prices.

She turned back onto the main road.

There were probably a dozen reasons for Shea and Moose to stop by Dolphin Isles. Kitty would ask Shea about it the next time she saw her.

13

||||||

Kitty went home and showered, then drove into the office and picked up her mail. She tried to fiddle with her Quicken account but she couldn't keep her mind on the figures. Normally, Becky manned the office on Saturdays while Kitty dealt with clients, but it had been weeks since she'd shown a house. Just a few years ago, she'd been so busy that even Pilar had complained they never saw her on the weekends. But all that had changed when Dolphin Isles came to town. Now, those same potential clients were being shown homes with names like the Calypso and the Blue Lagoon while Walt Walters smiled on. Kitty tried not to seethe whenever she thought of it.

Maybe some sustenance would help her concentrate.

She went next door to Hank's Bakery (it was purely coincidental that her real estate office was in the same strip mall as a doughnut shop), picked up a couple of Danish, made a pot of coffee, and tried to work on the accounts, but it was no use. She couldn't think.

What she needed was something to take her mind off her dismal business and her pending eight-thousand-dollar air conditioner bill, not to mention the unforgettable Thong Incident. But there was only one thing that would help her do that. She needed to go shopping.

She pulled out her checkbook, looked at the balance, then tossed it back in her purse in disgust. Thank God for credit cards. She would hit the outlet mall in Destin, buy a new outfit—something that made her feel skinny—then treat herself to a nice dinner in an air-conditioned restaurant.

With business so slow there was no sense in keeping the office open. And besides, what was the use of having an answering machine if you didn't use it? She grabbed her purse and was about to shut off the lights when Moose came strolling in. He wore tan slacks with a light blue shirt and a red tie with little yellow polka dots. Moose still weighed the same as when he played college football, 250 pounds of rock-hard muscle. Plus maybe an extra five pounds of belly fat. He'd never been a slob, but lately, he was dressing like he'd just stepped off the cover of *GQ*. Kitty would bet that Shea had recently gotten him a subscription.

"You look great. What's up?" she asked, giving him a hug.

"I was driving by on my way to visit a client and saw your car. Got a minute?" he asked in his Moose the Financial Advisor voice. It was different from his Moose the Friend voice. Kitty had learned a long time ago to distinguish between the two. Since she wasn't in the mood to talk money, the situation called for diversionary tactics.

"Hungry?" she asked, offering him a Danish. "I have two of them."

He gazed longingly at the sugar fest dangling under his nose. "No, thanks. I'm supposed to be on a diet."

Moose with willpower was not a good sign.

"Me too." She laid the uneaten Danish next to her computer and steeled herself for the lecture to come.

"I guess you know what I'm here to talk about."

"That bad, huh?" Kitty kicked off her shoes and hopped onto the edge of her desk. Her feet dangled a few inches from the ground. She stared down at her bare toes. Before she went to the mall she'd get a pedicure. It just so happened her office was next door to a nail salon (also a lucky coincidence). Maybe she'd get her toes painted fire-engine red.

"I know I sound like a broken record, Kit, but it's only because I care about you. Your credit cards are almost maxed out and now you're about to wipe out your emergency savings on this new air conditioner."

"Not having an air conditioner *is* an emergency."

"The house belongs to your mother. Why isn't she paying for it?"

"You know how scatterbrained my mom is. I don't want to bother her with those little details."

"Eight thousand bucks isn't a little detail."

"I can't live without an air conditioner, Moose. Besides, you'd be proud of the way I've been economizing. I've decided to fire my personal trainer and I've even given up on pedicures." She lifted her foot in the air and wiggled her unpolished toes to prove the point. Of course, she still planned to get her feet done. But she was serious about firing her trainer.

"You make me feel like an ogre."

Kitty picked up the discarded Danish. "Go on," she urged. "It'll make you feel better."

Moose snatched the Danish from her hand and plunked it back down on her desk. "I'm serious. First you move into your grandmother's old house and start sinking money into it. Money that you don't have, by the way. All the while, I've yet to see a For Sale sign in the front yard of that old house."

"You say 'old' like it's a four-letter word. It's a great house with lots of character and—"

"I'm not disputing that it's a great house. Hell, if it was in better shape and a couple hundred thousand dollars cheaper, I'd recommend you buy it yourself. If you had the money, that is."

"So you think I should buy a house?"

"You're probably the only Realtor I know who doesn't own her own house."

"Don't remind me," she said gloomily. "I should have bought that three bedroom on Emerald Drive five years ago when I had the chance. I guess I just figured there would be plenty of time." Or that she'd get married and be buying her first house with her husband.

"There's still reasonably priced real estate on the market. You could always buy a place at—"

"If you say Dolphin Isles I'm going to scream."

He shrugged. "Those houses make great rental properties. In a few years when the market turns around, you're looking at a nice little profit there."

"Please don't tell me you're buying a house in Dolphin Isles."

Moose made a face. "You know I'd never buy a house from anyone but you."

"I know. I mean, I'd never have thought that in a million years." She laughed in relief. "It's just that I saw Shea's car parked there this morning, and I have to admit, I was curious."

He frowned. "You saw the Navigator at Dolphin Isles? Had to be someone else. Shea was taking the girls to dance class. At least, I think that's what she said."

"You must be right." Although, she'd been positive it was Shea's car at the time.

Moose picked the Danish off the desk and studied it. "Is this cheese?" he asked.

Kitty nodded.

"I guess just one can't hurt." He finished it off in three bites. "Anyway, I didn't come by to harp on you." His tone turned sympathetic. He was morphing into his Moose the Friend voice. Kitty didn't know if this was good or bad.

"Promise me you won't get mad," he began.

"What are we, back in fifth grade?"

"Your mom called me last night."

"*My mom called you?*"

"At first, I thought she was looking for financial advice, so I thought, okay, this is cool, and then out of the blue, she goes in for the kill."

"The kill?" Kitty asked weakly.

Moose's gaze searched her desk for the other Danish.

"Spill it like a man," she said.

"She asked me if the For Sale sign was prominently displayed in front of the house."

"And you said?"

"Well, it's kind of tricky. She sort of snuck it in between

asking about T-bills and CDs and I guess I was distracted and sort of told her there wasn't a sign up."

"Moose!"

He cringed. "You have to tell her sometime, Kit. Or better yet, just put the damn sign up and get it over with. You can't afford the house, and that's that."

She nodded numbly.

"I'm sorry," he said, looking sheepish.

"It's not your fault."

He gave her a hug. "I'll call you soon." He eyed her open checkbook on the desktop. "Be a good girl."

Kitty flopped into her chair and stared at the empty computer screen in front of her.

This was a disaster. Up until now she'd managed to keep her mother in the dark, but she was only delaying the inevitable. If her mother was determined to sell the house, then she'd find a way to make it happen. Kitty wouldn't even put it past her to contact another Realtor. The only bright spot in this whole mess was that the market was painfully slow right now, and despite the run-down condition of the house, the size and location put it in a price range way above Whispering Bay's average buyer.

Which meant it would probably sell to someone who would turn it into a vacation home. Some . . . out-of-towner who'd only come down on the occasional weekend and leave it neglected the rest of the year. Or worse, rent it out to an endless string of vacationers.

No.

Gram's house deserved someone who loved it. Someone who'd cherish it and take care of it and not remodel it according to the latest trends a la *Coastal Living* magazine.

She fished around the bottom of her purse until she found Ted Ferguson's business card.

He picked up on the second ring. "Ferguson here."

"Mr. Ferguson—I mean, Ted? It's Kitty Burke. I've decided that . . . yes, I'd *love* to be your broker."

14

The three of them sat in beach chairs overlooking the blue green water of the Gulf of Mexico, Pilar on Kitty's right, Shea on her left. Nick and Moose were pretending to supervise the kids while they built sand castles. But what they were really doing was building the castles themselves. It was fun to occasionally glance over to see who was one-upping who with the tallest turret or the deepest moat.

It had been a typical Fourth of July. After a long afternoon at Pilar's house filled with various relatives, screaming kids, an eclectic mixture of Cuban food, hot dogs, chips, and one too many beers, they had packed their gear and hightailed it to the beach in time to secure their regular spot to see the fireworks. It was the first time today the three of them had had a chance to really talk.

The sun had almost finished setting, but Shea still wore her Oakley sunglasses. She also wore a hat and had just finished slathering on her umpteenth application of sunblock. "He said you *sucked* in bed?" Shea said, sputtering out a spray of soda.

Pilar whacked her on the back, dislodging the Oakleys off Shea's nose.

"Not exactly," Kitty said, calmly taking a sip of her Diet Coke as if her best friend hadn't almost choked to death. "He said I didn't rock his world. There's a difference, you know."

Nick glanced over at them. "Who sucks in bed?"

"Kitty," Pilar said, not bothering to glance at her husband.

"Oh. Well, I happen to know for a fact, that's not true." He winked at Kitty, making her giggle.

Moose laughed too, but Shea silenced him with a look that immediately sent him back to digging sand.

"Seriously," Nick said, his green eyes meeting Kitty's gaze, "the guy sounds like a real asshole."

"Watch your language," Pilar admonished, nodding toward the kids.

Nick shrugged and went back to his castle building. He was a runner, lean and agile, with cropped blond hair and a brooding sensitivity that befitted a man who taught high school English. Their son, Anthony, had Pilar's dark hair and flashing brown eyes, but even at three, it was obvious he had inherited Nick's personality. Kitty glanced away. She wished Pilar hadn't told them about Nick's vasectomy. It was weird knowing the two of them were in some sort of sexual power struggle.

"How's Anthony doing with potty training?" Shea asked.

"So far, no accidents with number one. But number two is a different story altogether."

Shea nodded. "I've read boys can be stubborn about that."

"The only good part about the whole thing is that Anthony

refuses to go to the ladies' room if Nick is there to take him into the men's."

Shea sighed in envy. "Lucky you. Although, I guess I can't complain. After all, I did have Elise. Maybe you should hire her to help you." Elise was a toilet-training expert Shea had brought in from Pensacola. She had stayed with them twice now. Her expertise had only been needed a few days with Casey. But Briana had proven more stubborn and Elise had had to stay over a week the second time.

"My mother would go crazy if I paid someone fifty bucks an hour to potty train Anthony. But enough of that. I want to hear the rest of Kitty's story. Did you really demand he give you back your thong?" Pilar asked her.

"Oh yeah. I stormed over to Pappas and Son Plumbing, called him a liar and a pervert, then demanded he return my thong. All in all, a stellar performance."

"Is that when he turned into a prick and said you were lousy in bed?" Pilar asked.

"He never said I was lousy in bed!" Where were they getting that from?

"Whatever," Pilar said. "Just cut to the nitty-gritty."

"I asked him to hand over the thong, and he looked at me like I was Glenn Close from *Fatal Attraction*. Can you blame him? I mean, it was a pretty far-fetched idea," Kitty said, raising a brow at Shea.

"It was the most logical conclusion based on the facts I was given," Shea said. "Besides, I only suggested he took it. *You're* the one who ran with it and had to confront him. We told you it was a bad idea."

Pilar cradled her chin in the palm of her hand. "Let's get

this straight. Your thong was folded on top of the dryer along with the towels?"

"I guess somehow it ended up on the floor in the bathroom. He must have scooped it up with the wet towels."

Shea readjusted her sunglasses. "Why would he do your laundry?"

"Maybe because he didn't want me to wake up and not have a clean towel?" Kitty suggested.

"Did he use fabric softener?" Shea asked.

"He doesn't wake you up to say good-bye and he doesn't leave a note, but he leaves you an apple and does your laundry," Pilar mused. "What does it mean?"

"I can't get Moose to pick up his dirty socks, let alone do a load of laundry. It just doesn't sound right. Maybe this Steve character is a metrosexual."

Pilar's eyes lit up. "Or a stray."

Kitty shook her head. "A what?"

"A straight guy who acts gay," Pilar said. "I just made that up."

"No you didn't," Shea said. "I think I've heard Dr. Phil use it before."

"Then Dr. Phil stole it from me."

"How could he have stolen it from you if you just made it up?"

"He's not a metrosexual *or* a stray," Kitty said. "He drives a pickup truck and he's worked construction. Besides, if he was one of those he would have made eggs Benedict or something fancy instead of just swiping an apple from my refrigerator."

"Maybe he's a healthy stray," Pilar said.

"I still say there's something not right here. The guy has no sense of humor," Shea concluded. "Good thing you discovered that before things went any further."

"Definitely." Pilar nodded.

"We were never going to go any 'further,'" Kitty said. "It was a one-night stand." How many times did she have to tell them that? And so what if Steve hadn't found the whole thing funny? If the situation had been reversed, she seriously doubted she would have been laughing. In fact, she would have probably thrown something at him.

"The whole one-night stand thing just isn't you," Pilar said. "Thank God you'll never have to face him again."

"Yeah," Shea agreed.

Kitty bit her bottom lip to keep from responding. Shea and Pilar were right about one thing. She definitely wasn't cut out for quickie liaisons. She didn't have enough energy left to tell them Joey knew she had slept with Steve. She'd save that nugget for another day.

She took a deep breath, filling her lungs with the warm salty air. There was something about beach air that made you feel alive. So what if it was hot and humid and there were bugs the size of small carnivores? There was no other place on earth she'd rather live than Whispering Bay.

"I can't wait till tomorrow," Kitty said, digging her toes into the damp sand.

"What happens tomorrow?" Shea asked.

"She gets her new air conditioner, dummy," Pilar replied. "You know, Kit, you can spend the night at our house. I swear, Nick jacks the thermostat down to seventy degrees at night."

"Thanks, but people have survived for thousands of years without air-conditioning. One more night isn't going to kill me. Actually, I have something else I'm pretty excited about."

Shea and Pilar glanced at one another. "Oh?" Shea asked.

"I'm meeting with Ted Ferguson at nine a.m. sharp. I've decided to rep him."

Pilar furrowed her brow. "So you're going to go through with it?"

"Why not? As far as I can see, it's a win-win situation. If I make a big enough commission off this, I could probably afford to buy Gram's house."

"I'm not crazy about the condo thing," Pilar said. "But it would be cool if you could buy the house."

"Are you sure that's smart?" Shea asked. "Moose says you need to start investing in a retirement fund."

"I wish you and Moose would stop worrying about me."

"You're a single woman living on an income that can fluctuate as easily as the wind blows. We just want to make sure you're financially secure."

"It's just that we love you, so naturally, we worry about you," said Pilar.

"I love you guys too. But you can stop worrying. I can take care of myself." She glanced back at Nick, who was patiently helping Anthony line up a row of seashells around the moat to their castle. A part of Kitty didn't want to know, but a bigger part of her couldn't help asking. "Are you and Nick still fighting?"

Pilar took a sip of her bottled water. Her gaze followed Kitty's line of vision. "Nick and I don't fight. We politely disagree. Did you see him this afternoon huddled up with my mother in the kitchen? I swear if he told her about the vasectomy, I'll strangle him."

"I'm sorry," Kitty said. "I just don't understand—"

"Look, can we not talk about this?" Before Kitty could respond, Pilar added, "I think we should cancel Bunco this week."

"Cancel Bunco?" Kitty and Shea both said in unison.

"It's a holiday week. I already know for a fact Mimi won't be in town. And Lorraine called me yesterday to say she can't make it either. That means we have to get two subs. And you know how I hate playing with subs. We can't talk about anything good."

The Babes played according to Vegas rules. What happens at Bunco, stays at Bunco. Subs couldn't be counted on to keep the gossip to themselves. And gossiping while rolling the dice was half the fun.

"Playing with subs is better than not playing at all," Kitty said.

"Besides, according to the rules, all three of us have to agree to cancel. And since it's at my house, I say we play," Shea said.

Pilar sighed. "Okay, but if another Babe cancels, then we skip Bunco this week. Deal?"

"Deal," Kitty said. She'd just have to make sure no one else canceled. She'd personally call the rest of the Babes to make sure they were coming.

"Uh-oh." Shea propped her sunglasses on top of her hat. "Prick alert. Over by the orange umbrella."

The Pappas clan was setting up camp down the beach, Joey and Christy and their two kids leading the way. Gus was there, and Joey's sister, Angela, who lived in Pensacola, along with her husband and their brood. It was like a scene right out of *My Big Fat Greek Wedding*. It was too much to hope that Steve would be missing in action from this little patriotic family gathering, because there he was, being all helpful hauling a cooler, dressed in nothing but navy blue swim trunks and flip-flops.

So much for her theory on never having to see him again.

Pilar whistled low under her breath. "And I thought he looked good *with* his clothes on."

Kitty slumped in her chair and slid her baseball cap over her face. But it was too late. Gus spotted them and shouted out a hello. There was no choice but to wave back. Steve ignored her and set down the cooler.

Four days, a yoga class, and a five-mile run this morning hadn't been enough to make her forget what a fool she'd made of herself in the Pappas and Son Plumbing parking lot. When she'd fallen on her ass, she must have also twisted something in her neck, because there was a now-seemingly permanent crick there that wouldn't go away. Maybe it was one of those psychosomatic things. Maybe the only thing that would cure it would be to apologize to him. It certainly couldn't hurt.

"Do you think I should go over and say hi?" Kitty asked. "After all, Gus is my plumber."

"Not on your life," Shea said. "If you go over there, then you're going to have to say something to the prick. And whatever you say won't be right, and then you'll feel like shit."

"I already feel like shit."

"So you want to feel even worse?"

"Shea's right," Pilar said. "It will only be awkward. Best to just leave it alone." Pilar eyed her up and down and smiled wickedly. "Of course, with the way you look in that bikini, he'll probably forgive you anything."

Kitty had to admit, the black Maya Bay halter top bikini had been an inspired buy. She usually preferred a suit with a little more ass coverage, but Shea had convinced her to try it on when the two of them had gone bathing suit shopping last spring, Shea's rationale being that they should go for it since they probably only had a few more good bikini years left anyway. Shea had on a red-and-white-polka-dot number that Moose had initially demanded she return, his rationale being that no wife of his was going to expose so much of her assets in public. Shea had argued that if that's the way he felt, then he should never have bought her those assets in the first place. Naturally, Shea won out.

"This *is* a great suit, isn't it?" Kitty said.

"I told you, didn't I?" Shea replied smugly. She eyed Pilar's faded blue tankini of last season. "If you'd come shopping with us like you'd promised, then I would've guided you into a similar purchase. But, no, you had to work on a Saturday."

Pilar sniffed. "Some of us have a life beyond shopping."

A beach ball flew through the air, landing at their feet. Kitty looked up to see Joey Pappas heading their way.

She snatched the ball and threw it to Joey before he could reach them.

"Thanks!" Joey yelled.

"Nice save," Pilar muttered.

Kitty watched as Joey headed back to the shoreline where the Pappas kids and Steve were awaiting the return of the ball. After a few agonizing seconds, Steve glanced her way. He nodded curtly in their direction, then turned to talk to his cousin.

Kitty's stomach slid to the sand. Four nights ago, the man had had his face between her thighs. Now, Steve could barely stand to look at her. She stood and wrapped a sheer black bathing suit skirt around her hips.

Pilar grabbed her by the arm and pulled her back in her chair. "Where are you going?"

"I'm going to apologize to him."

Shea shook her head. "We already told you that's a bad idea."

"It doesn't feel right to leave it like this between us. I need to feng shui my life."

"One yoga class and you're talking crazy," Shea said. "Seeing Steve today was a fluke. After a few weeks he'll be gone and you'll never have to think of him again."

"What are you going to do? Walk over there and apologize to him in front of his whole family? 'Sorry for calling you a pervert, dude. And by the way, thanks for giving me an orgasm and doing my laundry,' " Pilar mocked. "Didn't you learn your lesson the other day? We told you not to confront him on the thong thing, and look how that turned out."

"You're right," Kitty said, feeling both let down and relieved. He would probably throw sand in her face, anyway. Not that she would blame him.

"I'm always right," Pilar said. "Remember that."

"Except Jeff. You were wrong about him," Shea reminded her.

"Will you stop with that already!" Pilar said.

Nick walked up with a sleeping Anthony in his arms, interrupting whatever comeback Shea was planning on. "I think he's done," Nick whispered to avoid waking his son.

"Poor baby," Pilar said. "He's going to hate missing the fireworks."

Moose came up behind Nick, a look of exasperation on his face. "Casey is eating sand and vomiting it back up."

Shea grabbed a bottle of water and rinsed out Casey's mouth.

"Maybe we should call it a day," Pilar said wistfully.

"Let's go back to our house," Nick suggested. "If we leave now, we'll get home in time to see the fireworks from the deck."

"Good idea," Shea said. She folded her beach chair in two and began rolling towels and stuffing them in her bag.

Kitty glanced at Gus and his family. They were a boisterous group, laughing and having a good time. She should go back to Pilar's house and watch the fireworks and try to forget all about Steve. Shea was right. Seeing him today was a fluke.

But was *this* how she wanted him to remember her? A semi-lunatic who not only didn't rock his world but was too wimpy-assed to go over and speak to him?

She couldn't leave.

Not without apologizing.

She just *couldn't*.

If it turned out badly as Shea and Pilar predicted, she wouldn't tell them. On the other hand, if Steve accepted her apology and they ended things on a friendly note, she would love to tell Shea and Pilar, "I told you so."

"I'm tired," Kitty said, avoiding Pilar's gaze. "And I have to get up early for my meeting with Ted. I think I'll just go back to my house."

"The offer to spend the night is still open," Pilar said, sounding disappointed.

"Thanks. I'll keep that in mind."

15

||||||

Kitty waited till Pilar's car was long gone from the parking lot before she backtracked to the beach. "Hi," she said, glancing around the Pappas clan.

Everyone smiled and said hello.

Except Steve. He didn't look too friendly, but so far, no sand in her face. She would take that as a good sign.

"Join us," Gus said, pulling up an empty beach chair.

"No, thanks. I don't want to interrupt." *Might as well bite the bullet.* "Do you have a minute?" she asked Steve.

Gus and Joey exchanged a look.

Steve gave her a look that said she had him by the short and curlies. He couldn't very well turn her down without raising some brows.

They walked down the shoreline in silence. Families huddled around coolers while kids with flashlights chased crabs along the sand. A group of teenagers was playing volleyball in the dark. It took a while to find a spot where they wouldn't be overheard.

"Is this okay?" she asked, indicating the empty stretch of beach. "I promise, I didn't lure you here to go wacko on you again."

He put his hands on his hips and stared at her.

"That was a joke," Kitty said.

He nodded impatiently.

"Look, I'm sorry about the other day."

"No problem."

"I've never done that before. Stalked some guy down and accused him of stealing my underwear."

"So, I'm the lucky one?"

"I guess so," she said, hoping he would smile or do something to indicate he had forgiven her. "And thanks for doing my laundry." She figured she'd leave out the orgasm part.

"Like I said, no problem." He glanced down the beach. They were too far away to see clearly, but he was staring in the direction where his family was drinking sodas and making jokes. Kitty didn't blame him for wanting to rejoin them.

She had thought apologizing would make her feel better. But Pilar and Shea were right. She felt worse than ever.

"I really didn't think you'd taken my thong. I mean, not at first. Not that that's an excuse or anything."

His eyes locked onto hers. "Then what made you think it?"

It was hypocritical to expect him to accept her apology and not tell him the truth. "I did the very thing I accused you of with Joey. I told my friends about the other night. And . . . well, they sort of suggested it."

He didn't seem angry. Or even surprised. "Which one thought it first? The hot one or the sharp one?"

She couldn't help but smile at his description of Shea and Pilar. "What am I, then?"

"I thought you were the nice one."

Ouch. That wiped the smile from her face.

"I *am* nice," she said, fumbling to find the right words. "The truth is . . . you hurt my feelings."

He hurt her feelings? Where had that come from?

She tried to lighten the conversation. "You ruthlessly had sex with me twice and you never rang me again."

His mouth twisted. It was the definitely the beginning of a smile. "What is it with you and movies? Didn't Hugh Grant say that to Andie MacDowell in *Four Weddings and a Funeral?*"

"Wow. You're not supposed to know that. It's a chick flick."

"Yeah, but it had Andie MacDowell in it and there was nothing better on cable last night." He glanced down the beach again.

She wasn't ready to go back. Not yet.

"The truth is you were right. It was all too fast for me. I've never had sex with someone I've only known a few hours. Maybe that messed with my head. I don't know. I just know that while it might not have been great for you, it was the best sex I've had in a long time. Probably the best I've ever had, actually."

He inhaled sharply.

"You were right about something else too. I *was* pissed. I've *never* woken up alone before. But instead of admitting I was mad, it was easier to think you were a shit who steals women's underwear."

Even in the dark, she could tell there was a subtle change in his expression. "You had every right to be mad. I shouldn't have left without saying good-bye."

For the first time in days, it felt like the crick in her neck was gone. "So actually, it's all your fault."

This time he did smile.

But she wanted to make him laugh.

And then she realized what she really wanted was a repeat of the other night. "Can I ask a question? Did you leave your snake on purpose?"

"What do you think?"

"I think you left it on purpose so you'd have an excuse to come back." She held her breath while she waited for his answer.

"You have good instincts. Maybe you should listen to your gut more, instead of your friends."

"They were only trying to help."

He shrugged.

"Can I ask another question? Were you ever going to call me?"

His gaze never wavered. "I hadn't planned on it."

"Oh." So much for her instincts.

"Then you showed up the next day in those black heels, and I changed my mind."

"Because you liked my shoes?"

"Because I liked what was in them."

"And then I called you a pervert."

"And a liar. Don't forget that." He wasn't glancing down the beach every few seconds anymore. Instead, he was focusing on her legs, and her hips, and all the rest of her. Like Pilar said, she did look pretty damn good in this bikini.

Listen to your gut, Kit.

She reached up, put her arms around his neck, and kissed him. She didn't know who was more startled—him or her.

Steve shook his head. "I must be crazy." Before she could respond, he kissed her back. Only his kiss involved major tongue action. It was slow and deep and sent shivers down her spine.

"Oh my God," she whispered. "I think I just saw stars."

"It's fireworks."

"I saw those too."

He placed his fingers beneath her chin and tilted her head up. The night sky burst with green- and blue-colored lights. "It's the Fourth of July fireworks."

"Oh."

He kissed her again. This time, she heard music.

Steve jerked his cell phone from the pocket of his swim trunks. "This better be good."

Kitty caught her breath as Steve listened wordlessly to the caller on the other end.

"Thanks, Dave. I owe you." He flipped his phone shut. "I have to go."

"Now?"

"Sorry. It can't be helped."

He turned and began walking down the beach without further explanation. She had to take extra-long strides to keep up with him. He didn't try to hold her hand, or offer up a reason for his sudden turnaround. He was more distant now than when she had first approached him to apologize. Fireworks exploded in the air above them. She felt ready to explode too.

Damn it. He couldn't get her all worked up and not follow through. Wasn't there some kind of rule against that? If not, then there should be.

She grabbed his elbow, forcing him to halt in his tracks. "What's so important that you have to take off right now?"

"It's family problems. Nothing you want to hear about."

"Try me."

He hesitated. "That was my old business partner on the phone. My stepson ran away from home. I promised my ex I'd help if I could."

"Terrie? Is that what the call was about the other day?"

"Yeah."

"Poor baby. He must be scared out of his mind."

"That 'poor baby' is eighteen. And it's his mother who's scared out of her mind."

"Oh."

"I haven't seen the kid in almost a year. But I've always liked him."

"Of course you have to help."

Steve flipped his cell open and glanced at the screen. "It's almost nine fifteen." He looked up at the sky. The fireworks show was now in full swing. "I hate to ask, but I need a favor. Nathan's on a Greyhound headed to Mobile. There's a layover in Panama City. If I leave now, I just might make it, but I didn't drive here. We all came in Angela's van. Do you think you could give me a lift to Gus's so I can get my truck? I don't want to drag the kids away from the fireworks."

"What time is the bus scheduled to arrive?"

"Ten."

"You'll never make it to Panama City in forty-five minutes if we have to drive back to Gus's. Not tonight. The streets are too crowded. Why don't I drive you to the bus station myself?"

"I don't think that's a good idea."

"I don't mind. Besides, I owe you after the other day."

"You don't owe me anything. We had a good time for one night. Let's forget about the rest."

He wanted to forget about that incredible kiss down the beach?

It was as if she had never apologized. Never dug up the courage to humiliate herself by telling him he had hurt her feelings. It was as if the last thirty minutes between them had never happened.

He might not have thrown sand in her face, but she still felt like something sharp landed in her eye. She blinked hard. "If you want to get to Panama City in time to catch your stepson, then you're going to have to book it. It's either me or the van. I guarantee you'll never make it if you have to go all the way back to Gus's to get your truck."

His jaw tightened. "You're right. I'll take the ride. Thanks," he added.

"No problem," she said, purposely repeating that annoying expression of his. But if he caught the sarcasm in her voice, he didn't show it.

16

Kitty drove east on Highway 98. Steve sat next to her in the passenger seat staring gloomily ahead. "Can't you drive any faster?" he asked. It was the first thing he'd said since they'd left the beach.

"I could, but if I get stopped by the cops, you're paying for my ticket."

He eyed her bikini top. "There's not a cop alive that would give you a ticket. Not while you're wearing that."

She still had the sheer skirt tied around her hips, but her face felt sweaty and her hair was tucked up in a baseball cap. Her five-dollar flip-flops came from the bargain rack at Wal-Mart. She didn't exactly feel like vamp material.

"Wow. What century are you living in? Ever heard of female cops? First off, I'm not planning on getting stopped by anyone. The last thing I need is the points on my insurance. And secondly, if we do get stopped, ticket or no ticket, it's going to waste too much time, so going faster isn't going to help."

"You're right," he said. "Sorry."

"And they say women are backseat drivers," Kitty muttered. She focused her attention back on the road, but every once in a while she couldn't help but sneak a peek at him.

Steve had put on a faded green Ron Jon Surf Shop T-shirt over his swim trunks. His dark hair was wind tousled and his mouth seemed permanently set in a grim line—which only served to emphasize that gorgeous bottom lip of his. There was no denying the man was a hunka-hunka burnin' love. But he was also moody and way too mysterious for her taste. And Shea was right. The guy had *no* sense of humor.

So what if he was a great lay? Like he said, they'd had fun for one night. Kaput. The End. Thank God they'd been interrupted back at the beach before things had gotten out of hand.

If by some chance she ran into him again, she could hold her head high. She'd done the right thing and apologized, and now she was doing him a favor. As far as she was concerned, the score was even.

Still, they were both adults. There was no reason to ignore one another. She would take the high road and initiate some small talk. "You like to surf?"

"Why do you say that?"

"Your T-shirt," she said.

He glanced down at his shirt like he'd forgotten what he was wearing. "I surfed some when I was a kid."

"I could never stay on the board long enough to make it any fun," Kitty said. "And the waves on the Gulf aren't much to brag about, not like on the Atlantic side." She eyed his Ron

Jon T-shirt again. It was worn thin like it had been washed a lot. "Is that where you're from? Cocoa Beach?"

"I grew up there, but I've spent the last ten years in Tampa."

"Where you worked construction?"

"Yeah."

Kitty sighed. Screw him. She had tried, but the strong silent type was definitely overrated.

An increase in traffic forced her to slow down. She concentrated on making the green light ahead of them, then turned right on Henderson where bumper-to-bumper traffic caused them to come to a standstill. The downtown area was crowded with pedestrians huddled by the marina watching the overhead fireworks show. The tiny Greyhound bus station was overrun with cars. Kitty parked in the nearest empty spot, which conveniently happened to be in the parking lot of a McDonald's restaurant. She normally didn't do fast food—not if she could help it—but it had seemed like another lifetime since that last hot dog at Pilar's. And besides, it was hard to pass up a McDonald's. She wondered if Ted's plan to bring Whispering Bay into the twenty-first century included the Golden Arches. Maybe on the way back they could grab something to eat. Not an entire meal. But definitely some French fries. Just this once.

She opened her car door. "If we run, we might catch him."

Steve reached across the seat and slammed her door shut. "Good idea. But I'll be the one doing the running. You stay here."

"In the car?"

"Yeah, and put the top back up."

"No way. It'll get too hot."

"You're not going out there dressed like that."

"This is a beach town. Everyone walks around in their bathing suit."

"I'm going to a bus station, not a snow-cone stand, and not everyone looks like you do in a bathing suit. Look, the kid's probably already here. I don't have time to argue, and I sure as hell don't have time to fight off any horny drunks."

A tiny part of her found his Neanderthal attitude flattering. A very tiny part. "Maybe some women get turned on by that caveman routine, but I'm not one of them."

He stared her down.

Kitty fidgeted in her seat.

He was really good at this staring-down thing. "Fine," she snapped. "Hand over your shirt, because I'm *not* staying in the car."

He yanked off his T-shirt, revealing a lot of naked male chest. A lot of muscled naked male chest.

Kitty let out an exaggerated sigh. It was a little disconcerting to be upstaged by your date. Not that a trip to the Greyhound bus station could be considered a date. "*I'm* going to be the one fighting off the horny drunks," she said.

Steve raised a brow.

"Off you," she clarified. "You know, maybe you should think about doing an 'Officer Bob' in your spare time. Till you find a job, that is." She batted her eyelashes at him.

"Right."

"I'm serious," she said, pulling his shirt over her head. "When I first saw you, I thought you were the exotic dancer." She almost said stripper. Pilar would be pleased by her political correctness.

He looked so incredulous, she almost laughed. "I mean, it did seem a little lame, what with the Village People construction outfit and all, but it was working for me."

He grinned. But it wasn't a nice grin. "Oh yeah, I remember now. That's when I caught you peeing in the bushes."

"Shit. I was hoping you hadn't seen that."

"Honey, I've seen a lot more of you than that."

There were a number of provocative responses she could make here, but there was no sense going in that direction. He'd made it pretty clear back at the beach he wasn't interested in a repeat of the other night.

"Just so you know," Kitty said, "I don't normally do that. Pee outdoors, that is. I mean, I *never* do that."

"That's not exactly true, is it?" When she didn't say anything, he added, "Hey, if it makes you feel better, I've done it myself a few times when I've had to. Everyone has."

Somehow, she couldn't imagine Nick whipping it out and taking a leak outdoors. Except if he was stuck in the woods or something, but Nick wasn't a camping kind of guy. Now Moose, definitely. She could see Moose relieving himself in the bushes if necessary.

Steve shrugged. "I thought it was funny."

"Do you mind if we change the subject?" She checked out her reflection in the car window. "Okay. I think this is worse. Now it looks like all I have on is a T-shirt with nothing underneath."

"It's still better than before." He took her hand. "C'mon, we're wasting time."

A few suspicious-looking characters lingered near the entrance to the terminal. A man wearing army fatigues staggered dangerously close to her. He was barefoot and had a blond beard that reached the middle of his chest. "Hey," he slurred. "Show me your tits." His breath was 100 proof.

Kitty reeled back from the stench. "Mister, I think spring break was over for you a long time ago."

"I still wanna see your tits," he said.

"Fuck off," Steve said to the bum. He tightened his hold on her hand and threw her an "I told you so" look.

Someone had a heavy hand when it came to the thermostat on the air-conditioning. Compared to the muggy humidity outside, the tiny bus terminal was near freezing. Kitty shivered. Steve drew her into his chest and rubbed his hands up and down her arms. It was an automatic thing for him, Kitty supposed, because he wasn't really paying attention to her. His gaze was focused on the faces of the travelers sitting on the blue iron benches.

A tall, thin kid with scraggly dark hair sauntered out of the men's room. "That's Nathan," Steve said, pulling her forward.

Nathan looked surprised to see them. Kitty thought she detected some relief too. "What are you doing here?" he demanded.

"Your mom's worried about you," Steve said.

"So she sent *you* to find me?"

"Not exactly. But I told her if I ran into you I'd say hi."

"Right. You just happen to be at the Panama City bus terminal at the exact same time as me? What kind of an asshole do you take me for?"

Maybe this was a good time for her jump in. "Hi there," she said extending her hand.

Nathan seemed to notice her for the first time.

Steve placed his hand on the small of her back. "Sorry, I

should have introduced you right off. This is Kitty Burke. She was nice enough to drive me here."

Kitty put out her hand. "Pleased to meet you, Nathan."

Nathan readjusted his backpack and shook her hand. Kitty noticed his cheeks went a little pink. He turned to Steve. "I'm on my way to Mobile and you can't stop me. I'm eighteen, so I'm an adult now."

"Good for you," Steve said.

"If you're not planning to stop me, what are you doing here?"

"What's in Mobile, Nathan?" Kitty asked, trying to deflect the hostility in the air. "School?"

"I'm going to work construction. I have a buddy out there with a job lined up for me."

"That sounds productive," Kitty said lamely.

"Nathan has a full scholarship to the University of Florida," Steve said to Kitty. "But according to his mother, he's planning to piss it away."

"You don't have a college degree and you did just fine," Nathan shot back.

"That's because I was a lucky asshole."

"I don't blame you for not wanting to go to U of F. I'm an FSU grad myself," Kitty said.

Nathan looked at her as if she were crazy. "U of F is a great school. It's pretty hard to get in, you know."

"So you got a place lined up to stay?" Steve asked.

"I plan to crash with a friend for a couple of days. Then I'm gonna get my own place."

"Yeah?"

"Sure. I got money in the bank. Four thousand bucks to be exact. It's what I made working with you over the summers."

"Maybe you should check your account again."

Nathan's nostrils flared. "What the fuck is that supposed to mean?"

"It means your mom wiped out your account."

"Bullshit! She can't do that."

"It's a joint account, isn't it?"

Nathan let his backpack drop to the ground. He paced the small terminal floor, making an agitated circle. After a few loops, he stopped. "I don't believe you."

Steve shrugged. "Try your ATM card."

"*Fuck.*" Nathan looked like he was on the verge of tears.

A middle-aged black man in a Greyhound uniform stepped inside the terminal. "Bus leaves in five minutes," he called out.

A young woman sitting on a bench next to the window picked up her purse and exited to the waiting bus, prompting the rest of the half dozen or so travelers to follow her lead.

"It's up to you," Steve said. "No one's stopping you. But I suggest if you want your money back, you talk to your mom. In person."

The driver looked at Nathan and nodded his head toward the bus. "You coming?"

"I guess not," Nathan said, shooting Steve a poisonous look. Steve didn't look too happy either.

Kitty didn't think she'd like to be in either of their shoes right now.

17

| | | | | |

The ride home was torturous. Nathan sat in the back, sulking, while Steve sat next to her staring out the car window. The silence probably shouldn't have bothered her so much, except that she was still hungry (they never did hit that McDonald's) and it was more than a thirty-minute drive home. The tension reminded her a little of one of Shea and Pilar's spats. She didn't want to try talking Steve out of his mood. She'd already tried that on the ride over. Maybe she'd have better luck with Nathan. Only she had no idea what an eighteen-year-old boy was into. And there was only one sport Kitty knew well enough to talk intelligently about.

"Do you like baseball?" Kitty asked Nathan, not expecting more than a grumble.

He met her gaze in the rearview mirror. "Sure," he said dubiously.

From that moment on it was cake.

Nathan knew more about baseball than anyone Kitty had ever met. He threw out stats like he was reading them off a computer.

"You're pretty impressive," Kitty said.

"So are you." He flushed at the quick compliment he'd tossed her. "I mean, I've never met a girl who knew the difference between a curveball and a knuckleball."

Kitty smiled. She liked being called a girl. "My mother's second husband was a big fan. We used to hit all the spring training games we could."

Nathan edged forward in his seat. "What happened to your real dad?"

"My parents divorced when I was ten. That's when my mom and I moved from Dallas to Whispering Bay. My dad's a pilot for American Airlines and a very cool guy."

"My dad can be cool too, sometimes. He's remarried and has two kids with his new wife. What about you? Is your dad remarried?"

"Nope. I think he likes being this middle-aged Hugh Hefner kind of guy. A girl in every port, that sort of thing."

"What about your mom? She still married to the baseball guy?"

"No. It didn't work out between them. She's on her third marriage, but she's happy."

They were almost on the outskirts of Whispering Bay. Kitty slowed the car down to thirty-five miles an hour.

"So, this is where you live?" Nathan asked.

"Yep. Whispering Bay, Florida. Population five thousand four hundred, give or take one or two."

"And you moved here from Dallas? Man, you must have wanted to hang yourself."

Kitty laughed. It reminded her of Josh Bailey's statement about being dead without a car. She'd forgotten how dramatic everything was for teenagers. "At first I was a little . . . shell-shocked, maybe. But we moved in with my grandmother, who was a very cool lady *and* knew a lot about baseball. I was lucky. On the first day of school I hooked up with these two girls who are still my best friends to this day."

"What do people do in this town? Like for fun?"

Kitty thought about it a minute. "There's the beach, of course. It's spectacular."

Nathan nodded, clearly not impressed.

"And, well, there's great shopping not far away in Destin."

"Is there a gym?" Nathan asked. "If I have to hang around for a few days, I want to work out."

Kitty frowned. "Not here in town. I belong to a club in Destin, but it's kind of a drive."

"That's okay, I guess I could just shoot some hoops or something."

Maybe now wasn't the time to tell Nathan there weren't any public basketball courts in Whispering Bay either.

"Okay, so here's the really important question," she said. "Yankees or Mets?"

Nathan snorted. "Yankees, duh."

Kitty shook her head and sighed. "Sorry, I'm a Mets girl all the way."

Nathan gleefully slapped the back of her seat. "Man! I knew you were too good to be true."

"Did you play in high school?"

Nathan's face fell. "I was a pitcher, but I screwed up my wrist last summer."

"Working construction?" She glanced at Steve, who was

now looking on with mute interest. She remembered Nathan saying something about working for Steve. She hoped the answer to her question would be no. But it might explain why the kid seemed a little antagonistic toward him.

"Nah, I screwed it up by slamming my fist into a wall."

Kitty frowned.

"Steve's right," he said grudgingly, "I can be an asshole sometimes."

This spurred Steve to finally say, "Everyone does something stupid at least once in their life. Some of us more than once."

Was he referring to his multiple marriages? Or something else?

She rolled her convertible into Gus's driveway and killed the headlights. It was after eleven and tomorrow was a workday. A faint light shone from somewhere in the back of the house, but otherwise the place was dark.

"Are you sure it's all right if I stay here?" Nathan asked.

"I've already okayed it with Gus," said Steve.

Nathan slung his backpack over his shoulder. "Will I see you around?" he asked Kitty.

"Probably not, so good luck."

He looked disappointed, which made her feel oddly pleased. She had liked him too.

Steve waited till Nathan was in the house. "Thanks. I owe you one."

"We don't owe each other anything. Remember? Besides, Nathan's great." She paused a moment. "Of course, it could never work out between us," she said. "The Yankees/Mets thing, you know."

She wasn't sure, but she thought she saw him fight back a smile. "He's a great kid."

"How long have you and his mom been divorced?"

"Officially, only a couple of months, but we separated over a year ago."

"Things just didn't work out?"

"Something like that."

"She must be pretty desperate." At the blank expression on Steve's face, Kitty clarified, "To take the four thousand dollars from his bank account."

"I have no idea if she did that or not."

"You *lied* to him?"

He shrugged. "Terrie wanted a chance to talk some sense into Nathan. And for once, I agree with her. Thinking that his bank account's been wiped out seemed like the best bet to keep him here so she can do that."

"Terrie's coming here? To Whispering Bay?"

"I don't keep tabs on my ex, but yeah, from what I could gather, she's on her way."

She waited for him to say more. Or to make his exit. But he just sat there.

"Well, it was fun," Kitty said. "If I don't see you again, have a good life."

"You kicking me out of your car?"

"Something like that."

"You have a bad habit of throwing my words back in my face," he said.

"Then maybe you should expand your vocabulary a little more."

He grinned.

Damn. One smile and she was melting into the leather upholstery. She needed to remember how he was capable of doing a one-eighty without so much as blinking.

"Are you busy tomorrow night?"

Kitty froze. Was he asking her out? She'd always hated that opener. It gave all the power to the other person. She could say yes, she was busy, and he could shrug and go on to option two, or she could say no, and it still didn't mean he was going to ask her out. Maybe she should play it cool and—

"No, I'm not busy."

"Maybe you'll let me cook you dinner."

"You want to cook for me?"

"I'm pretty good at it." He was pretty good at a lot of things. She tried not to think about those things as she mentally debated her answer.

Her heart began to thump. This was definitely a date. Wasn't it?

"You really went out on a limb tonight. It's just my way of saying thanks."

Okay, so it wasn't a date. No need to suddenly feel so disappointed. "I thought we agreed we didn't owe each other anything," she said.

"That's only when you think you owe me something. When I think I owe you something, then it's different."

She had to laugh at his messed-up, testosterone-laden logic. "What year did you graduate high school?"

"Huh?"

"It seems strange that we've . . . you know, and I really don't know anything about you."

"Right." He hesitated a moment before saying, "Technically, I never graduated high school."

"Oh."

"I dropped out when I was sixteen, but I got my GED a

few years later. If you want to know how old I am, just ask me outright."

"Okay, how old are you?"

"Thirty-seven."

"And you work construction, but you're in between jobs, and you've been married three times," she said, trying not to wince. "Any kids?"

"One stepson. And you've met him. Anything else?"

"No, I guess that's it."

"All right then." He went to open the car door.

"Wait. I still have your shirt."

She started to pull off the shirt but he shook his head. "Keep it. It looks better on you than it does on me. So, we on for dinner or not?"

It was a simple enough question. Why was she having trouble giving him a simple answer? It was just dinner, for God's sake. To thank her for giving him a ride tonight.

Did she want to have dinner with Steve Pappas?

She thought about it a minute. Besides being moody and unpredictable, given the way he'd lied to Nathan, he was maybe even a little ruthless too. But tonight had also proven he could be a decent guy. If he didn't care about Nathan, he wouldn't have gone to all the trouble to keep him from making a potential life mistake. Gus obviously thought the world of Steve. And Gus was an excellent judge of character. On the other hand, Steve was family, so maybe Gus couldn't really be impartial where his nephew was concerned.

But then, there was Shea and Pilar's opinion of Steve. She knew what they would say. They would tell her to say no thanks, and drive off. There was no future with an out-of-work non-plumber with three failed marriages who was only going to be in town temporarily. Plus, there was the fact that he really wasn't interested in her. After all, she didn't rock his world, did she? So it *really* couldn't be a date. She should just say no . . .

"Sure," she said. "I'd like to do dinner."

"Good. I'll come by around seven."

She watched as he made his way into the house.

There. That was easy enough. She would have a simple dinner with a casual acquaintance (forget the fact they'd had sex—it was already out of her mind) and they would part on friendly terms. No animosity. No beating herself up over the Thong Incident. And the best part was that there would be no reason to avoid Gus for the rest of her life.

It was the perfect way to end her relationship with Steve Pappas. Her chi was well on its way to getting back in sync.

18

||||||

She should have spent the night on the couch at her office. Or at Viola's. Or at Pilar's. She should have spent the night anywhere but in her unair-conditioned sweatbox of a house.

She woke up at two in the morning and took a cold shower. At three, she got up and ate half a carton of Rocky Road ice cream. Low fat, that is. At three thirty, she fell asleep but was awakened an hour later by an erotic dream involving a faceless man, the pink feather boa, and what was left of the ice cream. Okay, so maybe it was Steve's face, but that was only normal considering he was the last man she'd had sex with.

What was wrong with her? She'd read about this phenomenon in women. How they hit their sexual prime in their thirties. Kitty had just never felt so thoroughly primed before.

It must be the heat.

She slid out of bed and put on a pair of gym shorts and

Steve's Ron Jon T-shirt. Maybe a run would get her mind off her raging hormones.

An hour and a half later, she tossed the sweaty T-shirt into her laundry basket. Wearing a T-shirt that reminded her of Steve hadn't been the smartest move if she wanted to get her mind off sex.

She showered again and dressed for her nine a.m. meeting with Ted Ferguson and Earl Handy. In between eating the ice cream, her erotic dream, and her five-mile run, she had finished going over the material Ted had sent over. His vision for the condos was exactly as promised. The renderings showed a series of two- and three-story buildings spaced far enough apart to allow for lots of landscaping. She couldn't help but feel a twinge of pride. Of all the Realtors he could have chosen, Ted picked her. Professionally speaking, this could be the most important day of her life.

She decided on a sleeveless light pink cotton shift, her pearls, and her brown sling-back mules. It was too hot to blow-dry and straighten her hair, so she let it air-dry and twisted the brown curls into a knot at the nape of her neck. She looked like a head shot for a box of Betty Crocker yellow cake mix. But it would work. There would be no four-inch stilettos at this meeting. At the last second, she added her grandmother's flamingo pin to the outfit—for good luck—then slipped her house key under the doormat so the air-conditioning people could get in. If all went according to plan, she'd be coming home to a cold house. Maybe tonight she could actually get some sleep.

She made a quick stop at the Bistro by the Beach. It was an eclectic little place that served just about any kind of coffee you could dream of. They also made the best spinach-and-onion bagels on the Gulf coast. Not coincidentally, the Bistro was owned by one of the Babes, Frida Hampton. She and her husband, Ed, lived above the cafe in a two-bedroom apartment. Ed was a struggling artist who moonlighted as a barista for the breakfast and lunch crowd. With the exception of the napkins, no paper products were used. The place was environmentally correct in just about every way.

Frida and Ed were busy serving up coffee behind the counter. Kitty ordered her usual grande cafe latte, no foam, one Splenda, along with an assortment of muffins. Not that she was planning on eating any of them herself. It was strictly for the clients. In business, little touches like that made a big difference.

A light sheen of perspiration shone above the V of Frida's white T-shirt. She expertly plucked up a muffin with a set of tongs and stuffed it into a paper bag. The motion revealed the small dice tattoo on the inside of Frida's wrist. Frida's tattoo had become a sort of joke among the Babes. They had all vowed to get a similar one for the twentieth anniversary of the group. Not that anyone took it seriously. Kitty had never considered herself a tattoo kind of girl, and the fad did seem to be going out of vogue, but still, some days she wondered if it wouldn't be fun to get a tiny one. Somewhere that no one would ever see it, of course.

She spotted Viola and a few of the Gray Flamingos sitting at a table overlooking the water. They looked like they were up to something serious. Probably another petition in the works. Kitty caught Viola's attention and waved to her. Viola smiled and waved back.

"Business looks good," Kitty said, gazing around the crowded tables.

"It's a holiday week," Frida said, filling the bag to the brim. "There's an art show in Destin this weekend. I'm hoping we get some business from that too."

Kitty hesitated a moment before saying anything. But what could it hurt to hint good times were just around the corner? She leaned into the counter and lowered her voice. "Keep this to yourself for now, but I happen to know there's a big deal in the works that could bring some of that tourist money right here to Whispering Bay."

Frida placed the palm of her hand on her lower back and stretched out her upper body. "What kind of deal?" she asked, her blue eyes narrowed.

"I can't say just yet—not until it's firmed up—but it's the kind of deal that could turn this place into a gold mine."

Frida made a face. "I'll believe that when I see it."

The tiny remark stung, but Kitty did her best to hide her irritation. It was only natural Frida would be skeptical. She would be too if someone had thrown out that bit of cryptic information at her.

"You're on for Bunco at Shea's this week. Right?" Kitty asked.

"Wouldn't miss it," Frida said.

Kitty smiled. Pilar's prediction of gloom and doom about this week's Bunco wasn't going to come true. So far, everyone Kitty had talked to was going to be there. Except Mimi and Lorraine, but they had already known that.

She was on her way out the door when she ran into Pilar's parents. Isabel grabbed her and pulled her into a hug. Kitty had to quickly maneuver the muffin bag and her latte to keep from dropping them. Isabel always smelled like Estée Lauder mingled with a slight hint of talcum powder and hair spray. There was no better smell in the world than Isabel Diaz.

"Why haven't you come to see me?" Isabel demanded in her slightly accented English. "It's been weeks since you've been in my house."

"Only two," Kitty said. "And we just saw each other at Pilar's yesterday."

"Two weeks is too long," Isabel replied. "And yesterday doesn't count. We were surrounded by people and we didn't get a chance to visit properly."

"Maybe if you make me some *ropa vieja*, I'll come visit," Kitty teased.

Isabel's dark eyes brightened. "If that's what it will take, then I'll make some right away."

Antonio shook his head. "She'll make it for you, but not for me." He kissed Kitty on the cheek. His thick mustache tickled her skin. "Isabel is right, two weeks is too long."

"I don't make *ropa vieja* for you because you're on a diet," Isabel said to her husband. "Antonio has been diagnosed with borderline diabetes," she told Kitty. "What can I do? He wants to eat rice three times a day."

Kitty wagged her finger at him. "What are you doing here at the Bistro, then?" She jokingly looked him over for hidden pastries.

Antonio held up a cup of coffee and an English muffin. "Low fat, low sugar, and low taste," he grumbled.

She eyed his red polo shirt and plaid Bermuda shorts. "Aren't you going into work?" Pilar's father was one of the two dentists practicing in Whispering Bay.

"We're on vacation," he said.

"That's wonderful," Kitty said, "where are you going?"

"To visit the children, of course," Isabel said. "We'll start with Silvia in Tampa, then make our way down to Antonio Jr. in Miami, then come back up and visit Carlos in Orlando."

Antonio let out a deep sigh. "Why couldn't they all stay here, like Pilar?"

"Who's going to take care of your patients?" Kitty asked.

"Dr. Walker is going to work in any emergencies," he said, referring to Whispering Bay's other dentist. "The rest will have to wait till I get back."

It was Isabel's turn to sigh. "Antonio needs to retire, but he refuses until he finds someone to buy the practice."

"No one wants to move here," Antonio said, shrugging. "I guess Whispering Bay isn't the most exciting place for a young dentist fresh out of school."

Kitty took a sip of her cafe latte to try to hide the smug smile she felt coming on. She'd already told Shea and Pilar the good news, and she'd just hinted prettily heavily to Frida. Isabel and Antonio were like her second parents. There couldn't be any harm in telling them too. "All that could change pretty soon. I've heard a rumor that some new development is coming to town. And that means more business and more people. All of which means Whispering Bay is going to look pretty attractive to outsiders."

"What kind of development?" Isabel asked.

"Condos," Kitty whispered.

Isabel and Antonio looked stunned. "In Whispering Bay?"

"I know what you're thinking. But I've heard the developer has a high respect for the environment. It's all going to be very tastefully done. Nothing gaudy or overcrowded."

Isabel smiled weakly. "If you approve, then I approve."

Antonio didn't say anything.

Kitty fought back a wave of disappointment. She was going to have to get used to reactions like this. It was natural people would be skeptical. She had been too, at first. But once they realized development was the way of the future, they would come around. And when they started seeing the financial windfalls the condos would bring, they would cheer Ted on.

"So, do I have a date with some *ropa vieja*?" Kitty asked, walking them out the door.

"I'll call you when we get back to town," Isabel said, giving her a kiss good-bye. Her face clouded over like she had just remembered something unpleasant. "Has Pilar said anything to you about this new craziness of hers?"

Kitty stilled. "Craziness?"

"This vasectomy business!" Isabel whispered fiercely.

Antonio suddenly found the fern to his right fascinating.

Kitty swallowed hard. "Did Nick tell you about that?"

"No!" Isabel said, batting her hand through the air. "Silvia told me."

Kitty nodded, relieved it hadn't been Nick. Not that she really thought Nick would have told his mother-in-law something so personal.

Kitty hated getting in the middle of Pilar and her family, and she had a definite opinion when it came to Nick's vasectomy, but she knew Pilar wouldn't appreciate her sharing it with Isabel. "Pilar told me a little bit about it. But you know, I try not to give advice about things I don't know much about."

"Pah! What do you mean? You're Pilar's closest friend."

"But I'm not married and I don't have children. I also don't have a high-powered job like Pilar's. I'm really not sure how I would feel if I were her."

"Your job is important," Isabel protested. "You're the most successful Realtor in the city. And you drive that fancy car! Don't tell me you're not doing well," she added proudly.

Considering all the debt Kitty was in, "well" seemed like a relative term. But she would die before she let Isabel discover how stupid she was with money. "I just think there are some things that should be kept private. Even among good friends."

"You're like a sister to Pilar. If she was going to jump off a bridge, wouldn't you stop her?"

Put that way, what Isabel said made sense. Pilar was making a big mistake. Kitty was sure of it. How many times in her life had Pilar come through for her? Too many to count.

"I can't make any promises about the outcome, but I'll talk to her again," Kitty said.

Isabel looked relieved. "*Gracias, hija.*" She gave Kitty another kiss, then she and Antonio drove off, leaving Kitty only ten minutes before her meeting with Ted Ferguson.

No way could be she be late a second time.

She jumped in the car and drove like a madwoman all the way to the office. Luckily, Becky was already there and had coffee brewing.

"Cutting it a little close, aren't you?" Becky asked.

Kitty opened the brown paper bag and arranged the muffins on a silver serving platter next to the coffeepot. "I ran into Pilar's parents at the Bistro and got sidetracked." She eyed Becky's white cotton slacks and red-and-white-striped shirt. Becky was twenty-four, reed thin, and could make sackcloth and ashes look like they belonged in *Vogue*. "You look very nautical this morning. How was Disney World? Oh, and I almost forgot, how did your showing go last week?"

Becky's eyes lit up like a pinball machine. "Disney was awesome. Brad and I had a great time. And . . . I think I might have made a sale."

"That's great! Why didn't you call me?" Kitty rejuvenated her cafe latte with a hit of the fresh brew. She was about to take a sip when Becky let out a large shriek. Kitty had to clutch her mug to keep from dropping it.

"I can't keep it in a second longer!" Becky cried, flinging her left hand in the air. A huge diamond nestled in a platinum setting made Kitty's eyes bulge.

"Holy shit!" She grabbed Becky's waggling fingers to get a better look. "This must have cost a fortune."

"Brad's been saving ever since we graduated from college. He didn't want to finance it and start our married lives with that kind of debt hanging over our heads."

Kitty placed her mug on the table and gave Becky a big hug.

"It was *sooo* romantic," Becky said, wiping away a tear. "We were standing at the bottom of Cinderella's Castle, along with about a kazillion other people waiting for Tinker Bell to fly down, when Brad just dropped to his knee and proposed. You should have seen the looks on people's faces! Everyone around us was cheering and clapping and snapping pictures." Becky sighed. "I'll never forget it. Not as long as I live."

Kitty smiled. "Sounds like Brad's a pretty romantic guy."

"Isn't he?" Becky's dreamy expression sombered. "You know, Kitty, I really appreciate everything you've done—encouraging me to get my Realtor's license, showing me the ropes and all. I know this isn't the right time, but I just hate keeping this inside. I've accepted a job with Walt Walters at Dolphin Isles."

"What?" Kitty asked, laughing weakly. "I thought you just said—"

"I'm sorry, but sales have been so slow lately, and Dolphin Isles is starting construction on a new subdivision. I took a client over there to look and she absolutely fell in love with the place. I know we have to split the commission with them, but there wasn't anything else in town she liked.

"Brad and I signed a contract with Walt to build our own home. You should see the model. It's gorgeous! Three bedrooms, two baths, a fenced-in yard. Plus it comes with sod and a sprinkler system. Brad and I could never have afforded anything like that right now, but Walt gave us such a good deal. And afterward, he offered me a job right on the spot. Brad said I'd be a total dope not to take it."

Kitty stuffed a blueberry muffin in her mouth. She didn't care if was low fat or not. "Of course," she mumbled. "When are you going to start working for him?"

"Well, that's the thing," Becky said, making a face. "He wants me to start right away and I'd be stupid to drag my feet on this. You know?"

Kitty nodded. The rent on her office was eight hundred a month, plus utilities and upkeep. She'd hoped once Becky started selling, they could split the costs. She was a selfish bitch for thinking of money at a time like this. But there it was.

"I hate to leave you," Becky continued, "but I don't want to lose this opportunity. I hope you understand."

Kitty nodded again, willing her hand not reach out for another muffin.

"I've already cleaned out my desk," Becky said.

"You have?"

"Like I said, Walt wants me to start right away. It's the post–Fourth of July sale. The theme this month is 'Sail away to the home of your dreams.'"

"Cute." Of course, it wasn't cute at all, but she didn't have the heart to let the wind out of Becky's sails.

"I got this new outfit to match. Isn't it adorable?"

Before Kitty could come up with a response, the door opened and Ted Ferguson walked in. He wore navy blue slacks and a blue and orange golf shirt with a University of Florida logo on the pocket. His hair was wet and slicked back like he had just gotten out of the shower. Kitty could smell his Polo cologne from across the room.

He looked Kitty over with a critical eye like she was a prize hen at the county fair. "You look perfect," he proclaimed. "Let's go."

Kitty blinked. "Where to?"

"Mexico Beach. I have a meeting set up with Earl Handy at his house."

"But I thought we were going to meet here."

"Don't worry," Becky said, pushing her toward the door. "I'll lock up and drop the keys off later."

Kitty glanced at the silver platter by the coffee machine. There was enough starch there to supply a Chinese laundry for a month. "Wouldn't you like something to eat before we go?"

Ted looked over the assortment of muffins. "Who in their right mind eats carbs in the morning?"

Becky shook her head. "Not me."

Ted threw her a sharp glance. "Smart girl."

19

| | | | |

A man who appeared to be in his early fifties ushered them into the living room of the one-story, cream-colored stucco home. He had red hair and reminded Kitty a little of Ron Howard before he went bald. Or Howdy Doody, depending on which way he turned his head. He introduced himself as Vince Palermo, Earl Handy's son-in-law. Earl's only daughter, Lenore, had divorced and remarried a few years ago, but this was Kitty's first time meeting Vince.

Kitty sat in a comfortable leather chair opposite Ted, careful to keep her knees together and her hands in her lap. Something about being in Earl Handy's house made her feel ten years old again.

Vince and Ted talked college football while she glanced around the terra-cotta-tiled room. Pictures of sailboats and ocean views covered the walls. A black-and-white photograph of Earl as a young man holding up a marlin hung above the fireplace mantel. The smile on his face was triumphant, like he was king of the world.

It was a nice room. Simple, but inviting.

After about ten minutes, Earl shuffled in slowly, using a cane. Kitty hadn't seen him since her grandmother's funeral last year. He seemed frailer than she remembered.

"What's this all about?" Earl asked gruffly.

"Hey, Dad." Vince tried to assist Earl into his chair.

Earl batted Vince away with his cane. "Thought I only had a daughter. Didn't know I'd sired a son at my age."

Somehow, Vince's complexion turned ruddier. "Would you like something to drink?"

"Got any milk of magnesia?" Earl asked.

Kitty pressed her lips together to keep from laughing.

Earl narrowed his eyes at her. "Who are you?"

She stood and nervously smoothed down the wrinkles in her linen shift. She hadn't anticipated Earl not remembering her. "I'm Kitty Burke, Mr. Handy. Amanda Hanahan's granddaughter?"

Earl looked taken aback. "Tall, scrawny kid, with the freckles?" He eyed her over. "Maybe not so scrawny anymore. I saw you at your grandmother's funeral. You cried, but you didn't make a spectacle of yourself." He motioned for her to sit back in her chair. "What are you doing here?"

"I'm Mr. Ferguson's Realtor."

Ted rose from his chair and held out his hand. "We've talked on the phone, sir."

"I talk to a lot of people on the phone."

"This is about the land deal, Dad—um, Earl," Vince said. "Remember?"

"I'm not senile. At least not yet." He ignored Ted's outstretched hand and pointed to his University of Florida golf shirt. "What year did you graduate?"

"Actually, I never attended the University of Florida," Ted began, "but I'm a great supporter—"

"Never mind," Earl growled. "Let's get on with it. I need to crap and that might take me a couple of hours. Don't want to waste the whole morning."

Vince cleared his throat. "Ted is interested in buying beach-front property in Whispering Bay. He's made an offer—a good one—and I don't think we should turn it down."

"Of course you don't think we should turn it down. So what's in it for me?" he asked, looking at Kitty.

She glanced at Ted, hoping for some direction. He urged her on with an apprehensive smile. "Well, money, of course," she said, sounding like a dope.

"I got plenty of that," Earl snapped. "What do I need more for?"

Vince started to speak, but Earl cut him off. "You're going to get it all eventually. What's a few more years? See that snapshot?" he asked her, pointing to the picture of him holding the marlin. "Caught that guppy right out of the ocean."

She smiled. "I remember the fishing tournament you used to host every year."

"Those were good days." Earl turned to his son-in-law. "Maybe I'll donate the land to one of them conservation groups. The ones that want to save the frogs. Or the turtles. Can't remember which. They're always sniffing around here."

Kitty held her breath. It wasn't such a bad idea. Of course, that wouldn't get her the big commission she was counting on.

Vince's face turned scarlet. "I thought you were against that," he sputtered.

Earl grinned. For a second, Kitty could have sworn she was looking at the same Earl from the marlin photo. Give or take fifty years. She actually felt a little sorry for Vince. "My grandfather bought that land back at the turn of the century. Last century, that is. It's been in my family for over a hundred years. I sure as hell ain't giving it away to no frog lovers."

She wasn't sure who looked more relieved, Vince or Ted. "I think you'll find the price I'm offering extremely generous, sir," Ted piped in.

"Like I said, I already have enough money," Earl said, dismissing Ted. Earl frowned at Kitty like he was expecting something from her, only he wasn't getting it and was disappointed. It reminded her of the way her high school chemistry teacher used to look at her when she hadn't finished her homework. She hated feeling unprepared. She knew Earl's reputation for being a straight shooter. What did he want from her?

"I know what you're thinking, Mr. Handy. I hate the idea of condos on the beach too." The words came out before she could stop them.

Oh God. Why had she said that?

"I'm not planning to build high-rises, sir," Ted said, throwing Kitty a split-second glare. "If you've looked over the paperwork, you'll know what I have planned is a string of tasteful, low-rise condos. Very modest and completely in tune with the native landscape—"

"Yeah, yeah . . . I've heard it all before." Once again, Earl looked to Kitty. "If you hate the idea of condos on the beach so much, what are you doing here?"

Good question. What *was* she doing here? Ted didn't need her for this deal—unless he was looking for someone to screw it up. Kitty had looked over the papers he had sent over. His partner, Teresa, had done an excellent job. Why wasn't she here instead?

"Give me one reason I should sell to this fella," Earl continued, pointing a gnarled finger at Ted.

Earl wanted a reason to sell? Okay, she'd give him one.

"I'm not going to lie to you, Mr. Handy. I'm here for only one thing. The commission. I really, really need the money."

That silenced the room.

Earl's cheeks began to twitch.

Kitty looked up at the marlin photo again. "And . . . even if *you* don't need the money, wouldn't it be nice to have some sort of control over what happens to the land your grandfather left you? Or would you rather leave the control to someone else?" she asked, glancing at Vince, who was glaring at her like his head was about to explode.

Earl gave a satisfied laugh. "You're smarter than the rest, Ferguson. I'll give you that. Tell you what. I'll look over the paperwork. If I like the figures, I'll sign. Don't come back here unless you bring *her*"—he pointed his cane at Kitty—"with you." He stood, balancing his weight with the cane. Vince ran to his side. "That's what I got the stick for," he said, waving Vince away. "Now, you'll have to excuse me, but I've got a date with the john." He nodded to Kitty and shuffled out of the room.

Vince and Ted shook hands and slapped each other on the back.

They were almost to the car when Ted grabbed her by the waist and swung her around. "I knew you were the perfect broker for this deal. You were fantastic! Who would have thought the old guy would fall for the greed angle?"

The greed angle?

It happened so fast Kitty didn't have time to respond. His mouth came down on hers in a hard kiss. It couldn't have lasted more than a couple of seconds. Three, tops? She wasn't sure. She only knew the whole thing left her dumbstruck.

"Sorry. I shouldn't have done that." He shook his head and smiled ruefully. "I just get so pumped up whenever I score big like this. How about we celebrate with dinner tonight?" His right hand lingered on her hip, his fingers pressing through the thin cotton shift.

"How about we wait until the contract is signed?" she eked out, stepping out of Ted's reach.

"Negative thoughts produce negative results." Before she could respond to that cheesy line, Ted added, "Earl's old-school. His word is as good as gold. I guarantee you he's going to like the numbers."

She forced a smile. "I'm old-school too. Until the contract's signed, anything can happen. I say we celebrate when the ink's dry."

"Whatever you say," he responded pleasantly.

She folded herself into the passenger seat of his black Lexus, careful to keep her skirt tucked under her thighs. She was aware of Ted's gaze on her legs. Or maybe she was just imagining it because of the kiss. Kitty only knew she was very glad she hadn't worn the stilettos again.

Ted talked all the way back to Whispering Bay, throwing out figures and projected construction start dates. All very proper stuff. Kitty began to relax. He hadn't made a pass at her. Not really. It was like he said, he'd just gotten carried away with the moment.

She made an occasional comment, but she mostly stared out the window. She thought of Frida and the Bistro and Antonio's dental practice and her own real estate business and Walt Walters and Dolphin Isles. Walt would prosper from Ted's condo business. The entire town would.

Ted had offered Earl a good deal. Kitty should feel proud of her role. Instead, she felt like ripping into a Snickers bar.

It was probably the change thing. Pilar was always telling her things couldn't stay the same forever; progress was inevitable. In a few years, Whispering Bay would look different. But that was good. Right? Life wasn't stagnant. If you wanted to stay ahead, you had to get with the program.

20

▐ ▐ ▐ ▐ ▐ ▐

By the time she got back to her office it was mid-afternoon. It was strange not having Becky around. Kitty wished her the best, but she would miss her. Maybe she should advertise for another assistant. Or maybe she would go it alone. She'd have to think about that. At any rate, Ted was right about one thing. Today's business deal called for a celebration.

She should call Shea and Pilar and maybe they could get the rest of the Babes to—no, that wouldn't work. Steve was coming over to make dinner and she hadn't told anyone about it. Not that anyone needed to know she was having dinner with Steve. Certainly not Shea and Pilar. They would only make a big deal about the whole thing and tonight wasn't a big deal. It wasn't even a date. She would tell them if it was a date. But it wasn't.

Speaking of which . . . what was she going to wear? Nothing fancy, of course. She would wear something casual. Something for the hot weather. Like her white cotton shorts. They made her legs look tan, which drew attention away from her butt (sort of like an optical illusion), which was a plus. Of course, today they were installing her new air conditioner, so it would be blessedly cool in the house and she could pretty much wear anything. Still, the shorts were a good idea and—

The phone rang, jolting her from the fashion show going on in her head. Finally! A client. She answered in her most professional voice. "Kitty Burke."

"I can't believe I got you on the first ring," said her mother.

Oh no. "Hi, Mom. What's up?"

"Nothing much. I'm bored out of my mind. Larry and I were supposed to drive up to Savannah to visit friends and play golf, but Pam hasn't gone into labor yet, so the whole family is basically being held prisoner by her uterus."

"Mom, I doubt Pam's uterus is that manipulative."

"You know what I mean. When I suggested that her doctor induce labor, she gave me that look she loves to give me. Like I'm some child who needs things explained slowly. She told me she doesn't believe in messing with Mother Nature. That when it was time for her baby to be born, then it would be."

"I think that's reasonable," Kitty said carefully.

"I don't understand the younger generation. What good is modern medicine if you don't take advantage of it? She's probably not going to get an epidural either, so we'll have to listen to her do that *awful* deep breathing thing for hours on end."

"You're *not* going to be in the labor room with her, are you?"

"She wants the whole family there. Like some sort of backwoods cabin birth."

The thought of her mother and Larry's ex in the same room made Kitty pause. Pam was a much better woman than she was.

"Anyway, I was looking through some catalogues for a new bathing suit cover—I did tell you that Larry and I are going on a cruise in a few weeks? And I found one that was just so adorable—"

"Mom? A client just walked through the door," Kitty lied, not feeling one bit guilty. Her mother could go on for hours. "I have to let you go."

"Oh well, of course. Business comes first. By the way, hon, I spoke with that lovely Moose the other day . . ." Her mother paused. "And he told me the strangest thing about the house."

Kitty had been expecting this. "There's a good reason I haven't listed the house yet—"

"I know what you're going to say, darling. You think we should renovate first. But Larry's come up with a much better plan. He thinks instead of sinking money into the house, we should tear it down. It's the land that's really valuable, you know."

Tear the house down? Was Larry on drugs? Not that Kitty would blame him. He did, after all, have to live with her mother.

"Katherine, are you still there?"

"I'm here." But she wasn't paying attention to whatever her mother was saying anymore. Her mind was too busy spinning in circles. Should she go ahead and tell her mother she planned to buy the house? The deal with Earl wasn't set in stone. He'd only promised to look over the numbers. But on the other hand, Ted seemed pretty confident. She couldn't let her mother tear down the house. She couldn't even let her *think* of it. "Actually, Mom, I was going to tell you that I have some fantastic news. I have a buyer."

There was a moment of stunned silence. "Why didn't you say so up front? That's wonderful! How much are they offering?"

"Well . . . we're still negotiating and I don't want to jinx it. But it's going to be good," she added, hoping that would placate her mother.

"Have you checked them out? It's a legitimate offer, right?"

"Oh yeah, it's very legitimate."

"You don't know how relieved I am. Even though the house is paid off, there're still the taxes and the insurance, and I hate to ask Larry for money for that sort of thing. When do you think you'll know for certain?"

"A few days. A week at the most."

Surely by then they'd have settled the deal with Earl. Then she could count on her commission and make a formal offer. In the meantime, it was best not to tell her mother the offer was coming from her. She'd just ask too many questions Kitty couldn't answer right now.

And if for some reason something went wrong with the deal . . .

No. Ted was right. Negative thoughts produced negative results. She would just have to make sure that no matter what, the deal with Earl came through.

21

Kitty drove home to find the Vance Air-Conditioning van blocking her driveway. Definitely not a good sign. They should have been done by now. She parked on the side of the street and went in to investigate. The sauna at her gym was more comfortable than the inside of her house.

"I was about to call you," said the technician, seeing the expression on her face. He was young and had a shaved head. Kitty remembered his name was Matt.

"Is there a problem?"

"The wiring in this place is ancient. Jake is a whiz with these old houses, but he's working in Panama City today. I think we're going to have to call it quits and start again tomorrow."

"Tomorrow?"

"Sorry, I know that sucks," he said, digging a handkerchief out of his back pocket to mop the sweat off his head, "but there's not much we can do until Jake gets out here."

The heat must be frying her brain, because all she could do was nod in a daze. She didn't have the energy left to ask how much extra this delay would cost. Matt and the other technician picked up their tools, loaded up their van, and rode off into the sweltering sunset.

Kitty pulled off her shoes and collapsed on the living room sofa. Last night had been miserable and it looked like she was in store for a repeat. She could always spend the night with Shea or Pilar, or even with Viola. But then, there was her not-a-date with Steve. He was supposed to be here at seven to cook for her. That was now out of the question. They'd melt away. She'd just have to call him to cancel. *No reason to be disappointed,* she told herself.

She had just pulled out the phone book to look up Gus's number when the doorbell rang.

It was Steve. He wore a pair of khaki shorts and a navy blue polo with deck shoes. There was a small cooler and a plastic grocery bag in his hands.

"You're early," she said.

"You don't sound happy to see me." He walked into her living room and grimaced. "It's hotter than a four-balled tomcat in here."

"That's one way of putting it." Kitty led him into the kitchen. "It's not that I don't want you to cook me dinner," she said, "but as you can see, my air is still out."

"We could go somewhere else," he offered.

"Like where?"

He thought for a moment. "Let me make a call." He pulled his cell phone from the back pocket of his shorts and slipped out the kitchen door to the backyard.

Apparently he needed privacy for the call. Which was fine

with Kitty because she used the opportunity to play detective and peek in the grocery sack. Inside were two bottles of wine, a bottle of olive oil, a head of garlic, an onion, a small can of tomato paste, and a bag of orzo. She was about to scout out the ingredients in the cooler when he stepped back into the kitchen. "I'm impressed," she said. "Whatever you're planning to make looks good."

"You can be impressed later. I have a place we can use, but we need to be there in an hour and it'll take almost that long to get there."

"Where are we going?" she asked.

"It's a surprise."

She wasn't sure if she liked the sound of that.

"Give me five minutes," Kitty said, dashing to the shower.

She washed and shampooed her hair in record time. Every few seconds she glanced at the bathroom door, half expecting Steve to pop in like the other night. Which was silly. It was called a one-night stand because you only did it one night. She dried off and threw on a white tank top and jean skirt (on second thought, the white shorts *did* make her butt look too big). Her hair was wet, but there was no time to do anything about it.

They got in his truck and turned east on Highway 98. She readjusted the vent to let the cold air-conditioning blast on her face and drew her fingers through her hair, feeling the fat sausage curls shape and grow. The truck had been a nice surprise. Not that it was a junker. The outside was in excellent condition. But she hadn't expected the inside to be so clean and comfortable. Either he was a neat freak or he paid someone to detail it all the way down to Q-Tip precision, in which case, he was still sort of a neat freak. Maybe Shea was right about the metrosexual thing.

"What's so funny?" he asked.

"Huh?"

"You're smiling."

"I was just thinking this was a great truck."

"My ex hated it."

Kitty shot him a sideways glance. "Why?"

"She thought I should drive something smaller, sexier, I guess."

"I know it's a cliché, but personally, I've always thought bigger is better."

He muttered something under his breath and shook his head.

Kitty laughed and laid her head back on the seat. The rest of the drive was spent in comfortable small talk. It was the first time she'd been with Steve that she hadn't felt slightly on edge.

They drove into Mexico Beach, where he pulled the truck into the private driveway of a two-story Tuscan-style house directly on the beach. A For Sale sign was posted on the well-manicured lawn. There was a car in the driveway and a woman standing next to it.

Kitty straightened to attention. "What's this?"

"We're going to hang out here for a few hours." He killed the engine and eyed her. "That okay?"

Kitty inspected the house. The red-tiled roof contrasted brightly against the waning early evening sky. Purple bougain-villea vines accented the columns leading to a dark mahogany-wood door.

Okay? The place was gorgeous.

"I think I could tolerate a few hours here," she said.

The woman came forward to greet them. She was young, with straight blonde hair that fell to her waist. A pair of sunglasses rested on top of her head. She wore a crisp, sleeveless white shirt and a beige cotton skirt that fell a few inches above her knee. It must have been ninety-five degrees outside, but her makeup was still impeccable. Kitty immediately hated her.

"You must be Steve Pappas. I've heard a lot about you," said the blonde, extending her French-manicured hand. "I'm Caroline Estes. But everyone calls me Caro. I'm new with the company."

He shook her hand. "Thanks for meeting me out here on such short notice."

"Anytime." She eyed him up and down like he was a prize filet and she was a butcher. "I hear you're an avid fisherman."

"I try."

"I think you'll find the waters around here pretty friendly."

Kitty couldn't help the choking sound that came out of her mouth.

Caro finally noticed her. Her big blue eyes widened at the sight of Kitty's flip-flops and still-damp hair. "And, you are?"

"Sorry, I should have introduced you. This is Katherine Burke." Steve paused. "My Realtor."

Caro looked confused. "But I thought—"

"She's looking at property in Whispering Bay for me," Steve said without missing a beat.

Kitty blinked and tried not to give anything away with her expression. She wondered if this was how Bonnie felt when she and Clyde had walked into a bank right before robbing it.

"Oh," Caro said, smiling with regained composure. She took a small leopard-skin case from her purse and handed Kitty a business card. "What company are you with?"

Kitty glanced at the card. Malibu Barbie was a Realtor? She wondered if Walt Walters had sniffed her out yet.

"Actually, I'm a broker. I work for myself. I'm afraid I don't have my cards with me." *Ha.* As if she'd have given Caro one of her *Help me help you* cards, anyway.

"No problem. I'm sure I can reach you if I need to," she said to Kitty, but her gaze was glued on Steve. Subtlety was obviously not one of Caro's strong points. "I had no idea there was anything . . . exciting going on in Whispering Bay."

"You'd be surprised," Kitty said, trying to keep from yanking out a chunk of Caro's golden hair. Surely it wasn't natural. Neither the color nor the hair itself. Kitty searched (discreetly, of course) for the telltale extension line.

Caro pulled a set of keys from her purse and handed them to Steve, along with one of her business cards. "I can be reached twenty-four-seven."

"Thanks."

"Anytime," she said. "Just call when you want me to pick up the keys."

"I'll drop them off at your office." There was a finite ring to his tone. A subtle dismissal at which Kitty couldn't help but cringe. She wondered if Caro would notice.

"Sure," Caro said, her shoulders slumped. Malibu Barbie wasn't so dense after all. Kitty almost felt sorry for her. The key word being *almost.*

She waited till Caro's car was out of sight. "Does she think you're interested in buying this place? And why on earth would she leave you the keys?"

"My natural charm?"

"This is a multimillion-dollar house. No one is that charming. What we're doing is verging on the illegal. You're misrepresenting yourself to that poor girl."

"Let me worry about that."

She should demand they get back in the truck and leave. That's what she *should* do. But the truth was she didn't want to. There was something incredibly exciting about having a non-date in a house you had conned your way into.

What the hell was happening to her?

Steve opened the front door. Kitty had been a Realtor long enough to have developed a decent poker face, but this was too much. "Oh my God," she said, trying not to laugh.

22

IIIIII

A large gold mirror, adorned at the corners with two cherubs aiming arrows at one another, hung above a glass table in the foyer. A black-and-white zebra-striped sectional sat in the center of the living room where a rhinoceros head gazed down from the top of the stone fireplace. The room was accented in lots of gold and strong pinks. It was a mixture of Victoria's Secret meets Versailles meets the Serengeti.

"At least it's air-conditioned," said Kitty.

Steve stood in the middle of the living room and shook his head in disgust. She followed him as he walked through the rest of the downstairs, into a large study with a big oak desk, a master bedroom and bath, and finally into the kitchen. With the exception of the foyer and the living room, the rest of the house was tastefully decorated. The kitchen was painted a rich gold color. Copper light fixtures and stone countertops complemented the Mediterranean feel. There were lots of shiny silver kitchen appliances that screamed, "only serious cooking here, please." He placed the food on the counter and began opening drawers, taking out equipment.

"Weird, huh?" she said. "It's like the entrance to the house was decorated for shock value."

He laid the contents of the bag onto the kitchen counter and began furiously dicing the onion.

"Something wrong?" she asked.

"Nope."

She sighed. "Are you going to get all moody on me again? 'Cuz if you are—"

He looked up, surprised. "Sorry. I was just a little . . . taken aback by all that out there." He took two beers from the refrigerator with a familiarity that made her eyes narrow, screwed off the caps, and handed her a bottle. "You think I'm moody?"

"Um, yeah." She took a sip of her beer. "You've been in this house before." She tried not to make it sound like an accusation.

He shrugged. "I helped build it."

"So you know the owner?"

"Yeah." He selected a large skillet from an overhead rack and splashed olive oil in the bottom.

A part of her felt like she'd been had, but it was a relief to discover they weren't crashing some random house. Caro's leaving him the keys made sense now.

"How long has the house been on the market?"

"Too long."

"The front rooms are hideous, but that's easily solved. It's a gorgeous house."

"What do you like about it? Besides the location. That's a given."

"The exterior is beautiful. I feel like I've been transported to southern Italy."

He nodded, urging her on.

"I can't comment on the upstairs, since I haven't seen it yet." She paused, thinking how to put it best. "I like the way the house is laid out. A lot of people make beach houses too narrow because they're trying to save land. But this is a house someone would really live in. Not the type of house you'd use just for vacation or to rent out. Take the study. Someone really works in it. And this kitchen," she added, waving a hand in the air, "the owner of this kitchen can really cook. Or at least they like to pretend they can."

He smiled at that last part. "The house hasn't sold because the asking price is too high."

"How much?"

"Four million."

"Yikes."

"The owner's stubborn. But eventually they'll have no choice but to lower the price. Then the place will sell and Caro's company will make a nice fat commission. Like I said, I'm not worried about her."

"Good, then neither am I."

He went back to his dicing, but he seemed more relaxed now.

"Where did you learn to cook?"

"My mother died when I was fourteen. My older sister was already married and out of the house, so it was just me and the old man. He worked sixty, seventy hours a week. I learned to do just about everything to keep a house together."

"Like laundry?"

"Yeah, like laundry," he said with no hint of sarcasm. Kitty felt that last vestige of tension between them ebb away. It looked like the Thong Incident was a thing of the past.

She thought about what it would be like to lose a parent. Fourteen seemed a terrible age. But then, there was probably no good age for that. "Is that why you dropped out of high school? To help out at home?"

"I dropped out of high school because I was an idiot." He paused from his chopping. "Figuratively, not literally."

She smiled.

"After my mom died my old man drowned himself in work. I started smoking dope and cutting classes. I thought I knew more at sixteen than he did at fifty."

"Where's your dad now? Still in Cocoa Beach?"

"Nah. He lives in a retirement community near St. Pete about ten minutes from my sister."

"Is he a plumber, like Gus?"

"Electrician." He took a bundle of plastic-wrapped chicken breasts out of the cooler and patted them dry with a paper towel. "How about you? Did you graduate from college?" Before she could answer, he said, "Let me guess. You were the valedictorian of your high school class and you majored in . . . finance."

"Finance." She laughed. "That's a good one."

"Was I right about the valedictorian part?"

"There were only ninety-four kids in my high school graduating class, so it wasn't that big a deal. And I majored in marketing."

"I wouldn't have guessed that."

She raised her brows.

"'Help me help you find the house of your dreams'?"

She sniffed. "For your information, that tagline has gotten me a lot of business."

"If you say so."

"Just because business isn't exactly hopping right now doesn't mean I haven't been successful in the past."

"I didn't say you weren't successful, but it wasn't because of that tagline. I can see how someone would want to buy a house from you." He stopped what he was doing to give her a slow perusal. "You're attractive, smart, not too aggressive. And most important, you know how to push the right buttons."

She felt herself flush. "What do you mean?"

"Look at Caro. She's attractive, probably smart, but she's way too aggressive. She's working on the wrong buttons."

Kitty's heart began to pound. "Really? I hadn't noticed."

He locked gazes with her. "Yeah, you did."

Neither of them looked away for a long time. Finally, Kitty had to back down. It was either that or jump him right there in the kitchen. Considering he was working over a hot stove, the latter wasn't a safe choice.

"Maybe I did notice her flirting with you. Just a little," she admitted, feeling her face go even hotter. "So, um, what are the right buttons?"

He took a long drag of his beer. "I'll let you figure that out."

She cleared her throat. Maybe it was best to change the subject. "How's Nathan?"

"He's cooled down some," Steve said, placing the chicken breasts in the skillet. "I'm going to let him and his mom duke it out. Meanwhile, he's going to hang out at the beach and figure out the meaning of life, that sort of thing."

"When he does, let me know. I've been trying to do that for thirty-five years."

"Joey tells me you've never been married. Just never met the right guy?"

"Something like that." She sipped her beer and watched as he expertly maneuvered the pan over the hot stove with the flick of his wrist. "What did Joey think about us?"

He glanced at her. "I didn't ask him. Do you care what he thinks?"

A few days ago she would have said yes. It was natural to worry about what other people said behind your back. Especially a big mouth like Joey. Surprisingly, right now she couldn't care less what Joey thought. But she did care what Gus thought. She wasn't *that* evolved. "Does Gus know about the other night?"

"Not from me."

"I didn't mean to imply that you'd actually tell him." Maybe she should change the subject again. "Tell me about your first wife, the stripper."

She didn't expect him to answer, so it surprised her when he said, "That really rattled you. Didn't it?"

"You meant it to."

He ignored her barb. "What do your friends think of me?"

"I don't know what you mean," she said, trying to sound innocent.

"You give them the lowdown on our night together and they had no comment other than they thought I was some sort of underwear thief?"

Busted.

"Okay, I told them you've been married three times and they think you're a loser."

Instead of looking offended, he laughed. "What do you think?"

"I think you've made some mistakes in the past."

"And I don't plan on making a fourth one."

"Good, because I don't plan on *being* the fourth one."

"Glad we got that out of the way."

"Don't worry. You're not my type."

He grinned, like he didn't believe her.

"Well, you're my type for *that*," she said, flustered. Why did he keep looking at her like she was naked or something? She fiddled with the neckline to her shirt. "But you're not the type of guy I'd go for in a long-term relationship."

"What kind of guy is that? Just out of curiosity's sake."

"Preferably one who hasn't been married before, but at my age, I know that might be hard to find, so one divorce would be okay, but multiple divorces? Well, no offense, but if you haven't gotten it right after a couple of tries, you're pretty much doomed in the marriage department."

"No offense taken." He began cleaning off the counter, tossing away garbage. "You still want to know about my first wife?"

"Sure." She tried not to sound too eager, but for some reason, she really did want to know.

"I was eighteen with no high school degree, working whatever construction jobs I could find, getting drunk every night with my buddies. Then one night, I walked into a strip joint and met the woman of my dreams."

She snorted.

"What can I say? I was horny. And stupid. Plus, it royally

pissed off my old man, which back then was an added bonus. The marriage lasted about a month. It was a real wake-up call for me. After that, I got my GED and joined the army."

"You were in the army?"

"Special Forces. Don't mess with me, or I might have to kill you."

She laughed.

"That's where I met Sarah, wife number two."

"She was in the army?"

"Yeah. She was a nurse."

"What happened there?"

He shrugged. "Not much to tell. We were stationed in Germany together and it seemed like a good idea at the time. After a couple of years, she wanted kids. I wasn't ready and she got tired of waiting. I don't blame her. I was a crummy husband and still not very smart when it came to women."

Crummy husband. She wondered what sort of criteria he based that on.

"What about Terrie?"

"Terrie was my payback for Sarah. If you believe in karma, that is." He drank down his beer. "I got out of the army and started working construction. After a couple of years I got my contractor's license and I joined up with an army pal of mine, Dave Hernandez, to form our own company. Terrie worked in real estate. She was divorced so she knew all about past failed relationships and we hooked up. That seemed like a good idea too. But it wasn't."

"How did Nathan take your divorce?"

The question seemed to surprise him. "Okay, I guess. I thought he and I were buddies, until the attitude he gave me at the bus station the other day."

"So the two of you stayed in touch then?"

He frowned. "Sure. I mean, sort of."

Men. They were so obtuse.

She sighed. "What happened to your company?"

He hesitated before answering. "Dave and I parted ways."

She got the feeling there was more to the story. But she didn't want to press him. He'd already opened up a lot more than she'd expected. "I'm sorry."

"Shit happens."

He said it so sheepishly, she had to laugh. It was strange, being in this beautiful house, watching Steve cook and talk about his ex-wives. She looked out the window above the sink facing the Gulf. This morning she'd been in another house just a few miles down the beach helping cement the deal that was going to save her ass. Financially, that is.

He opened the can of tomato paste and added it and some water to the skillet. Using a dish towel for a pot holder, he gave the whole thing another shake, then turned the knob to lower the heat. "You're in a good mood," he said.

His comment startled her. He couldn't know her well enough to gauge her moods. "Maybe I'm in a good mood because I'm having a good time."

"Maybe." He tipped his head in the direction of the patio. "This chicken needs to simmer about thirty minutes. Grab the wine and let's head outside."

It was dark now, but the recessed lighting along the edges of the wooden deck provided a soft illumination. Kitty leaned against the railing and watched as Steve opened the wine and poured out two glasses. A gentle breeze lifted the hair off her shoulders. Add in the sound of the waves lapping against the shore and the smell of salt in the air and the scenario was ridiculously intimate. He couldn't have set up a more romantic scene if he'd tried.

She thought about his comment about her being in a good mood. He was right. She was happy. Other than the air-conditioning fiasco, today had been stellar.

She probably shouldn't talk about it. Ted had warned her to keep the condo deal on the lowdown, but Steve didn't live in Whispering Bay, so the condos weren't going to affect him one way or another. Besides, she was too excited to keep it in a second longer. "I had some great news today. I'm just this far"—she brought her thumb and index finger to within a half inch of each other—"from closing on a big deal."

"What sort of deal?" he asked.

"I don't want to bore you with the details," she said, remembering the glazed looks in some of her former boyfriends' eyes whenever she talked too much about her job. Not that Steve was her boyfriend. Which would make him even less likely to be interested.

"It wouldn't bore me."

She took a sip of the wine. It was perfect. Not too sweet, not too dry. She mentally added "ability to pick out a good bottle of wine" to his list of talents. "Okay, well, remember what you said about me being smart and successful? That's not exactly true. I mean, I'm smart, just not with money. Instead of investing my money when real estate was hot, I overspent."

"Is that why you can't afford to buy your grandmother's house?"

"Moose says—"

"Moose?"

"My financial advisor."

"You have a financial advisor named Moose?"

"He's an ex–football player." At the look on his face, she added, "It's a long story. He's also a good friend of mine and he's married to my best friend, Shea."

Steve nodded. "The hot one."

Kitty narrowed her eyes. "Just how hot do you think she is?"

"It's just a general observation. Leggy redheads with fake boobs aren't my type."

"Oh yeah, what is?"

"Leggy brunettes who know how to put a little bit of shake in their ass."

Holy crap.

She chugged down her wine.

"Slow down." He took the glass from her hand and placed it on the wooden railing. "I don't want you drunk."

"Why not?" she squeaked.

"Because then I couldn't do this." He leaned in and kissed her.

She kissed him back, but before it went too far she broke it off and took in a lungful of the sea air to clear her head. "Hold on. I thought I didn't exactly rock your world."

"You rocked it enough," he said, moving back in to kiss her.

She placed her hand against his chest, fending him off again. "I did?"

"I was an ass to say that," he admitted. "But at the time, you weren't being very nice either."

"If you're just saying that to get laid, it's not going to work."

He began nuzzling her neck. "What do I need to say then?"

Damn it. She hated when he did that. Not because she

didn't like it, but because she couldn't think. "I . . . I don't know," she gasped, curling her fingers in his hair.

He stopped kissing her neck. "How about this? I think you were terrific with Nathan the other night in the car, and for like five crazy minutes, I was actually jealous of the kid because you were paying so much attention to him. How about I've spent the whole day thinking about tonight and what I was going to cook to impress you."

She gulped.

"And that all I've thought about since we stepped foot in the house was getting you out on this deck"—his voice dropped to a harsh whisper—"and fucking you until neither of us could walk straight."

Double holy crap.

"That would work." She threw her arms around his neck, nearly knocking him off his feet.

He laughed, then lowered himself into a chair and pulled her onto his lap, straddling her legs around him. He pushed her denim skirt up till it bunched around her waist then cupped her bottom in his hands. Did he really mean he wanted to have sex right here? Outside, on the patio?

She nervously glanced out into the dark, toward the ocean. "What if somebody walks by?"

"So what? Let 'em look the other way."

She felt a tiny surge of excitement, but she still hesitated.

He sighed. "Even if someone did walk by, it would be too dark to see anything. If you're worried about it, then we'll just have to bring down the noise level. I can be quiet if you can." This last part felt like some sort of challenge.

"Of course I can be quiet."

He grinned. "You're on."

He pushed aside the crotch to her panties to slide a finger up inside her. Then he kissed her again. His tongue moved in and out of her mouth, keeping up the same rhythm he used with his finger. He withdrew, circled her clit, then dipped back inside. She squeezed her eyes shut and concentrated on not making any noise.

But it wasn't easy.

"You know what I like?" His voice sounded far off, like an echo in a cave.

"What?" she asked, vaguely wondering what he was referring to.

"I like the look on your face right before you come."

Her eyes flew open.

They were nose to nose, her body wrapped around his. His forehead shone with perspiration. She could feel the sweat running down her back.

"You close your eyes real tight and look all worried, like it's not going to happen for you." He stopped the in-and-out motion and concentrated on her clit, flicking his finger back and forth.

She couldn't help herself. She let out a half moan, half laugh.

"Then there's the thing you do with your mouth."

"My mouth?" She arched her hips forward, urging him to press harder.

"You suck in your bottom lip and bite on it some and it gets all rosy and kinda sexy-looking. But you know what I like the best?" he asked, reaching his other hand beneath her shirt. He found her nipple through the thin satin of her bra and tweaked it. "I like the way you laugh."

Instinctively, she giggled.

Damn it.

But two could play at this game.

She eased down the zipper to his shorts and placed her hand over his erection. Steve drew in a sharp breath. Kitty had to fight back her smile.

She slid her hand down to cup his balls, giving them a gentle squeeze, then slid her hand slowly back up and down again. She repeated the motion over and over. "You know what I like?" she began. "I like—"

"My back pocket," he rasped.

"I like your back pocket?"

"Condom . . . in my back pocket."

She straightened, nearly dislodging herself off his lap. "You keep a condom in your back pocket?"

"Only when I think I might get lucky," he said, catching his breath like he'd just run a marathon.

Lucky? She wasn't sure she liked that. But then, where he was concerned she *had* been easy. It looked like their relationship was well on the way to becoming a two-night stand.

He tilted his hips, rubbing the tip of his penis against her wet clit.

Hell, who cared?

She found the small foil packet and tried to rip it open, but she couldn't get a good grip on it. She brought it up to her mouth and tore the edge with her teeth, then tried to roll the condom on, but her fingers weren't cooperating. Finally, Steve had to take over.

He circled her waist with his hands to steady her and tried to slide inside, but her panties were in the way. "Rip them off," she croaked.

He laughed and reached his big hand down between them.

She heard the lace tear and tried to stifle her moan.

"Don't hold back on account of me," Steve said.

He was right. Who cared if someone heard them? It was private property and—

He drove into her.

In the end, she wasn't sure who made more noise. Him or her.

Probably it was her.

He leaned his head against the back of the chair and held her close, the two of them plastered in a sweaty heap.

She sighed, too exhausted to move. "This time I heard sirens."

His hand lingered on her back, slowly stroking up and down. "Huh?"

"I said, this time I heard—"

He jerked his head up. "Fuck," Steve swore under his breath.

"I thought we just did that."

He tossed her to her feet and threw on his shorts. "It's not sirens. It's the damn fire alarm!" he said, flinging back the patio doors.

A huge gust of smoke burst out into the warm night air.

23

Steve ran to the kitchen with Kitty hot on his heels. Or as fast as she could, considering her skirt was still bunched around her hips and she was somehow missing her flip-flops.

The dishcloth he had used to handle the pan was lying across the stove in flames. He turned off the burner and reached beneath the kitchen sink to retrieve a fire extinguisher. Within seconds, white frothy foam covered the stove top and half the adjoining counter.

"Open the windows," he said, choking back a cough.

They aired out the house and cleaned up the kitchen, but no matter how hard Kitty scrubbed, a large black soot stain refused to budge from the cabinet above the stove.

"Forget about it," Steve said, taking the cleaning rag from her hand and tossing it into the sink.

"I feel terrible. I shouldn't have distracted you while you were cooking."

"It was worth it," he said, grinning.

She frowned. "This cabinet is custom-made. It's going to be expensive to replace. And the entire downstairs is going to need to be aired out really well or else the smoke smell is going to linger."

"I'll take care of it in the morning."

"Are you sure? Caro could get in a lot of trouble for this."

"I'm sure."

"But—"

"It's no big deal. I told you, the house belongs to a buddy of mine." The relaxed mood they'd shared earlier was gone. "Sorry about dinner," he added.

"I'm really not hungry anymore," Kitty said, feeling deflated. He thought ruining a kitchen cabinet in a house that didn't belong to him was no big deal? It was so . . . irresponsible. At least she had the grace to feel guilty. "Maybe under the circumstances we should go home."

He nodded, his face a combination of resignation and something else she couldn't put her finger on. "Let's take a walk on the beach first. It'll be good to get some fresh air."

Steve was right. After being in the smoky house, it felt good to be outside. They walked along the shore, sucking in the salty, damp air. She wondered briefly if he was going to hold her hand or try to kiss her. But he didn't. They walked in silence broken only by occasional chitchat.

They stopped on the deck before heading back inside the house. Kitty found her torn panties on the floor, next to the chair.

"Sorry about that," Steve said.

She shrugged. You couldn't compare her ten-dollar panties with an expensive cabinet. She wadded the panties and stuck them in her purse. No way was she going to toss them in the trash for Caro to find.

It was weird. One minute they'd been having hot sweaty sex and the next it was like they were polite strangers. Maybe this was the way they were supposed to act. Sophisticated and all cool about it.

Only she didn't feel sophisticated or cool. She felt let down. Pilar and Shea were right. She wasn't cut out for one-night stands. Which could only mean she would doubly suck at this two-night-stand thing.

24

Shea picked up the dice and blew three consecutive puffs of air into the palm of her hand. They were rolling for threes and it was her standard good-luck gesture. One puff of air for each number she wanted. Shea rolled again but her method didn't work and her lucky streak ended, so Brenda scooped the dice from the table. A huge whoop of laughter erupted from table number two. Shea craned her neck to see what the fuss was about.

Despite the fact they were missing Lorraine and Mimi, Bunco had gone on as scheduled. Kitty had almost choked on her martini olive when she'd found out Christy Pappas was subbing tonight, which wouldn't have happened (the near-choking part) if Shea had made her secret frozen margaritas. But Shea had refused. Her rationale being that they shouldn't repeat signature drinks two weeks in a row. So instead, they were drinking dirty martinis. The martinis were a little strong for Kitty's taste, but by her third one, she'd loosened up.

So what if Christy Pappas was subbing? And so what if big-mouth Joey had probably told his wife that he'd seen Steve's truck parked in front of Kitty's house at six in the morning. It's not like Christy was going to announce it or anything.

"So, Kitty, are you dating my cousin-in-law?" Christy yelled across the living room. Being married to big-mouth Joey must be rubbing off on her.

"Is that the guy who unclogged your toilet last week?" Frida asked.

"I saw him at Corbits buying beer," Tina said. She eyed Kitty. "Is there something going on between you two?"

The room went quiet.

"Hey, we're supposed to be playing here," Brenda yelled. Rolling resumed, but no one spoke. They were all too busy looking at Kitty, especially Shea and Pilar, who were gazing at her with unholy interest.

"Going on between who?" Kitty asked. When in doubt, play dumb.

"Between you and Gus's nephew. The plumber guy," Frida said.

"Plumber?" Christy asked, clearly confused.

Pilar began coughing loudly.

"I thought I saw his truck in front of your house yesterday," said Brenda. "Around dinnertime."

"No offense, Christy, but I hear he's been divorced three times," Tina said. "The rumor is his wife caught him cheating on her." Last year, Tina had suspected her own husband of cheating and had enlisted the Babes in a plan to expose him.

The whole thing had turned out all right, since Tina's husband wasn't cheating (it was a gambling problem). He was now in counseling and went to weekly meetings of Gamblers Anonymous.

"It's true, he's been divorced three times," began Christy. "His last marriage has only officially been over a few months, but I don't think it had anything to do with him being unfaithful." She didn't say it with much conviction though. She shrugged. "Joey has been pretty tight-lipped about the whole thing."

"Are you going out with him, Kitty?" Brenda asked, frowning.

"Not exactly," Kitty said. She rolled three sixes. "Bunco!" she yelled, grabbing for the dice. According to Bunco Babe rules, anyone who picked up the dice from a Bunco roll automatically doubled their score. She laughed and pumped her fist in the air, expecting the rest of the room to cheer her on, but no one was paying attention to her roll.

"What do you mean, not exactly?" Tina asked.

Liz's brow scrunched up. "If he's recently divorced, then that would make you his transition person."

"I'm not his transition person," Kitty said. "Because I'm not going out with him." Which wasn't exactly a lie. She didn't think having sex with someone twice qualified as a relationship. Not in Steve's mind anyway.

"Good," Tina said. "You deserve better than that."

The Babes, and even Christy, nodded in agreement. "Don't get me wrong," Christy said, "Steve's a terrific guy, he just . . . well, he has a lot of baggage."

Shea picked up the dice and rolled two more threes, giving them a total of twenty-one. She let out a victory yell and rang the cowbell to signal the end of the game. The Babes switched tables and started rolling for fours.

"I heard a pretty cool rumor the other day," Brenda announced, smiling mysteriously.

Yes! A change of subject. Anything was better than having the Babes talk about Steve Pappas. "What sort of rumor?" Kitty asked.

"I hear they're going to build a Publix in town."

The Babes all murmured in appreciation. Publix was Florida's premier supermarket but the closest one was in Destin.

"Who did you hear that from?" Frida asked.

"Andy golfs with Bruce Bailey." Andy was Brenda's husband. "And since Bruce is on the city council, plus is vice president of the bank, I figured he should know."

"No offense against Corbits but they don't carry any gourmet spices and their vegetables are always wilty," said Christy.

"Why would Publix come to Whispering Bay all of a sudden?" Tina asked.

Frida glanced at her. Kitty hadn't gotten permission from Ted to spill the beans yet, but she'd already alluded to the condo deal twice. Once to Frida and then to Pilar's parents. And Shea and Pilar already knew all about it. So what could it hurt to drop a heavy hint to the Babes? "I've been hearing rumors that a big-time developer wants to expand his business here in Whispering Bay," said Kitty.

"What sort of business?" Brenda asked.

Kitty tried for a nonchalant shrug. "Condos."

"I knew it!" said Frida, crossing her arms over her chest.

"You don't sound happy," Pilar said.

"I'm not."

"Neither am I," said Liz. "One of the reasons Paul and I

moved here was so that we could raise our kids in a quiet community. A place where they could ride their bikes anywhere. Once the condos come, traffic is going to go crazy."

Several of the Babes nodded.

Kitty downed the rest of her martini. "Isn't that a little extreme? I mean it's just a few condos."

"Today it's a few condos, tomorrow we'll be another Miami Beach," Frida grumbled.

"Well, it's only a rumor," Kitty said. Good God. Maybe they should have kept talking about Steve Pappas. "Let's take a break." She stood and stretched out her legs.

"Good idea," Shea said. "I need another drink." She followed Kitty into the kitchen and closed the door. "That didn't go over so well." She poured herself another martini.

"Should you be drinking if you're trying to get pregnant?"

"Wow. I've never heard you sound so preachy before. It just so happens I started my period today."

Shit. Kitty wanted to bite her tongue. "Sorry."

The kitchen door burst open and Pilar marched in. "You haven't started talking without me, have you?" She looked at the expressions on their faces and frowned. "What's going on?"

"Shea got her period today," Kitty said, sending Pilar a "be nice" message with her eyes.

To Pilar's credit, she managed a sympathetic face. "That just means you and Moose get to have more sex," she said.

Shea gave them a noncommittal look. "I guess so. The thing is, I've been thinking about maybe going back to work too."

Pilar's eyes lit up. "Thatta girl! Whispering Bay is in desperate need of a top-notch interior designer."

Shea rolled her eyes. "I'm not sure yet." Her voice picked up in enthusiasm as she said, "I'm interviewing a nanny next week. Her name is Hilda and she comes highly recommended from a couple who also uses Elise."

"Elise the toilet trainer?" Pilar asked.

"Elise the child elimination expert," Shea corrected.

Kitty giggled. "She sounds like a kiddy hit man."

"Ha-ha," Shea said, clearly not amused. "But whether I decide to have another baby or go back to work, I definitely need some child-care help."

"Good idea," Pilar said. She turned to Kitty. "So what's Brenda talking about? Was this Steve character really at your house yesterday?"

"I tried calling you," Shea said. "But I got your voice mail."

"I meant to call you back," Kitty said, "but I've just been so busy with this condo deal. Speaking of which, what's up with everyone's reaction? I thought at least Frida would be happy. More people in town means more business for the Bistro."

"I don't think Frida looks at it like that. So Steve wasn't at your house yesterday?" Pilar asked again.

Kitty thought about the best way to answer. "He came by the house to bring me a bottle of wine as a thank-you present. Remember the Fourth of July? After you guys left the beach, I went over to say hi and the two of us talked a little."

Pilar and Shea gave each other the look that Kitty hated.

"I apologized for the thong thing and then I gave him a ride to the bus station in Panama City. His stepson had run away from home and he was helping his ex by going after him."

Shea shook her head. "Runaway stepson? Man, Christy's right. The guy has a lot of baggage. Do you think it's true about him cheating on his ex?"

"How should I know?"

"You *are* telling us everything, aren't you?" Shea asked. "It's just us now, so you don't have to pretend anymore."

"I get a really bad vibe from this guy, Kit," said Pilar. "He's not kosher. First, he's a plumber, then he's not. And then there's this thing about him cheating on his ex. Where there's smoke, there's fire. Plus, the fact he's only been divorced a few months isn't good. Liz is right. You'd be his fauxship."

"His what?"

"His transition relationship gone bad," Pilar clarified. "And you'd only end up getting hurt."

Sometimes Kitty really hated the words Pilar made up. She took the martini from Shea's hand and tossed it back. She should tell them to relax. That she wasn't involved with Steve. Except for some occasional earth-shattering sex, that is.

She looked at their faces. Besides her parents, Shea and Pilar were the two people in the world she loved the most. She told them everything.

But she didn't want to tell them any more about Steve Pappas. If she did, she'd have to tell them about the dinner in Mexico Beach and how they had white-lied their way into a four-million-dollar house and then ended up having sex on the back deck and almost setting the place on fire. She wondered if Steve had gotten the cabinet fixed today. It would probably have to be special ordered. Her stomach ached just thinking about it.

She didn't want to tell Shea and Pilar about Steve's ex-wives and she didn't want the two of them dissecting their nonexistent relationship or asking a bunch of personal details about him. Details she didn't really know anyway.

Just this one time, what she did know, she wanted to keep all to herself.

So she did something she hadn't done since the sixth grade when she accidentally ran her bike over Shea's new Madonna album.

She lied to them.

"I've already told you everything. Now let's go back and play Bunco."

25

||||||

Kitty spent Saturday morning at her office, wrestling with her Quicken account. Her listing on Ocean Avenue hadn't gotten any nibbles so she'd scheduled an open house for tomorrow. She hated doing open houses. Especially in the summer when it was so hot. The traffic usually consisted of curious neighbors, but clients always loved to hear she was spending her Sunday afternoon working for them. In Kitty's opinion, the only way to spend a Sunday afternoon was sitting in her beach chair by the edge of the Gulf, sipping a cold brewski while reading a novel.

The loud beep of the fax machine made her jump. Ted's attorney/real estate shark Teresa had been faxing Kitty mountains of paperwork every day. Just hours after the meeting with Earl Handy, Ted's company, Ferguson and Associates, had made a formal offer for the beachfront property. They'd given Earl four days to respond and time was up. Kitty was anxious to see if Earl would accept the offer or if he would try to up the price. From what Kitty knew of Earl, he would definitely counteroffer.

The fax machine froze and a button began to blink. She scooped up the two pages that had gone through. One was the cover sheet from Teresa and the other was blank.

Damn it. The machine was out of paper.

She scoured the office cabinets but there was no paper anywhere. Even her computer printer had only a few sheets left. Becky had always taken care of office supplies.

Kitty looked at her watch. It was almost one and her stomach was making scary animal noises. She'd close up, get a bite to eat, and then head over to Al's Office Supplies.

She was locking the door to her office when Steve's truck pulled up. He wore a pair of dark slacks and a collared shirt—sort of corporate casual. She'd never seen him in anything other than jeans or shorts. Or naked. *Don't think about that . . .*

"Want to grab lunch?" he asked. He seemed in a good mood. All smiles and acting friendly. She wanted to ask if he'd gone by the house in Mexico Beach to take care of the cabinet, but she didn't want a return of the tenseness that seemed to follow that conversation the other night.

"Lunch?"

"Yeah, it's the meal you eat between breakfast and dinner."

"Ha-ha."

He grinned. "So what do you say?"

What did she say? She'd love to go to lunch with him. Or dinner. Or breakfast.

Or better yet, dinner *and* breakfast.

"I'd love to, but I need to make a run for office supplies."

"I could tag along," he offered.

She glanced around the small parking lot. No sign of Brenda or any of the other Babes. Still, it was best not to take any chances.

"Sorry," she said, regretting the fact she didn't have time to suggest they eat lunch in another town, "but I have a busy afternoon." As soon as she said it she almost changed her mind, but Whispering Bay was just too small. If she was lucky enough to avoid running into one of the Babes, then she'd run into someone who would *tell* one of the Babes. Somehow, the whole thing would come back to bite her in the ass.

"Then how about dinner?"

His persistence was flattering. It was more than flattering. It was making her feel all hot and flustered. And downright desirable. This was looking a lot like a date.

"You buying or making?" she asked, trying to sound casual.

"Whichever you prefer."

Kitty thought about it a minute. Her new air conditioner had been installed yesterday so there was no reason Steve couldn't comfortably cook for them. But if Steve made dinner at her house, there was no doubt in her mind they'd end up in bed again. Did she really want that?

Hell, yes.

She was on the verge of asking him to cook for her when her mother's voice suddenly niggled in her ear whispering about the cow and the free milk analogy. He'd been so sure the other night they'd end up in the sack together that he'd put a condom in his back pocket. Maybe for once, her mother was right about something. She shouldn't make it so easy for him.

"How about we go out? Maybe in Panama City?"

"I know just the place."

She studied his face. "Are we celebrating something?"

"Maybe. I just got some encouraging news."

"A new job?"

"Even better." In his circumstances, what could be better than a new job? "I'll tell you all about it tonight. Pick you up at six?"

"Sounds good." She got in her car, trying very hard to remain composed while he watched her drive away. Maybe he'd gotten a job in the area. Which would mean he was staying in Whispering Bay. Which would mean that one of the strikes against him was potentially lifted. Maybe tonight was the start of a real relationship. Something that could lead to a permanent thing between them.

She forced her mind to steer back into reality. His "good news" could mean he'd gotten a job anywhere. Maybe he was even getting back with his old partner from Tampa. It was best not to get her hopes up. And it was probably best not to even *think* about sleeping with him again. She'd already determined she wasn't a two-night-stand kind of girl. It did crazy things to her mind.

She headed to Al's Office Supplies, stocked up on paper, then made a quick detour through Dolphin Isles. She just couldn't help it. The petty, insecure part of her had to see what was going on. She turned onto the subdivision's main road and slammed on her brakes.

Parked in front of the Calypso model home was Shea's white Lincoln Navigator.

26

Walt Walters stood in the foyer of the model home, talking on his BlackBerry. He must have spied her coming up the walkway because he didn't look surprised to see her. He put one finger in the air to signal he'd be right with her.

It was the first time Kitty had been inside the Calypso, Dolphin Isles's newest furnished model. From what she could see, it looked identical to the other floor plans. A large foyer that opened into a great room with vaulted ceilings, lots of white tile and white walls. As a matter of fact, there was lots of white everywhere.

Walt finished his call and clipped the BlackBerry onto his belt. "Looking for a job, Kit?"

As if. "No, thanks, business has never been better."

"Really? Well, that's super. Just super." He crossed his arms over his chest. "That Becky is a real spitfire. She's already sold her first home. You must be really missing her."

"I've always been a one-woman operation, Walt. Much simpler that way. But I'm thrilled for Becky. She's a nice kid."

Walt smiled like he didn't believe her. He wore black slacks and a bright yellow cotton polo shirt with a Dolphin Isles logo over the front pocket.

"Let me guess," Kitty said, pointing to his outfit. "The theme this week has something to do with bumblebees?"

"We're undergoing new management and this is the official company look," he said, ignoring her barb.

She picked up a brochure from the foyer table. *Dolphin Isles, brought to you by TNT Properties* was printed in minuscule letters at the bottom of the back flap. "Who's behind this TNT? Ever met any of the bigwigs?"

"I talk to the owner on a near-daily basis," Walt said, which was a smooth way of not directly answering her question.

"Sure you do."

Walt's eyes got all slitty. "As a matter of fact, TNT is planning a big expansion. There's talk I'm up for head salesperson for the whole enchilada."

"Oh? What's next? Dolphin Isles Two: The Revenge?"

Walt stuck his hands in his pockets and smiled his smarmy Grinch smile. "Something like that."

Great. Just what Whispering Bay needed. Another Dolphin Isles.

She was saved from responding by the sound of the front door opening. It was Nathan. Walt's BlackBerry buzzed. He slinked off into a corner of the living room to answer it, giving her an opportunity to speak with Nathan privately.

"It's Mets Girl," Nathan said. "I thought that was your car out there." It was the first time Kitty had seen Nathan in town.

He wore board shorts, a threadbare Hawaiian Tropic T-shirt, and a Yankees baseball cap.

"Oops," Kitty said, knocking the baseball cap off his head, "sorry about that."

Nathan grinned and picked up the cap, then hastily hand combed his dark hair back from his face.

"What's up?" Kitty asked, trying not to stew over what Walt had just told her.

"I'm getting a job working on-site here."

"What about college?"

"My mom and I had a long talk. She's cool with me taking a year off school." Nathan's face screwed up. "You know, that was all bullshit about her taking the money from my bank account." He shrugged. "Steve sort of apologized to me, though."

"He did?"

"Well, not in so many words. But he's going to—"

Her cell phone went off. "Excuse me," she muttered, fumbling to find her phone in the chaotic mess of her purse.

Walt shook his head, silently admonishing her as he motioned to the BlackBerry now re-clipped to his belt. Kitty ignored him and picked up the call on the sixth ring. Ted's number flashed across the screen.

"Where the hell have you been?" Ted boomed.

"Excuse me?"

"I expected after today's catastrophe you would have at least had the smarts to call me first. Meet me at your office. *Now.*"

No need to get all riled up, she told herself, taking a deep breath. This was just Ted being Ted again. Earl must have come back with an outrageous counteroffer. With an outward calm she really wasn't feeling, she snapped her phone shut and placed it back in her purse.

"Anything wrong?" Walt asked. Like he cared.

"Of course not. It was just one of my clients calling to tell me how much he appreciates my attention to detail." It sounded ridiculous, even to her, but she had to save face.

She turned to Nathan. "I have to go, but before I do, I need to warn you. This is the *last* place on earth you want to work."

Nathan looked confused. "It is? But—"

"Trust me," Kitty said. "I wish I could say more but I have to go." She was almost out the door when she remembered her mission. "The white Lincoln Navigator parked out front—I think that belongs to the Mastersons. Have you seen them?" she asked Walt.

"Who?" Walt asked with mock innocence.

"Never mind," Kitty said, her keys in hand. She didn't have time to play games with Walt Walters. She had to save her energy for Ted and Earl.

She made the five-minute drive to her office in three. Ted was outside waiting for her. "I'm afraid I don't know the latest development," Kitty said, hearing her voice shake a little. "I was out getting office supplies when you called."

Ted flung a piece of paper at her. "Read this."

It was Earl's counteroffer. Kitty quickly scanned the page until she found the glitch Ted was so furious about. She'd been right. Earl had counteroffered with a ridiculously high amount.

"I'm sure it's a mistake. A typo or something." She pulled her cell phone from her purse. "Let me call Earl and see what's going on." She got an answering machine with a male voice she didn't immediately recognize. It must be Vince. Instead of leaving a message, she hung up. Earl seemed like the sort of person who would respond better face-to-face. He was practically a recluse. He had to be home.

"I'm going to see Earl right now and straighten this out."

"You better, because I can't afford to pay this much for the land. Not without going for additional financing, and that might take a few months."

A few months? By that time, her mother and Larry would have bulldozed the house.

"Don't worry," Kitty said, looping her purse over her shoulder. "I'm prepared to do whatever it takes to make this deal happen."

27

A woman with short cropped gray hair answered the door. She was thin and wore jeans and Birkenstock sandals. Her face was tanned and unlined. "Whatever you're selling, we're not interested." Her tone was more businesslike than rude.

"Mr. Handy knows me," Kitty said, fishing inside her bag. She found a crumpled business card at the bottom. "I'm a real estate broker."

The woman grudgingly slipped on a pair of glasses with rainbow-colored frames she kept on a chain around her neck. "'Help me help you find the house of your dreams'," she read. "Isn't that a line from that movie . . . what's it called?"

"*Jerry Maguire*," Kitty supplied. *I've been meaning to change that!* she wanted to scream. Instead, she smiled and tried again. "May I please see Mr. Handy?"

"You're Amanda Hanahan's granddaughter, aren't you? Earl told me about you. I'm DeeDee," the woman said, "Earl's housekeeper-slash-nurse-slash-companion. I see to it that Earl takes his medication and doesn't piss anyone off enough to kill him."

If her nerves weren't in danger of exploding, she would have laughed. But the fact that Earl had mentioned her to his nurse was encouraging. "Is Mr. Handy available? I really need to talk to him."

"He's watching *Perry Mason* reruns. Might not be the best time to interrupt him."

"He'll want to see me. It's a business emergency."

DeeDee sighed. "Come on in."

The smell of onions and beef wafted through the air, making Kitty's mouth water. She never did get to eat lunch.

"That's my beef stew simmering," DeeDee said, noticing Kitty's reaction. "If you want, I could fix you up a bowl. We could eat it in the kitchen and you can talk to Earl later."

"I'm sorry. I can't wait."

DeeDee shook her head. "I'll tell Earl you're here. But don't say I didn't tell you so."

She returned a few minutes later. "He says to come on back. It's the part in *Perry Mason* where you find out who the killer is, so I suggest you keep your mouth shut until he talks first."

Kitty followed her down a short hallway into a den. Earl was sitting in a recliner, his bare feet propped up, totally engrossed in his program. After a couple of minutes, Earl scowled at the set and turned it off with the remote. "Anyone could've seen that ending coming a mile away. I hate it when you can figure out the killer in the first fifteen minutes."

Kitty nodded sympathetically. Her grandmother had loved *Perry Mason* too.

"I guess I know why you're here," Earl said.

Fuck. That could only mean that outlandish figure wasn't a glitch like she'd prayed.

"I wanted to clear this up in person." Kitty automatically folded her hands in her lap. "I understand that you'd want to try to up the offer, but the amount is somewhat unreasonable. Don't you think?" She waited for Earl to respond. "I don't think you're going to get a better offer than ours, Mr. Handy."

"Already have."

"*What?*"

Earl raised his chin a notch and wiggled his nose in appreciation. The beef stew smell had reached the den. "DeeDee's a damn pain in the ass, but she can cook. Want to stay for supper?"

"Um, maybe. First we need to clear this up. I thought we had a deal," Kitty said.

Earl's gaze sharpened. "And I thought you were smarter than that. A deal's a deal when the paper's signed. And even then a good ambulance chaser can get you out of it. One of the few things the buzzards are good for."

She tried not to look rattled. "May I ask what the other buyer has offered? Have you checked their financing? Maybe it won't go through," she added hopefully.

"Vince already checked it out. Fella's good as gold." Ted had used a similar expression to describe Earl's word. The irony of it wasn't lost on Kitty.

"I thought you said you had enough money."

"I said that? Well, I was wrong. You can never have enough money."

Now she understood DeeDee's statement about Earl pissing people off. Kitty would happily stand at the front of the line to wring his neck.

"Bottom line," Kitty said. "How much do you want?"

Earl pondered this a minute. "I'd be willing to negotiate something lower than my counteroffer."

"We can do five percent over our original offer," Kitty said. "But not a penny more." God, please, let Earl take the offer.

"Other fella's offered me more than that."

Kitty frowned. "Has it occurred to you that it's pretty coincidental to get two offers for that land in the same week?" Walt Walter's words suddenly came crashing into her head. "By any chance, did the other offer come from a company named . . . TNT?"

Earl shifted in his seat. "As a matter of fact, it did."

Kitty narrowed her eyes in satisfaction. "Mr. Handy, are you familiar with the Dolphin Isles subdivision in Whispering Bay?"

"Dolphin like Flipper?"

"It's a neighborhood of grotesque cookie-cutter slapstick homes that will get wiped out by a weak hurricane wind and it's owned by TNT. Is that the sort of construction you want on the beach?"

Earl looked taken aback.

He was weakening. She could see it. If only there was something she could use to convince him how important this deal was. She remembered the way his face looked when he'd talked about Gram, and how he'd mentioned her to DeeDee. Maybe he'd even been to Gram's house before. After all, it was one of the oldest residences in Whispering Bay. "Mr. Handy, how well did you know my grandmother?"

Earl's eyes went soft. "She was my first girl," he admitted. "Damn fine woman. Even if she did marry that fella from Alabama."

Kitty jerked up in her chair. Earl and her grandmother had been sweethearts?

It was shameless. But she had to use it.

"I know I told you that I wanted this deal to go through because of the commission. But it's not just because I want money, Mr. Handy. I want the commission so I can buy my grandmother's house."

Earl's eyebrows shot up. "The one on Seville Street?"

Kitty nodded. "My mother wants to bulldoze it."

"God damn it!"

It was just the reaction she was hoping for. "And if this deal falls through, that's exactly what will happen."

Earl stared at the blank TV for a few seconds before he let out a deep holler that startled Kitty. "DeeDee!"

DeeDee poked her head in the door. "Who died?"

"Get Vince on the phone. Now!"

DeeDee raised her brows at Kitty. "I don't know what you said to him, but you're *good*."

Ted was ecstatic. "Only five percent?" he asked over the phone.

"Yep." She had to keep her answers short or she would burst out in a wave of giddy gibberish. "Earl signed the contract right in front of me."

"Fantastic! How did you pull it off?"

Kitty paused a moment. "Let's just say . . . I pushed the right buttons."

28

Steve picked her up at exactly six. She wore a lime green halter dress that faked some cleavage. She'd thought about wearing the black pumps, but at the last second decided against them. They were too dressy and way too obvious. Instead she went with a pair of four-inch wedgies that were almost as flattering. It was nice not to have to worry how tall she'd appear in the shoes. Steve's height was a definite advantage there.

"You look great," he said, helping her into his truck.

"Thanks. So do you." Like earlier, he was dressed in dark slacks, but these were made of a richer material, maybe a wool-silk combo? It was a great Armani rip-off. And for the first time, she noticed he wore cologne. Okay, so yes. This was *definitely* a date. If she'd known that, she'd have worn the black stilettos.

They drove into Panama City Beach to a quaint seafood restaurant Kitty had never been to. The atmosphere was intimate and the waiters all wore tuxes. She tried not to appear shocked at the prices.

"So what are we celebrating?" she asked. "You mentioned a new job today."

"I was a little premature this afternoon." He didn't seem too upset though.

"I'm sorry."

"Something else will come along. It always does."

Maybe it was a bad time to bring it up, but she had to know. "I still feel terrible about that cabinet. Were you able to replace it?"

"It's on order."

"I'd like to split the cost with you. After all, it was my fault too."

"It's not a problem," he said.

"What about Caro? Is she going to get in trouble?"

"I told you, I know the owner pretty well. It's no big deal."

Steve turned his attention to the wine list. Kitty supposed he didn't feel like talking about it anymore. Not that she could blame him, poor guy. The cabinet must have cost a small fortune to replace, and then to find out the job he was counting on wasn't going to happen . . . She decided then and there to pay for dinner. Steve would probably put up a weak protest, but she'd convince him it was the practical thing. And after today's deal, she could definitely afford it.

The food was delicious. The service impeccable.

Steve watched her slurp up the last of her lobster ravioli. "I like a girl with a healthy appetite."

She blushed. "I never got around to lunch today," she said, pushing her plate away.

"Big office-supply trip?"

"I had some serious damage control to do on a deal."

He studied her face. "You don't look happy about it."

"I'm over the moon, actually. It's just that . . ." She hesitated, but Steve seemed to know a little about the real estate business. Maybe he was the perfect person to talk to about this. "I think I took unfair advantage of a personal relationship."

"All's fair in business."

"I thought that was love and war."

"That too."

Kitty glanced around the restaurant and lowered her voice. "Normally, I wouldn't have done it, it's just that with the commission off this deal, I can afford to buy my grandmother's house now. And then there's this company here in town that drives me nuts. TNT Properties. They're despicable."

Steve took a sip of his wine. "What do they do? Run some sort of child-slavery ring?" he joked.

"Worse," she muttered.

"Worse than child slavery?"

"They came to town two years ago and built this subdivision called Dolphin Isles. Have you seen it?"

"I believe Gus does their plumbing."

"Then that's the only thing over there that isn't substandard. It's awful. Row after row of these crummy little identical houses with almost no yard. No soul, no character. Who would want to live in a place like that?"

"Someone who wants to own a new home?"

"Do you know how many existing homes are currently on the market in Whispering Bay? Over two hundred. Most of them built in the fifties and sixties. Houses built during a time when people took pride in what they did." She frowned. "Nathan was at Dolphin Isles today, looking for a job on-site. I told him not to bother."

He scowled. "Isn't that his decision?"

"The only experience he'll get there is learning how to build a crappy house."

"Sounds like sour grapes to me. I think you're just pissed because this place has cut into your business."

Kitty flushed. "You work construction. Don't you take pride in what you build?"

"Of course I do."

"Then you should understand what I'm talking about. It's companies like TNT that are responsible for the decline of America."

He snorted. "The decline of America? That's a little melo-dramatic, don't you think?"

Kitty felt her face go hot. "No, it's not. And thanks to me, or rather my newest client, we just saved Whispering Bay from more crappy TNT development."

His eyes narrowed. "What client?"

"It's sort of on the QT." Steve raised a brow at her. "You know, hush-hush," she explained.

"I know what 'on the QT' means."

Oh hell. She'd already blabbed to half the town. Other than Gus and big-mouth Joey, who was Steve going to tell? She'd come close to confiding in him about it the other night. Eventually the sale was going to be announced in the business section of the *Whispering Bay Gazette* and then everyone in town would be talking about it. And despite the Babes' predictions of gloom and doom, if companies like Publix were thinking of coming to Whispering Bay, the majority of the town would crown her a hero.

"I'm representing a developer who's going to build condos on the beach—Ferguson and Associates. TNT must have gotten wind of it because they put in a bid for the same piece of land. A ridiculously high bid that could only have been meant to choke out my client."

His jaw tightened. "So, by using this personal connection, you got the seller to agree to the deal at a lower bid?" He paused. "That's pretty impressive." He didn't sound impressed though.

"Like you said, it's all a matter of pushing the right buttons."

He gave her a chilly smile. "You despise a company like TNT for building affordable housing, yet you rep a company that wants to litter the beaches with condos?"

Kitty straightened in her seat. "I've seen the renderings for the condos. They're a string of tasteful low-rise buildings that mesh with the natural landscape."

"That's one way to spin it."

"Obviously, you're out of your league here." Kitty gulped down the rest of her wine.

"You think TNT Properties is guilty of shoddy workmanship and the decline of American values, but you use a personal relationship to throw a deal your client's way. A client who's going to build some 'tasteful' condos on the beach? Maybe I'm out of my league, sweetheart, but at least I'm not fooling myself. I know a spade when I see one."

She almost choked on her wine. "I thought you of all people would understand why I did it. What was all that gushing over my grandmother's house about?" she asked, her voice rising to a near shout. An elderly woman at the next table turned to stare at them. Kitty lowered her voice to a hiss. "Do you even like old houses? Or was that just a ploy to get me into bed?"

"I didn't have to *get* you into bed, you practically fell into it."

She took a deep breath and counted to ten. "Obviously we're not going to agree. Maybe we should call it a night."

"Good idea." Steve motioned to the waiter for the bill.

"Did you enjoy your meal?" the waiter asked in a pleasant voice.

"Yes," they both answered in unison without looking up.

Kitty made a move for the bill, but Steve was faster. "What do you think you're doing?" he demanded.

"You're out of work and you have a kitchen cabinet to replace. Remember?"

"Anyone up for dessert?" the waiter asked, his tone more cautious now. "We have a delicious cherries jubilee on the menu tonight."

Steve pulled out his wallet and flung an American Express card on the table. She'd love to fling her own card down too. But it seemed childish. Plus, she suddenly remembered her credit cards were nearly maxed out. "I'm the one who invited *you* to dinner," he said. "Remember?"

"I'll take that as a no on the dessert," said the waiter. He scooped up the card and made a quick exit.

Neither of them said a word the entire ride home. Steve pulled into her driveway but before he'd even turned off the engine, she'd already scrambled out of the truck. She could open her own damn door, thank you.

"It's been wonderful knowing you," she said stonily, keeping her eyes trained on the rearview mirror next to his head. She had no desire to ever look Steve Pappas in the face again. "Please tell Nathan I wish him the best of luck in his endeavors."

Wait. There was more. But she was going to have to relent on the "never looking him in the face again" thing. What she had to say next, she wanted to make sure he heard. So she looked him directly in the eye. "And in case you haven't figured it out by now, for some bizarre reason, Nathan admires you. So don't let him down."

She slammed the car door a little too forcefully (she really hadn't meant to slam it at all) and made as graceful an exit as possible under the circumstances.

Once inside the house, she opened the refrigerator freezer and ripped into the Snickers bar she kept hidden behind the ice maker.

How dare he criticize her?

What did he know about real estate or business or anything important? He was just some thrice-divorced loser out-of-work construction worker who happened to be occasionally charming and really good in bed.

Shea and Pilar had known that all along. Why hadn't she listened to them?

She picked up the phone and dialed Pilar's number.

29

It was like one of those hokey MasterCard commercials. Pink-and-black-polka-dot thong from Victoria's Secret: ten dollars. Early morning breakfast at the Bistro by the Beach with your best friends: twenty bucks. Looks on their faces when you tell them about the latest bump in your love life: priceless.

Shea's cheeks were red with indignation. "First he said you sucked in bed. And now he's called you *greedy*?"

"Pretty much," Kitty said. Actually, it had been Ted who'd called her greedy, but Shea and Pilar didn't have to know that part. Steve might not have said the G word, but he had certainly alluded to it. And she could hang up trying to explain the whole sucks-in-bed/didn't-rock-my-world statement because they were apparently *never* going to get that one right.

Pilar shook her head. "I still can't believe you went out with him. We told you he was bad news."

"I know, I know. I should have listened," Kitty said miserably.

"Did you really tell him you thought Dolphin Isles was responsible for the decline in American values?" Shea asked, wide-eyed.

"Yep."

Pilar glanced at her watch. "I have to leave by eight. Don't let me stay a second longer."

"You've already reminded us three times," Kitty said. "What are they going to do if you're late for once in your life. Fire you?"

Pilar ignored her.

"I don't agree with Steve the prick," said Shea. "But you have to admit he has a point. It seems sort of, well, hypocritical to be so down on Dolphin Isles when you're representing a company that's going to be putting up condos."

"Whose side are you on?" Kitty demanded.

Shea rolled her eyes. "Yours, of course. I'm always on your side. It's just weird how the two of you got into this argument anyway."

Kitty sighed. "Speaking of Dolphin Isles, what were you doing there Saturday?"

Shea looked startled. "At Dolphin Isles? When?"

"Around one thirty. I had to have a close encounter with Walt Walters. He denied you were there, but it was so obvious he was lying—"

Pilar's watch went off. She stood and smoothed the nonexistent wrinkles from the skirt of her Ann Taylor suit. "Gotta go. Despite popular opinion," she said, glaring at Kitty, "I can't keep Hillaman, Soloman, and Kaufman waiting."

"Don't you ever get bored wearing the same thing every day?" Kitty asked.

Pilar frowned. "This is a brand-new suit."

"Well, it looks like all the others you always wear," said Shea.

"Well, it's not." Pilar gave them both a peck on the cheek. "I'm glad you told us about last night, Kit."

Shea nodded enthusiastically. "That's what we're here for. To keep each other uplifted in times of crisis. How can we help if we don't know what's going on?"

Pilar waved to Frida, who was working behind the bagel counter. "See you Thursday!"

"Seven sharp!" yelled Frida. "I have something special planned."

"That's right," said Kitty. "It's Frida's turn to do Bunco this week."

"Yup. Right here at the Bistro. I always love it when Frida hosts."

Only three more days till Bunco. It couldn't get here soon enough for Kitty. She needed to unwind big time.

"So you never answered my question," she said to Shea. "About Dolphin Isles."

Shea shook her head. "There must be another white Lincoln Navigator out there with FSU tags, because it wasn't me."

Kitty stared at her a minute, then slowly took a sip of her coffee. In the twenty-five years she'd known Shea she'd seen just about every expression on Shea's face. But she'd never seen this one.

There was no doubt about it. Shea was lying to her.

30

BUNCO at the Bistro was always a blast. Frida would set up the playing tables in the middle of the restaurant and pipe music through the overhead stereo system. Just like the signature drinks, whoever hosted each week always picked out the food and the background music. Seeing who could come up with the coolest motif was part of the fun. Frida's choice in music always ran to something eclectic that no one else had ever heard. Tonight's theme was Japanese. The signature drink was sake, and sushi was on the menu.

"I don't think I've ever had sake before," said Brenda.

"It's pretty strong," said Liz. "Maybe we should have a designated driver for tonight."

"Ed has volunteered to drive anyone home who needs it," announced Frida.

Kitty took a sip of her sake. She'd been looking forward to Bunco all week. Especially after the disastrous date with Steve and then the strange lie she'd caught Shea in. She'd wanted to mention it to Pilar and find out her opinion, but Pilar had been so busy with work this week they hadn't been able to get together. Maybe after Bunco tonight the three of them could sit down and straighten it out.

Frida clapped her hands to get the group's attention again. "I have an announcement to make. In just a few minutes, we're going to be joined by some special guests. I told them to come around seven thirty, before we started playing."

Brenda and Lorraine gave each other a look. "You've invited outsiders to Bunco?" asked Brenda.

"They're not outsiders," Frida clarified. "And they're not going to stay for the Bunco part. But I thought this could be a preview of something new. Instead of playing Bunco every week, maybe we should mix it up with something different."

The room went silent.

"Something different?" Shea finally repeated in a horrified voice.

"We've been playing together for ten years now, and frankly, it's getting a little old." Frida held up her sake. "Like the signature-drink thing. Every week we try to outdo each other. Wouldn't it be nice to take a break from that every once in a while? I think we should alternate Bunco with a community project or a book club every other week."

"A book club?" Shea said. "You mean, we'd sit around and talk about books?"

"That's right," said Frida. "As much fun as Bunco is, you have to admit, it's not very intellectually stimulating."

"I don't come to Bunco to become intellectually stimulated," said Tina. "I come to hang out with my friends and have fun."

"A book club can be fun too," Frida insisted.

"Are there dice involved?" Liz asked.

Frida narrowed her eyes. "You know there's not."

"What about prizes?" asked Brenda.

"The 'prize' is the knowledge that you're expanding your mind by discussing books with other people."

"Would we get to shout and laugh and act stupid like we do in Bunco?" Tina asked.

"What if we're discussing a sad book?" asked Shea. "Like the ones Oprah is always touting on her show. Oprah only likes books about the Holocaust or addictions. How are we going to have a good time if we have to talk about the Holocaust?"

Frida pressed her lips together.

"If we don't have signature drinks, then what do we serve?" asked Brenda.

"You drink wine at book clubs," Frida said.

"Let me get this straight," said Liz. "Instead of playing Bunco and having signature drinks and laughing and being stupid and getting prizes, you want us to sit around and drink wine and talk about the Holocaust?"

"Oh, never mind," Frida grumbled.

Just then the front door opened and in walked Viola and Gus, along with Mr. Milhouse and several other Gray Flamingos. Pilar's parents, Isabel and Antonio, were with them.

"What's going on, Mami?" Pilar asked.

"We've joined the Gray Pelicans," Antonio announced.

"That's Flamingos," Isabel corrected.

"I get those two birds confused all the time," chimed in Mr. Milhouse sympathetically.

"I've invited the Gray Flamingos here to talk to us tonight,"

Frida announced to the group. "I think you'll all be very interested in what they have to say."

Everyone took a seat, except for Viola, who was clearly in
charge. She glanced around the room and smiled sweetly.
"Thank you, Frida. Don't worry, this won't take long. I know
how my bridge group is, and I wouldn't want to keep you girls
from playing."

The Babes murmured in approval.

"It's no secret that over the past ten years, the Bunco
Babes have become one of this town's most influential groups.
That said, the Gray Flamingos are here tonight to ask for
your help."

The Bunco Babes were one of Whispering Bay's most pow-
erful groups? By the looks on the Babes' faces they liked the
sound of that. Viola obviously knew how to work a crowd.

"Now prepare yourselves, ladies; what I have to say will
come as a shock."

Kitty took a sip of her sake and edged forward in her seat.

Viola cleared her throat dramatically. "We have it on good
authority that Earl Handy plans to tear down the senior
center."

A few of the Babes booed and hissed.

Viola let the ramifications of her announcement sink in before she continued. "As most of you know, Earl owns the building and the land, but for the past twenty years or so he's leased
it to the city for a dollar a year. I'm not going to sugarcoat
things and tell you everything's peachy keen. The building is
falling apart. The roof leaks and the plumbing is atrocious. Although I can happily say that the plumbing situation is in the
process of being repaired. Pro bono," she added, flashing Gus a
smile. "But despite the problems, it's become our building. A

place for Whispering Bay's retired citizens to socialize and keep from feeling isolated."

"Why would Earl tear down the senior center?" Pilar asked.

"Yeah, it makes no sense," Shea added, throwing Kitty an uneasy look. "Where did you hear this?"

Kitty sat frozen in her seat.

"Josh Bailey let it slip," said Viola.

"Yesterday after pottery class I had a word with him," Mr. Milhouse said. "Damn kid never remembers to turn off the lights when we're through. You'd think electricity is free the way he wastes it. When I threatened to get him fired, he just laughed and said he was looking for another job anyway, on account of his daddy telling him the senior center wasn't going to be around much longer."

"I wouldn't put too much credence in a rumor started by a seventeen-year-old," Kitty said, relieved to hear this was the basis for their excitement. "Especially not one started by Josh Bailey."

"Rumors start for a reason," said Viola. "Whatever the case, we can't be too careful. We've got a petition right here demanding that the city council buy the senior center from Earl." She handed Kitty a clipboard. "As the granddaughter of one of the Flamingos' founding members, it's only right that you be one of the first citizens to sign this."

"Of course." Kitty took the attached pen and wrote her name on the first line in her large loopy writing.

Viola looked at the signature and smiled proudly.

"I doubt Earl Handy would ever allow someone to mess with the senior center," said Kitty. "The building is named after his mother, for God's sake."

Mr. Milhouse made a gurgling sound against the roof of his mouth. Kitty hoped his dentures weren't going to fall out or anything. "Earl hated his mother. She used to make him swallow a tablespoon of castor oil every morning before school. First day of second grade Earl messed his pants while we were standing in line for music. He's never forgiven her for it."

Kitty had to bite her tongue to keep from laughing. Maybe that's when Earl's obsession with his bowels started.

"I guarantee you the only reason Earl leases that building to the city is because he's getting some kind of tax write-off. Either that, or no one's shown any interest in buying it. Let someone with cold, hard cash come along and Earl will sell that land so fast it'll make your head spin," said Viola.

For one chilling instant, Kitty panicked. She tried to recall the exact description and dimensions on the contract regarding the beachfront property. She had gone over the paperwork Teresa had drawn up dozens of times, mostly to make sure the names were spelled right, but she was certain the land Ted wanted to buy only bordered the senior center. It most definitely did *not* include the section of land where the center was located.

Kitty had never thought about the ramifications of having the condos so close to the center.

What would Viola and the Gray Flamingos think of all that construction? She would have to talk to Ted about making some concessions. They could erect one of those walls that blocked out the noise—the ones they used on the highways. Or maybe, she could even get Ted to donate some money to the center to make up for the inconvenience the construction would cause. That would certainly keep the Flamingos happy. Ted might balk at having to spend money on something that didn't belong to him, but Kitty would just have to point out that it was in his best interest to keep the senior center as attractive as possible.

"I think you're all worrying over nothing," Kitty said. "I've met with Earl recently, and if anything, he seems reluctant to sell his land."

"Aren't you a Realtor?" asked Mr. Milhouse. "What would Earl be doing meeting with you if he wasn't considering selling?"

A few of the Babes glanced at Kitty.

"Rumor has it Earl's in seclusion over at that house of his in Mexico Beach. When did you meet with him?" he persisted.

Shit. When was she going to learn to keep her big mouth shut? She sucked at this "keeping things under wraps" stuff. "I can't give out details, not yet anyway, but my reason for meeting with Earl has nothing to do with the senior center." She made an X over her chest with her index finger. "Cross my heart."

Mr. Milhouse looked leery, but Viola nodded confidently. "If Kitty says Earl's not selling the senior center, then he's not selling the senior center. Still, it doesn't hurt to be safe. Now, if the rest of you ladies would like to sign this?" Viola motioned to the clipboard.

The Babes lined up and added their signatures below Kitty's. Frida invited the Flamingos to stay for sushi, but Mr. Milhouse nixed the idea.

They began to roll for ones, but Kitty couldn't keep her mind on the game. She had to go read the contract again and make sure she was right. Not that she doubted it. But still, it couldn't hurt. Her chi demanded it.

"I think I feel a little queasy," she announced at the end of game one.

"Oh no," said Brenda, "do you think the sushi's bad?"

Lorraine shook her head. "I knew we shouldn't be eating raw fish."

Frida rolled her eyes.

"I'm sure the sushi's fine," said Kitty. "I just need to go home and lie down."

"Ed can drive you," Frida offered.

"Thanks, but it's a two-minute drive. I'll be fine," said Kitty, avoiding any eye contact with Shea or Pilar.

But she'd only be fine once she was certain she was right about that contract.

31

Her hands gripped the steering wheel. What kind of contract only gave specs for a location? How was she supposed to know what was where? She was accustomed to a contract having a street address, for God's sake.

Don't panic, Kit. Just because the Flamingos were in an uproar didn't mean anything. She just needed Earl's assurance that everything was all right.

She glanced at the dashboard clock. It was almost eight thirty, Central time. Why did Mexico Beach have to have two time zones? What kind of freak aberration was that? She couldn't remember if Earl lived in fast time (what the locals called EST) or slow time, but either way it was too early for him to be in bed, wasn't it?

DeeDee looked surprised to see her. "You again?"

"I'm sorry to come by without calling. Is Mr. Handy still up?"

"I'm not some titty baby who's in bed by six," Kitty heard Earl holler from the living room.

DeeDee grinned and ushered her inside. "We were just working on a puzzle."

Earl sat at a table spread with what looked to be a thousand tiny puzzle pieces. "Want to join us? It's supposed to be the Eiffel Tower."

"Um, no, thanks." Kitty pulled a copy of the contract from her bag. "I was looking over the paperwork again and I had a quick question."

"You young people. All you do is work. Don't you have a husband or something?"

Kitty shook her head.

"Shame," muttered Earl. "So what can I do for you?" He made a face. "I'm not bringing the price down again. We've already signed the contract. Vince went over the roof when I told him we were going to turn down that TNT deal." Earl laughed. "It was worth losing that money to see his face turn purple."

DeeDee shook her head. "You should cut Vince some slack."

"What for?" Earl asked. "Getting him riled up is the highlight of my day. That and my visit to the john."

Kitty cleared her throat. "You'll never believe what happened tonight. I ran into Viola Pantini. You remember her, don't you? She's head of the Gray Flamingos."

"Bah!" Earl batted his hand through the air. "They're nothing but a bunch of geriatric losers. Except your grandmother of course," he added, looking contrite. "She was a fine woman. Just had her priorities a little mixed up, is all."

"They seem to think you're planning to tear down the senior center," Kitty said, laughing nervously. "I tried to reassure them that wasn't the case."

"Of course I'm not tearing down the center," Earl said.

Kitty nearly staggered in relief. "Thank God. I thought for a second there that—"

"I'm going to let Ferguson do that. It's his land now."

Kitty felt the blood drain from her face.

DeeDee looked at her strangely. "Are you okay? You look kind of sick." She pulled up a chair just in time for Kitty to plunk herself down. "I'm going to get you some water."

"Looks like she could use a whiskey instead," said Earl.

Kitty shook her head. "Water," she croaked.

DeeDee returned from the kitchen with a glass in her hand. "Here, drink up."

"I bet it's diet pills," Earl said. "Read all about it in *People* magazine. Don't know why a woman thinks she needs to be a stick to attract a man." He winked at her. "Personally, I like a woman with some hips."

"Thanks," Kitty responded weakly. Dear God. This was a disaster. What had she done? Why hadn't she bothered to look at the contract more closely? Why hadn't she gone along with the surveyor to actually visualize the land? Or more simply, why hadn't she thought to ask *exactly* where the ten acres was located? Earl owned a lot of land, yes, but she should have been more careful. She sagged back in her chair.

The truth was she could have read that contract until she'd memorized it and it wouldn't have made a lick of difference. Her specialty was selling homes. Not obscure parcels of land. She'd been stupid. And now the town's senior citizens were going to pay for her carelessness.

How was she going to explain this to Viola and the rest of

the Gray Flamingos? They would hate her. The whole town would.

"Mr. Handy, I know this sounds strange, but I need a favor."

"Another one?"

Kitty cringed. "Isn't there another section of land you could sell that doesn't have the senior center on it?" The instant she said the words she knew how ridiculous she sounded. Ted had probably scoped out that particular parcel for a reason. You couldn't just trade one piece of land for another. Could you?

"I've been giving Whispering Bay a free ride on that center for years now. The building's falling apart. Vince says it's nothing but a lawsuit waiting to happen. And for once, he's right." Earl frowned at her. "What are you worried about? It's not your fault. You bargained a good deal for that Ferguson fella. And you're going to get your commission, so everything's jake. You can't have it all, missy. Business is business." He studied the table for a second and slipped a puzzle piece in place. "Sure you don't want to stay and work the puzzle?"

"I'm positive," Kitty muttered.

She thought about the tagline to her business card. She now knew exactly what it should read. *Help me help you fuck everything up.*

32

She drove home and took a long, hot shower, put on a bath-robe, then slipped her *Bull Durham* DVD into her machine and curled up on the couch.

What had she been thinking to throw it away?

Thank God Shea had saved it from the trash.

Kitty was on her third rum and Coke (Diet Coke, that is) when the doorbell rang. She glanced at the clock above the mantel. It was after eleven. It had to be Shea and Pilar on their way home from Bunco. Thank God. She needed them now more than ever. She would explain the whole horrible mess and between the three of them, they'd find a way to fix this.

But it wasn't Shea *or* Pilar.

It was Steve.

She blew the bangs out of her eyes and tightened the sash to her bathrobe. "What are you doing here?"

"I was driving by and saw your light on."

"I've heard that line before."

"Can I come in?"

"No." She hiccupped.

He searched her face. "You're drunk."

"How can you tell?"

"Because you told me the first night we met you cry when you're drunk."

"I'm not drunk," she said, holding up the tumbler of rum and Coke. "I'm only slightly tipsy."

She caught a glimpse of her reflection in the mirror above the foyer table. Her hair looked like a bird's nest, sticking out in all directions, and there were tear tracks down her cheeks mingled with smeared mascara. She bent over and scrubbed her face with the hem of her bathrobe. "There. That's better."

He picked up the bathrobe sash and dipped the end into her drink then cradled the back of her head in his hand while he wiped at the smudges with the wet sash. Kitty had to admit, it felt sort of good.

"Why are you crying?"

She ignored his question and closed her eyes. "That feels nice. All cool and tingly on my face. I've changed my mind. Come on in."

"How much have you had to drink?"

"Just some sake and a few rum and Cokes."

He took the tumbler from her hand and swallowed some of the drink. "There's no Coke in here."

"Sure there is. At least, there was when I mixed it."

He grinned, then his gaze shot to the fireplace and his expression sombered. "Why does it smell like smoke in here?"

"Don't ask."

"Did you make a fire in July?"

"I burned my business cards."

"A little drastic, don't you think?"

She shrugged.

Steve placed his hand at the small of her back and propelled her to the sofa. "Sit."

Kitty flopped down and propped her feet on the coffee table. She stared at her bare toes. She never did get that pedicure.

"When did you eat last?" Steve yelled from the kitchen.

"Do you like my feet?"

He stuck his head in the doorway. "What?"

"Do you like my feet?" she repeated, lifting a foot to wiggle her toes in the air. "I think I have great feet."

"Yeah, I love your feet. When was the last time you ate something?"

"I had half a California roll four hours ago."

"That's it?" She could hear him rustling around in the kitchen, opening the refrigerator, rummaging through cabinets.

"I would have eaten more, but I had to go ruin a few hundred people's lives. Well, actually, I'd already done that, sort of by accident, but I had to make sure." When he didn't say anything, she sighed and stared at the television screen. It was the part in *Bull Durham* where Susan Sarandon was tied to the bed while Kevin Costner painted her toenails. That's weird. The last time Steve had come over the movie had been at the same exact scene. She flopped her head back on the sofa. "I've always wanted a man to paint my toes. Will you paint my toes?"

"Maybe." He walked back into the living room with a large glass of ice water and something wrapped in a paper towel. "First, eat this."

It was a peanut butter sandwich on semi-stale wheat bread. No jelly. "Yuck, I don't want this."

"Then you should keep more food in the house. This is all I could find besides some Lean Cuisines and an empty carton of Rocky Road ice cream."

He forgot to mention her hidden Snickers bars, except she suddenly remembered she'd eaten them all after their fight the other night. She grudgingly took a small bite of the sandwich. "Why are you here again?"

"To tell you I'm sorry. I was out of line. And that I'm glad you are going to be able to buy this house."

"No. You were right. About everything. I'm just as bad as TNT." She shook her head. "Worse, even. TNT might not have a soul, but I sold mine for two thousand square feet two blocks from the beach."

"Don't be so hard on yourself. This house has a lot of sentimental value for you."

"How can my mother even think of tearing it down?" She took a swig of the ice water to wash down the bite of sandwich.

"Kit, there's nothing wrong with going after what you want."

Steve didn't know the worst of it. He didn't know about the senior center. "It's not that simple."

"What's wrong, baby? You look miserable."

That did it.

She'd never liked being called baby before. But there was something about the way Steve said it that made her want to crawl into his arms. She didn't know if it was because of the crappy day she'd had, or the fact that he was being so nice—or maybe it was the sake and rum mixture—but suddenly it all became too much. She started crying again. Not little sniffly delicate tears, but great big slobbery ones. The kind that made her nose run and her eyes get red and puffy.

He sat on the couch and put his arm around her. "That bad?"

"I screwed up. Big . . . time," she said between sobs. "Thanks to me, the senior center is going to be destroyed and everyone in town is going to hate me." She buried her face in his shirt to dry her tears. "God, you smell good."

He tensed. "Maybe I should leave."

She pulled away. "And now you're freaked out because you think I'm throwing myself at you."

He choked back a laugh. "I think you're confusing freaked out and turned on." He shook his head. "I just don't want to take advantage of you during a weak moment."

She thought about it a minute. "You're not just saying that to make me feel better?"

"I'm always turned on by slightly tipsy beautiful women who throw themselves at me."

She studied the expression on his face. His eyes had that smoky look in them again. "I told you, I'm not throwing myself at you . . . You think I'm beautiful?" Before he could answer, she went on, "Can I ask you a question? Did you cheat on your wife?"

He narrowed his eyes. "Where did you hear that?"

Normally, she would have hemmed and hawed, but liquor always made her more direct. Before she could stop herself, she blurted, "We talked about it. At Bunco."

"Your Bunco group talked about me?"

"Just a little. But don't worry," she rushed, "I pretended I barely knew you. And Christy defended you. Sort of."

"Great."

She snuggled her way back into the crook of his shoulder. "You don't have to answer. About cheating on your ex. I already know. I don't think it's in your nature." She took another whiff of his cologne. "God, you smell really good. Did I tell you that already?"

"What's not in my nature?"

"Cheating. You're one of those honest guys who always tells the truth. No matter how ugly." She frowned. "Well, except for the lie you told Nathan about his mom swiping the money from his bank account. But you've always been honest with me. I mean, you made it pretty clear when we slept together that it was only going to be for the one time. And that you hadn't planned to ever call me again. And last night, you were right about everything. I'm just as greedy as TNT. Which leads me to my second question. Was last night a date?"

"You really have to ask?"

"Okay, so last night was a date." *Listen to your gut, Kit.* "And tonight's a booty call."

His shook his head slowly. "No, it's not."

She frowned. Her instincts hadn't counted on that.

"I'm not that lucky," he explained quietly.

The air whooshed from her lungs. "Maybe . . . you could be," she said, suddenly feeling shy. Which was ridiculous. His mouth and hands were intimately acquainted with every square inch of her. And vice versa. They'd had stand-up shower sex, for God's sake, not to mention in a chair on the back patio of a house that didn't belong to either of them.

He slipped his arm down her back and pulled her beneath him, landing them both horizontal onto her narrow sofa. "What are you doing?" she laughed, grateful for his playful turnaround.

He untied the knot on her bathrobe sash. "Checking out the panty situation."

"Sorry, it's plain white cotton. Hanes Her Way."

He slipped them off in one smooth move and tossed them on the floor. "Not anymore." His tone turned serious. "Let's go to Hawaii."

She giggled. "Is that some sort of kinky sex game?"

"No, but if you're interested, I'm sure I can come up with one." He slid down the sofa and began nibbling at her belly. "If you don't like Hawaii, we can go somewhere else. Name a spot. As long as it's warm and I can fish. How long will it take you to get ready? Two days? Two hours?"

She lifted herself onto her elbows and stared down at the top of his head. "I . . . I can't go to Hawaii in two days. Or even in two weeks. I have a business to run and houses to sell. And I have to figure out a way to fix the mess I made with the senior center."

The senior center. For a few glorious minutes, she'd forgotten all about it. "Do you think I'm a terrible person?"

He let out a long sigh. "You really want to know what I think?"

"I asked, didn't I?"

He came back up to cradle her head in his hands and leaned down close so that his face was just a few inches from hers. "I think you care too much what other people think. But it's one of the reasons I like you so damn much." He bent down and covered her mouth. His kiss was sweet and gentle, and Kitty suddenly felt like crying again.

But not because she was slightly tipsy.

"Can I tell you something?" she whispered.

He placed his mouth on her neck.

"That night at the beach, remember when I told you I saw stars when you kissed me?"

Steve nodded, trailing his lips to nuzzle the soft skin above her clavicle.

"It couldn't have been because of the fireworks."

His gaze shot up to meet her eyes.

"Because I'm seeing them again, and I know I haven't had *that* much to drink and—"

"Shut up." He slid his body down hers and dipped his mouth between her legs.

It was no use. She couldn't think. Not when he was doing that to her.

She leaned her head back and whatever she was about to say died on her lips and dissolved into a long, slow laugh.

Surprisingly, she didn't wake up with a headache. But she did wake up with something heavy draped across her waist. It was Steve's arm. She untangled herself and scooted to the edge of the bed.

How was she going to tell Viola that she was the Realtor in the condo deal? The deal responsible for tearing down her beloved senior center? There had to be a way out of this mess. There just had to be.

Maybe she could convince Ted not to build on the land the center was located on. The center couldn't take up more than an acre. What was one measly acre in the grand scheme of things? And the gesture would generate goodwill among the population in town that was already against the condos. She could even offer to give up her commission.

But giving up her commission would be mean giving up the house.

Maybe if she explained the situation to her mother . . . She couldn't afford a down payment, but Moose was the king of creative financing. And now that Becky was gone, Kitty didn't need the office. She'd economize by working out of the house. The office rent and utilities alone would save her at least a thousand dollars a month. Her heart began to thump. It was going to be all right. She could feel it.

She'd call Ted ASAP and get the ball rolling.

First, she'd wake up Steve and get him out of here.

She went to tap his shoulder, then stopped herself. She couldn't bring herself to wake him up. Not just yet. Instead, she took a minute to savor the view.

He was lying on his side, the bottom half of his body covered by the Pottery Barn sheet with the little red sailboats. His chin and lower cheeks were covered in dark stubble. The morning light crept through the blinds, exposing the silver strands along his temples. Why did gray always look better on men than it did on women?

There was no doubt about it, she liked waking up with Steve in her bed. She liked the way his feet stuck out from the bottom of the sheet and the way his arm curled over her pillow. She liked that he talked all through sex and how his voice got huskier as he got more excited. She liked the way he smelled, the way he tasted. And she especially liked the low growly sound he made in the back of his throat when he climaxed. She was even beginning to like his moodiness. He didn't pretend to feel something he didn't. He was a man who knew exactly what he wanted. And last night, he said he wanted to take her to Hawaii.

"You're a million miles away." His voice sounded rough and scratchy. "What are you thinking?"

She cleared her throat. "I was wondering how you stood on the whole Yankees/Mets thing."

He smiled like he didn't believe her. "Neither. I'm a Braves fan."

"Oh."

He rolled onto his back and scratched his belly. "You want to know what I'm thinking?"

She lowered her gaze over the part of him still covered by the sheet. "Let me guess."

"Come here and you won't have to guess."

The doorbell rang.

"Don't answer that." He threw off the sheet.

"Impressive," she said, waggling her brows up and down. "But I really should get the door."

"Ignore it. They'll go away." He pulled her back onto the bed and positioned her beneath him, pressing his erection against her thigh. "Stop wiggling."

"I thought you liked it when I wiggled."

He wrapped his mouth around her nipple.

"I can't go to Hawaii with you," she blurted.

He stopped what he was doing with his tongue and looked up at her. "Can't? Or won't?"

"I already told you, I have business to take care of. Besides, could you even afford it?"

"I can afford it." He turned his attention back to her breast.

The way this was going, if she didn't speak up, she'd find herself on a plane to Honolulu before the day was over. "Say I do go to Hawaii with you. What happens after that?"

"Why do we have to worry about that now?"

She was saved from responding by a persistent rapping on the front door.

"They're not going away until I get that." She searched the floor for her bathrobe and slipped it on.

Steve made an impatient sound. "Hurry back."

Kitty ran to the door and threw it open.

A middle-aged woman with chin-length blonde hair stood at her door. She had on bright red lipstick and wore dark sunglasses. Kitty must still be sleeping. Caught in the middle of one of those hideous dreams where something really great is happening, and then the whole thing twists into a nightmare.

She closed her eyes and opened them again.

Dana Hanahan Burke Lewis Cartwright was still there.

"What took you so long to answer? Are you all right?" her mother asked, walking into the house. She dragged a large black Samsonite on wheels behind her. "My car has been acting up lately so I had to rent a sedan. The air-conditioning isn't working properly. Either that or I'm having hot flashes again even though, thank God, *that* part of my life was over a few years ago, so I think it must be the air-conditioning."

She stopped talking long enough to pull off the sunglasses and kiss Kitty on the cheek. "Did I wake you up? I suppose it *is* early, but you know how I like to get on the highway before the traffic gets bad. And I assumed you'd be up already. What's that red truck doing in the driveway?"

"I . . . Mom, what are you doing here?"

"Visiting you, of course."

Kitty glanced out the front window. A blue Ford Escort was parked behind Steve's truck. "Where's Larry?"

Her mother's eyes clouded over, then she sniffed and raised her chin a notch. "I've left the son of a bitch."

33

"Mom, you aren't serious."

"I don't want to talk about it. I came here for some sun and relaxation."

"But you hate Whispering Bay!"

"Nonsense. It's my home. I was raised here." She sat on the sofa and patted the space next to her. "Sit down and tell me what's going on with the offer for the house and with you and . . . oh, you never told me what that red truck is doing out there."

"The truck belongs to me," Steve said. He was dressed, but his hair was rumpled and he still had that "just woke up and waiting to get laid" look in his eyes. He might as well have come out not wearing anything at all.

"You remember Gus Pappas, don't you, Mom?"

"Of course I remember Gus. But if this is Gus, then I want to know where he found the Fountain of Youth." Her mother batted her eyelashes.

Kitty rolled her eyes. "This is his nephew, Steve. He was fixing my clogged toilet." She turned and gave Steve a pleading look. "Thank you so much for making an early morning house call."

Steve ignored the pleading look. "You must be Kitty's mother."

Her mother did the eyelash batting thing again. "I didn't know Gus had a nephew living in town."

"He doesn't live in Whispering Bay," Kitty said quickly. "He's just passing through."

"I've been in Tampa for the past ten years, but actually, I've been thinking of moving to the area," Steve said smoothly.

Since when?

"I'm sure you won't have any trouble getting a job," said her mother. "Plumbers are always in demand."

"I'm not a plumber," he said.

"Oh?"

"Gus sent him over because . . . because he and Joey were busy with another call," explained Kitty. "We don't want to keep you any longer," Kitty said to Steve. Instead of a pleading look, she gave him a "get the hell out of here" glare. "Mom, will you please move your car?"

"I hope I see you again," her mother said.

Steve nodded. "Likewise."

Kitty watched out the front window as her mother moved the rental car. "That was close."

"What was that about?" Steve asked, sounding none too happy.

Kitty whipped around. "That's my mother!"

"You don't think your mother knows you have sex?"

"Of course she knows I have sex. She's not stupid. But this is different. She knows I don't have a boyfriend. What am I supposed to introduce you as? My encore two-night stand?"

"Tell her whatever you want. But don't introduce me as the damn handyman again."

"Gee, and here I thought you were a morning person."

He shoved a hand through his hair. "This isn't how I wanted *this* morning to go."

"Tell me about it. The last thing I need is my mother crashing my pity party."

"Call me." He sounded serious. "We need to talk."

"About Hawaii?"

He hesitated a moment. "Yeah, about Hawaii."

"Is that what you normally wear to answer the door?" asked her mother.

"What do you mean?"

"That bathrobe's a little flimsy, don't you think?" Her mother laughed. "I'm not that naïve, you know. So tell me all about him! He's absolutely delicious. And he looked like he wanted to stay. I can't believe how rude you were, practically shoving him out the door. The three of us could have had breakfast together."

"I already told you, Mom. Steve was here to unclog my toilet. I barely know him."

"My God, Katherine, a good-looking man just . . . what did you call it? Unclogged your toilet? I'll have to remember that one." Her mother bent over and scooped last night's underwear off the floor. She held up the plain cotton Hanes Her Ways in the air and shook her head in disgust. "How do you expect to nab him wearing *this*? Do you have no feminine instincts? No desire to go in for the kill?"

Kitty snatched her underwear from her mother's hand. "I have plenty of desire to kill. Mom, what's going on between you and Larry?"

"I already told you. I don't want to talk about it." Her brown eyes softened a notch. "Not yet anyway."

Kitty sighed.

"I'd rather talk about your 'plumber.' I like him."

"Of course you do. The two of you have a lot in common."

"Really?"

"Yeah, you've both been married three times."

"Currently available?"

"I'm going to ask you one more time," said Kitty. "What are you doing here?"

"Do I need a reason to visit my own daughter?"

"Some advance warning might have been nice."

"The house looks good," her mother said, glancing around the living room. "Did you paint?"

"I painted last month. I told you that on the phone. Do you like the color? Shea picked it out."

"Very nice. Very neutral. But, sweetie, I really wish you hadn't gone to the expense and trouble. Now tell me all about the offer! How much am I getting?"

"Um, I'm still negotiating. I've just been so busy lately. The air conditioner broke down and—"

"The air feels fine to me."

"That's because I had a new unit installed."

"Without consulting me?"

"It isn't like air-conditioning is an option in Florida."

"I'd just like to be kept in the loop."

"Got it. Now what's going on with you and Larry?"

"I told you, I don't want to talk about it."

"Tough. You're going to have to."

Her mother's chin began to quiver. "Pam had her baby."

"Why didn't you tell me? What did she have? Is she okay?"

"She had to have a Cesarean. Larry spent the entire night at the hospital. She had a girl. They named her Dorothy Ann, Dottie for short."

"Ah." Dottie was Pam's mother's name, Larry's first wife. "And they're both fine?"

"Of course they're both fine. This is the twenty-first century, not *Little House on the Prairie*."

"Mom!"

"I'm sorry, that sounded . . . cold. It's just that we were supposed to go on a cruise next week, and now Larry wants to postpone it, on account of Pam having surgery and needing her family to help out."

Kitty nodded.

"But I'm not family. Pam barely tolerates me. I don't understand what she has against me. You'd think I'd broken up her parents' marriage or something."

"You did break up their marriage."

Her mother looked stunned. "How can you say that?"

"Wasn't Larry still married when you started dating him?"

"He was separated!"

"I don't think Pam looks at it the same way you do."

"She's thirty-five years old. She needs to get over it."

And you're fifty-eight, Kitty thought. *You need to get over it too.* "So you picked a fight with Larry and walked out on him when his daughter's in the hospital? That's just peachy, Mom."

"I came here for some sympathy, but I guess that's too much to expect from my own flesh and blood." She sniffled. "Now do you understand why I'm so anxious for this house to sell? It's my inheritance. I'm going to take the money and finally do what *I* want. I'm going to buy my own condo and go on fabulous vacations. It's my last stab at independence. At any real happiness."

"Mom, I don't think the sale is going to bring you that much money."

"Of course it is. If you've priced the house right," her mother said, frowning.

Kitty's head began to pound. There was no way she could give up her commission and still come up with a big enough amount of cash to bankroll her mother's pre-divorce spending spree.

Which meant she would have to depend entirely on Ted's goodwill if she wanted to save the senior center.

34

Ted had arranged to rent out the back room of the Harbor House for the official celebration. Earl wasn't there, but Vince was, along with Bruce Bailey from the city council. Kitty had left her mother home soaking in a warm tub. They'd spent all weekend shopping, which, blessedly, had distracted her mother from asking too many details about the sale of the house. She'd managed to put her off, but her mother wasn't stupid. Kitty was going to have to tell her sooner or later that the offer was from her. Hopefully, her mother would be so giddy about the money, she'd overlook any former objections she had to Kitty buying the house.

She stood near the big picture window overlooking the ocean, talking to Ted's attorney, the infamous Teresa. Instead of the frumpy corporate type Kitty had pictured, Teresa was tall and slender with an olive complexion and dark shoulder-length tousled hair. She had the longest eyelashes and plumpest lips

Kitty had ever seen. She also had a killer gleam in her eye that had made Kitty pause before shaking her hand.

"I can't tell you how relieved I was to hear the deal was saved," Teresa said, waving off a waiter with a tray of shrimp puffs. Kitty noticed Teresa hadn't eaten anything all night. Instead, it looked like she preferred to drink her calories. "How did you pull it off?" she asked before taking a sip of champagne.

Kitty took a sip of her own cold champagne. Usually the bubbles tickled her nose, but tonight she felt more numb than tingly. "Dumb luck, I guess."

Ted came up and put his arm around Kitty's waist. "Did I just hear my name?" He wore a pristine white cotton T with dark slacks and a light summer jacket, a la retro Don Johnson from *Miami Vice*.

She thought about wiggling out of his reach, but alienating Ted wasn't going to get her what she wanted. Besides, it was just Ted's way of being friendly. "We need to talk."

He bent down to whisper in her ear. "Have I told you how hot you look tonight?"

"Um, thanks."

"What do you want to talk about?"

"Can we go somewhere private?"

"I was hoping you'd say that." Ted grabbed two fresh champagne flutes off the tray of a wandering waiter. "You don't mind if Katherine and I take off, do you, Teresa?"

Teresa narrowed her eyes. "Of course not." She gave Kitty an amused once-over before joining the crowd by the bar.

Kitty tried not to let it rattle her as she recalled the speech she had mentally rehearsed dozens of times this afternoon while shopping. Her mother had commented on Kitty's lack of enthusiasm for the sale at Banana Republic. But it couldn't be helped. It was critical she win Ted over to her way of thinking tonight. She could always go back to Banana Republic tomorrow.

Ted led her outside to the back deck facing the ocean. Normally, there would have been tables with customers here, but the deck had been cleared for the party. A string of tiny white lights ran along the edge of the railing. It was darkish and definitely private. *Not the best place to be having this conversation.* But she had no choice. A reporter from the *Whispering Bay Gazette* had been sniffing around earlier, hanging on Bruce's every word. He had even taken a photo of Ted and Vince shaking hands. The *Gazette* was a weekly paper that came out every Friday. Which meant she only had five days until the rest of the world found out about the deal.

"I have a favor to ask," she began.

Ted placed the champagne flutes on the wooden railing behind her and leaned in close. "Your wish is my command."

"Actually, it's not for me. It's more about keeping up public relations. There's a building on the land you bought that Earl leases to the city to use as a senior center. I want you to consider keeping the arrangement. Maybe even make some improvements to the building."

"Why should I do that?"

"To promote goodwill," Kitty said. "To keep this town happy."

Ted laughed. "The town is ready to crown me mayor. Didn't you hear old Bruce's speech?"

"Not the whole town. The Gray Flamingos will be furious. They won't take this lying down. They already know something is up thanks to 'old' Bruce. I would be surprised if they don't try to protest."

"Let 'em. I'm not afraid of a bunch of geriatrics."

Not the response she was expecting.

"Controversy is never a good way to start out a project." A trickle of sweat ran down her spine. Damn humidity. She shuddered to think what it was doing to her hair.

"Once jobs start falling off trees no one's going to remember the Gray Seagulls or whatever they call themselves."

"What harm could it do to keep one little building?" Kitty asked, trying not to panic.

"Number one, I need every bit of land I bought for this project. I've talked to the architect and he agrees we can probably add more units than we originally planned. It's going to increase profits substantially. And number two, that seniors building is a fucking eyesore. I'm in the process of trying to get funding for a strip mall and no one wants some run-down building with a bunch of incontinent shuffleboard players in their faces."

"Incontinent shuffleboard players?" she sputtered.

Ted leaned in closer, trapping her against the railing. Kitty could smell the liquor on his breath. And it wasn't champagne. "I say we forget about them and focus on why we came out here."

"We came out here so I could convince you that tearing down the senior center will be a PR nightmare," Kitty said, twisting her way under his arm to escape.

He grabbed her hand. "Not so fast."

Was he for real?

She yanked her hand from his grasp. "Look, Ted, I get it. You have no interest in playing nice with the Flamingos. But now it's time you get it. I have no interest in playing nice with *you*."

For a second, he looked stunned. Then he smiled in a way that made Kitty's blood freeze. "Just one kiss."

Her fingers instinctively reached for one of the nearby champagne flutes he'd placed on the deck railing. She'd gotten the creepo vibe from Ted before, but she'd chosen to ignore it. *Listen to your gut, Kit.* Right now, her gut was pissed. Before his oily lips could swoop in for the attack, she flung the contents of the flute willy-nilly into the air and hightailed it to the door.

Her last image of Ted was the incredulous expression on his face as the champagne dripped off his nose and chin rolling its way down his perfectly pressed MTV-cop white cotton T-shirt.

"What's going on?" Pilar said, slightly out of breath. "Your voice mail said it was an emergency." She slid into the booth and took the cappuccino Kitty handed her.

"Yeah, Kit, you sounded frantic," said Shea. It was Monday and Kitty had called an early morning meeting at the Bistro. Shea had arrived only minutes before Pilar, but Kitty had wanted to wait until they were both present to break the news.

"My mother's in town," Kitty announced. "She's left Larry."

"Since when?" Shea asked.

"Since Friday."

"Why didn't you call us sooner?" Pilar demanded.

Part of the reason she hadn't called was because of Steve. She wasn't sure she wanted to tell them she'd slept with him again. And she was definitely sure she didn't want to tell them about his offer to take her to Hawaii. For one thing, she hadn't made up her mind yet. He'd left her a message on her cell but she hadn't returned his call. She'd call him later. When she had a chance to figure things out. Plus, there was the thing with Shea lying to her. But right now, the drama with her mother was zapping all her energy.

"I haven't had a second to breathe," Kitty complained. "She's had me taking her all over the coast, shopping for clothes and looking for real estate. She wants to buy a condo. Preferably, somewhere where's there a lot of male *action*."

Pilar nodded. "Boytoys-R-Us." There was a lull in the conversation. "Adult singles community," she clarified.

"Oh," said Shea.

Kitty grimaced. "She actually told me she was looking forward to being a cougar again."

"Dear God," Shea muttered.

"Don't worry, Kit," continued Pilar. "She'll go back to Larry. Didn't she do something like this a couple of years ago?"

"Yeah, but a couple of years ago she didn't have her nest-egg money."

"What nest egg?" Shea asked.

"The money she's going to get from selling Gram's house."

"You sold Gram's house?" Pilar asked.

"Not exactly. At least, not yet," Kitty said.

"What's that supposed to mean?"

"I sort of told her I got an offer on the house."

"That's great!" said Shea.

Pilar gave Shea an exasperated look.

"Isn't it?" Shea asked, looking confused.

"The offer came from me," Kitty admitted. "With the money I'm going to make off this deal with Ted Ferguson, I can afford it." Just saying Ted's name now made her cringe.

"So what's the problem?" Pilar asked.

"The problem is that the land I helped Ted buy is the land the senior center's located on."

Shea and Pilar gave each other a look.

"I know, I know," Kitty said miserably. "How am I going to fix this?"

Pilar sighed. "You can't. Unless you can convince Ted not to tear down the center?"

"I already tried that. First he laughed, then he made a pass at me."

"Oh my God. What did you do?" Shea asked.

"I threw a flute of champagne in his face."

"That should make him come around," Pilar said sarcastically. "What an asshole."

Shea shook her head. "Why do all the rich, available guys always end up being jerks?"

"It looks like you're stuck," Pilar said.

"So the Gray Flamingos were right all along," Shea said. "Good thing they have that petition going."

"Is that supposed to make me feel better?" Kitty asked.

"We warned you something like this might happen," Pilar said.

"Yeah," said Shea. "I mean, it's not like you didn't already know what you were getting yourself into."

Pilar's watch beeped. She grabbed her cappuccino and stood. "Gotta go. I promised old man Hillaman I'd be in the office by eight."

"Is that all the advice I get?" Kitty asked. "I'm ready and willing to do *whatever* you two suggest."

Pilar's dark brows scrunched together. "What more can you do? Besides, compared to something like world hunger or ten-

sion in the Middle East, you have to admit, it's small potatoes."
She made her way out of the booth. "Remember, Bunco is at
my house this week. You're both coming over early to set up.
Right? I have an associates meeting at five, but I promise to be
home by six thirty."

"Isn't six thirty cutting it a little close?" Shea asked.

"No can help!" Pilar yelled on her way out the door.

That was it?

Kitty gritted her teeth. At least Shea hadn't cut out on her.
"I never asked you how the nanny interview went."

Shea's face dropped. "It was a total bust."

"You'll find someone. And you have at least nine months
till you really need a nanny, right?"

Shea dipped her finger in her mocha latte and licked off
some of the whipped topping. "I've been thinking. Maybe Pilar's right. Two kids are a handful, and like I said, I'd really like
to go back to work soon. Moose thinks it's a good idea. At the
very least, it would get me out of the house and talking about
something other than toilet training."

"I thought you liked talking about toilet training."

Shea gave a dispassionate laugh. "Things are just a little
strained right now. Moose and I are each other's first and only,
and after a while, it gets sort of old. You know?"

No, she didn't know.

First it was Pilar and Nick and the vasectomy thing, and
now Moose and Shea were having bedroom problems? Could
it have anything to do with Shea's car always being at Dolphin
Isles? Shea was hiding something. Kitty was sure of it.

Could Shea be having an affair?

With Walt Walters?

No way. It was too ridiculous to even think.

"So, what should I do about the senior center?" Kitty asked.

"I think Pilar's right. There's not much you can do. Cheer up! It's not the end of the world. And it's not like you did it on purpose." Shea paused. "Did you?"

"Of course not! What kind of question is that?"

"If I were you, I'd be more freaked about your mother."

"I guess I'll figure out something on my own," Kitty said, pushing her latte to the side. Things were bad if one of Frida's lattes couldn't tempt her.

Damn it. She hadn't called this meeting to be brushed off. Usually whenever she was in trouble, Pilar would come up with some brilliant scheme to fix it and Shea would know exactly what to say to make her feel better. But all they could talk about was themselves.

In the twenty-five years they'd been friends, Kitty couldn't remember one instance that Shea and Pilar hadn't come through for her.

Except today. When she needed them the most.

Apparently, the greatest crisis in her life was nothing more than a blip on the radar in theirs.

35

IIIIII

It had been two days since the worthless powwow with Shea and Pilar, and Kitty hadn't been able to come up with anything to fix the senior center situation. There was no use putting it off any longer. She needed to talk to Viola before she heard news of Kitty's involvement from someone else.

The back door to Viola's house was unlocked. The smell of fresh coffee lingered in the air. "Come in!" she cried cheerfully, waving Kitty into the room. "I have some exciting news! We've gotten over six hundred signatures on the petition!"

Kitty didn't have to ask what petition Viola was referring to. Her stomach began to ache.

"You don't look so good," Viola said, studying her face. "Did you eat breakfast?"

"Not yet."

"Help yourself to some muffins. I made six dozen to bring

to the Gray Flamingos emergency meeting Friday night." She looked up thoughtfully. "We're expecting a record crowd. Do you think I should have made more?"

Emergency meeting? "I have something I need to talk to you about."

Viola smiled. "I think I know what it is."

"You do?" Viola didn't seem upset. Maybe Shea and Pilar were right. Maybe things weren't so gloomy after all.

"Gus told me. He's not naïve, and neither am I. There's not a lot of red pickup trucks with Hillsborough County tags around here. I'd have to be blind not to have seen his truck parked in front of your house the other night."

Kitty felt a little dizzy. "I didn't come here to talk about Steve."

Viola poured her a cup of coffee and handed it to her. Kitty noticed she knew exactly how much cream and sweetener to put in. "Thanks."

"I didn't get married until I was almost thirty-four," said Viola. "Did you know that?"

Kitty shook her head. Bob Pantini had died of cancer when Kitty was still in high school. She didn't remember him all that well, except that he was a nice man, tall, and now that she thought about it, good-looking.

"I'd lived in Whispering Bay all my life, except when I went to school in Tallahassee to get my teaching degree. Most of my friends found husbands by the time they'd graduated college, but not me. I was picky," she said with a laugh. "Like Elizabeth Bennet in *Pride and Prejudice*. 'I am determined that nothing but the deepest love will ever induce me into matrimony,'" Viola quoted.

Kitty smiled. She knew the line by heart too.

"Did you know that I almost made the 1956 Olympic swim team?"

"No! Why haven't I heard that before?"

"I said 'almost.' Almost doesn't make you famous. I was nineteen, and the best in the state in the one-hundred-meter freestyle. But someone beat me out the day of the qualifiers and that was that. So I finished college, came back home, and started teaching at the high school. Back then, if you were twenty-two and unmarried with no prospects, people worried about you. By twenty-five, I was an old maid, and by thirty-three, I was practically shriveled up.

"And then, something happened that changed my life. Old Man Donnelly, that's what we teachers called the principal, retired. And come that September, who moves to town, but the most handsome man I'd ever laid eyes on. Bob Pantini. Straight from Brooklyn, New York." Viola chuckled. "He was tall, with a head full of dark hair and the most gorgeous green eyes you'd ever seen. He was thirty-eight and divorced and every available woman in town was after him from day one."

"But you're the one he liked," Kitty said.

Viola laughed again. "Unfortunately, it wasn't that easy. Most of our conversations lasted less than a minute. 'How are you today, Mr. Pantini?' 'Just fine, Miss Hayes, and you?' And that was it. Every once in a while, I'd catch him looking at me out of the corner of his eye during a staff meeting, and he always seemed to pop up in the teacher's lounge during my planning period. Once, we talked for an hour straight. He was the most fascinating man I'd ever met. He knew all about opera and literature. So different from the local men, most of whom worked at the old paper mill and were only interested in fishing and getting drunk on Saturday night. I told him how I had dreamed of being an Olympic swimmer, and I'll tell you, he acted pretty impressed. But he never asked me out. I figured he either wasn't interested in me that way, or he didn't want to date a teacher from his school."

"So how did you end up together?"

"On the last day of the term he called me to his office to go over my evaluation. He sat behind his big desk, looking all yummy in his white collared shirt and navy blue tie. I still remember the smell of his Old Spice aftershave. He was very professional through the whole thing. Told me what an asset I was to the school and how the girls all loved taking my classes. And I sat there, barely listening to a word he said, just itching to reach out and run the palm of my hand over that stubbled chin of his.

"Then he handed me the evaluation to sign and our hands brushed, you know, just a little." Viola's eyes got a far-off dreamy look in them. "It was like a surge of electricity shot between us."

Kitty felt her breath hitch.

Viola took a sip of her coffee and smiled mysteriously. "I was a little startled at first, embarrassed, really. I waited till my cheeks had cooled off to look at him, and when I did, he was blushing." She laughed again. "Here was this big, handsome man from New York City and he was blushing."

"Did he ask you out?"

"No," Viola replied, calmly. "I asked him out."

"You didn't!" Kitty cried, slapping the pine table with the palm of her hand.

"I realized then and there that I was too old to just sit back and do nothing. If I wanted that man, then I was going to have to make the first move myself."

Kitty nodded, fascinated. Why had she never heard this story before? "Was he shocked? That you asked him out?"

"It was the early seventies, not the turn of the century," Viola said. "Not an everyday occurrence, but certainly not completely unheard of."

Kitty smiled. "Go on."

"At first, I could tell he was taken aback. And I was mortified, sitting there across from him at that desk, waiting for his answer. Then he picked up a sheet of paper and handed it to me. It was a job offer from one of the high schools in Panama City. They'd heard what a good job he'd done here in Whispering Bay and they wanted to hire him. He asked me if I thought he should take it. That's when I knew the reason he hadn't asked me out before was because he was my boss. Bob was very professional, you know."

"So, you told him to take the job?"

"Of course not! You should never make it *that* easy," Viola said. "I told him maybe we should have a date first. See how things went."

"And they went great," Kitty supplied.

"You could say that." Viola's blue eyes twinkled. "He took me out to dinner, and afterward, we walked on the beach for hours. He told me all about his ex-wife and how after their divorce he had wanted to move somewhere new to start fresh. So he came to our little beachside town hoping to do just that. And I told him all about me and my family and how I loved teaching PE. And when he went to drive me home, I said 'No, take me back to your place.'"

"Really?" Kitty squeaked.

"It was bold of me, but we weren't kids and I knew five minutes into that date that I was going to marry that man. One thing led to another, and before I knew it, we were on his bed doing it."

Kitty's mouth dropped open.

"You should have seen the expression on his face when he realized I was still a virgin. I might have been a little fast with him, but you have to remember, I was raised Baptist in a small town in north Florida. You just didn't give it up until your wedding night, or at least until you had a ring on your finger and could figure out a way to not get caught. The pill was around then, but an unmarried woman in Whispering Bay didn't dare ask for a prescription for it, especially not when you taught public high school. And neither of us had been clearheaded enough beforehand to think about a condom. Safe sex back then meant using a padded headboard."

Kitty laughed. "Then what happened?"

"He asked me to marry him and I said yes. Of course, I had to come up with this elaborate made-up story to tell everyone when they asked how he had proposed. I couldn't very well say, 'Oh, Bob and I had sex on our first date, and then he asked me to marry him.' My daddy would have loved that one." A sentimental look came over her when she added, "Your grandmother was the only one who knew the real story of how Bob proposed. She thought it was a big hoot, you know."

"My grandmother knew that story?"

Viola shook her head. "Why is it that every generation thinks they're the ones who invented sex?"

Kitty shrugged, a little embarrassed. It was weird hearing all this from Viola. And to think that her grandmother had known the story too.

Viola took a long sip of her coffee and placed it carefully on the table. "We got married two weeks later. Since I was already pushing thirty-four, we decided to go for a baby right away.

"After trying for about a year, and believe me, we tried," she added with a wink, "we got worried. I went to the doctor and got a clean bill of health. He told us we were just stressed, to give it a little more time. Before we knew it, another year went by, and I began to suspect something was wrong. Bob had been married for four years that other time, and his first wife never got pregnant either. Back then, fertility problems weren't so commonly discussed. So we looked into adoption." Viola glanced out the kitchen window. It was the first time Kitty had ever seen such a wistful expression on her face.

"By that time I was thirty-six and Bob was forty. The first two agencies we looked into said we were too old to start a family. Can you imagine them telling a couple that today?" She shook her head. "We were stupid. Plain ass stupid. We gave up without a fight. And that," she said, giving Kitty a hard stare, "is the only regret I've ever had in my entire life. I've never regretted not making the Olympic team or waiting till I was almost thirty-four to have my first real orgasm, or even staying in Whispering Bay all my life. But I've always regretted not having a child.

"So what if we were considered a little old to be first-time parents? Bob would have been the best father ever. It would have been nice to have a son or a daughter. They would have been almost your age by now. I might even have been a grandmother. I'd have been a good grandmother." She sighed heavily. "But I've never been one to look back and cry over what could have been. That's just not me." She glanced at the clock and then at Kitty's uneaten muffin. "Eat! You're probably starving and here I am talking my head off."

Kitty took a little nibble of the muffin. "Viola, why did you tell me all this?"

"Sometimes we have to go out of our comfort zone to make things happen. I just thought you might need to hear that."

It didn't take a genius to figure out what Viola was getting at. But she had it all wrong. She and Steve were nothing like Viola and Bob Pantini.

"Viola, are you dating Gus?"

"I'm not sure if what we're doing would be called dating, but I guess you could call it that." Viola blushed.

Dear God. Kitty didn't want to take this any further. She smiled. She was happy for Viola. She really was.

"So if you didn't come here to talk about Steve, then it must be your mother. I've been so busy with this senior center project I haven't had time to go over and say hello, but I noticed she's moved in."

"She's left Larry."

Viola made a face. "What is it this time?"

"Basically, he's a selfish beast for wanting to spend time with his new granddaughter."

Viola sighed. "You know, your mother isn't the enemy, Kitty."

Viola's defense surprised her. "I know that."

"And your grandmother wasn't a saint. I loved her. She was my best friend, but she made her share of mistakes too."

Kitty suddenly remembered Earl's admission about he and her grandmother being sweethearts. She wondered what else she didn't know about her grandmother.

She eyed the empty muffin tins on the counter. By the time the Flamingos held their emergency meeting on Friday everyone in town would have read the *Whispering Bay Gazette*.

They would know about the condo deal and the destruction of the senior center and Kitty's role in the whole mess.

Kitty's stomach felt like it was being scoured in acid. She'd forgotten the sensation, but she'd felt it once before. On the day she and her mother had moved here twenty-five years ago. She'd been scared and lonely and angry then. But her grandmother had made it better. And then Viola had shown her how to bake sugar cookies and had let her play with Sebastian. And then, a few weeks later, she'd met Shea and Pilar. And everything had worked out okay.

But nothing was okay now.

She had a short reprieve. Two more days of blissful freedom. Two days before she became the town goat. She didn't want to give those two days up. She couldn't tell Viola about her role in the condo deal. She just couldn't.

"Can I help you make more muffins?" Kitty asked.

"You think we're going to need more?"

Kitty nodded. The Flamingos meeting was going to generate a lot more interest than Viola could even begin to imagine.

36

||||||

It was strange. Three weeks ago she hadn't even known Steve Pappas, and three days ago he was the last person she'd have gone to for advice. After she'd left Viola's house she'd gone into the office and tried to make sales calls, but she'd been too agitated to get much done. Her mother, sensing something was wrong, had even made Kitty's favorite childhood supper—fried chicken and mashed potatoes—but Kitty had only been able to get down a couple of bites. She'd excused herself from the table, laced on her sneakers, and gone for a run. Five miles later, here she was, standing on Gus's doorstep.

She rang the bell, catching sight of her reflection in the glass panel strip alongside the wooden door. Her face was flushed and her hair was pulled back in a sweaty ponytail. She wore Steve's Ron Jon T-shirt and a pair of navy blue nylon shorts, both of which were dripping wet.

Steve answered the door. "You look like hell," he said, ushering her into the air-conditioned living room.

"Gee, thanks."

"It's an expression. Personally, I always think you look fantastic. What I meant to say is that you look like you need a friend."

"That's exactly what I need," Kitty said. She'd never been in this kind of situation before. Shea and Pilar had always been there for her. But for some reason, they just didn't get it. Or maybe they did and they were just too busy to care. Either way, it was depressing to think of what was going on with the three of them right now.

She took a look around the room. She hadn't been inside the place since she'd sold it to Gus. He'd ripped out the old gold carpet and replaced it with Mexican tile. Most of the furniture looked brand-new, but Kitty recognized the La-Z-Boy chair Gus had insisted on bringing from the old house. Family pictures covered the walls. Pictures of Joey and Angela and their spouses and children.

"Where's Gus?" she asked.

"He took Nathan bowling. They just left."

"We're alone?"

"Yep."

Her skin tingled. It was probably the cool air-conditioning drying the sweat off her body. Or maybe it had something to do with knowing that she and Steve were alone. "Do you have a few minutes?"

"Are you kidding? I've left three messages on your cell, not to mention the half dozen times I've driven by your house."

She'd known about the messages, of course, but she hadn't

known about the drive-bys. Her heart seemed to skip a beat. "Why didn't you stop?"

He shrugged. "Your mom's car was always out front."

She couldn't blame him for that. "I'm sorry about pushing you out the door. It's like I said, I really don't know how to explain you to her." *Or to anyone else for that matter.*

"Come here." He led her down the hallway into the spare bedroom. On top of the queen-size bed was a large suitcase and several neat piles of clothes.

Her throat went dry. "You're leaving?" she asked.

He pulled out an envelope from the drawer in the nightstand and handed it to her. Inside were two airline tickets from Pensacola to Honolulu. One of them was in her name.

"Saturday morning for Hawaii. I'd like you to come with me."

She stared at the ticket. "*First class?*"

"Why not?"

"This must have cost a fortune. I . . . I'm not sure I can get away."

"We've already been through this. You can do whatever you want. Maybe you just don't want to."

"I want to," she said softly.

"Then do it."

She started to sit on the edge of the bed, then remembered her sweaty clothes.

"Go ahead," Steve said, reading her mind. He shoved the suitcase and the clothes off the bed. It all landed in an untidy heap on the floor.

He sat next to her and took her hand in his. She was suddenly glad she'd come here. It felt . . . right.

"I need some advice," she said. "About the senior center thing. In a couple of days, the whole town, including Viola—she's my next-door neighbor and the head of the Gray Flamingos—"

"I know who Viola is," Steve interrupted.

She nodded. Of course he did. After all, she was dating Gus. "They're all going to know that I'm responsible for this mess," she continued.

"How the hell are you responsible?" He sounded indignant. She winced.

"Sorry," he said, toning it down after seeing her reaction, "I just hate to see you this way. You're eating yourself up for nothing. It's business, Kit. Plain and simple."

"I know that," she said testily. "But I *feel* responsible. I can't help how I feel, Steve."

"Tell me about it," he said, reaching out to tuck an errant strand of hair behind her ear. His fingers lingered a few seconds longer than necessary, causing a shiver to run down her spine. "You're not the one who initiated this deal. You only helped broker it. Ted Ferguson was going to do this with or without you."

"That's what I keep telling myself. But it's such a cop-out. Like it or not, I'm an accomplice in this whole mess." She narrowed her eyes at him. "Hey, how do you know about Ted Ferguson? I've never mentioned his name before. Have I?"

He hesitated. "You mentioned his company, Ferguson and Associates. I'm familiar with him."

"Well, you were the one who said I should listen to my gut. And right now my gut is all torn up inside."

He sighed heavily. "Baby, I wish there was some way I could make this all disappear for you. The only thing I can tell you is

that the people who really care about you are going to understand. As for the rest of them? Fuck 'em.'"

Despite her mood, she let out a little laugh. Men always
seemed to be able to break things down into the simplest
common denominator.

He pushed her onto the bed, landing on top of her. "I know
a way to make you feel better."

"Oh no, we don't." She tried to rise, but she couldn't budge
two hundred pounds of Steve Pappas off her. "We can't do
this," she said. "We can't always end up having sex."

"Why not? It's what two people who are crazy about each
other do," he said, nuzzling her neck.

"We're crazy about each other?"

He pulled off his shirt. "Aren't we?" He tossed the shirt on
the floor. His shorts came off next. Kitty sucked in a breath.

"That's not fair," she said. "Getting all naked on me."

"Then get even," he said, tugging off her running shoes.

"But I'm all icky and sweaty."

"I like you sweaty." His gaze slowly ran up her legs, over
her hips and breasts, making her flush.

Maybe he was right. Maybe a little sex would make her feel
better. It certainly couldn't hurt right now. "Okay, you talked
me into it," she said, tearing off her clothes.

He smiled and raised her arms over her head, placing them
on the headboard. "Don't let go," he ordered.

She grabbed the headboard, too fascinated not to.

He eyeballed the discarded clothes on the floor. "I don't
have anything to tie you up with. Maybe an old T-shirt or
something," he said, more to himself than to her. "And I sure
as hell don't have any nail polish so this is going to have to
be a poor substitute for the whole 'tie me up and polish my

toes' fantasy you got going. But I can give you a rain check on that."

"Sure," she squeaked. She waited for him to kiss her, or touch her breast. Or something. But he just stared at her. She began to feel restless. And a little embarrassed. She squirmed beneath his perusal. Maybe he'd changed his mind. Maybe he did find her too sweaty and icky after all. "Is something wrong?" she asked, hearing the vulnerability in her voice.

"I was just going back to that first night we were together."

"Oh." She laughed nervously. "I guess you must be thinking that pink feather boa would come in handy right about now."

He trailed his fingers lightly down her throat and over her shoulder. "That's not what I was thinking." He clamped his mouth around her breast, gently sucking on her nipple until it got all stiff and pointy, then he started in on the other one. He took his time, lingering over them, his tongue hot against her skin.

Kitty sighed and went to reach for him, then remembered she was supposed to keep her hands on the headboard. The restless feeling she'd had before intensified. She rubbed the soles of her feet against the hard muscle on the back of his calves. She could feel the moisture pool between her thighs. She pushed her hips up and ground herself against his erection. "Steve . . ."

He glanced down at her, surprised by whatever he saw in her face. Kitty could only imagine it was the raw lust in her eyes. Not much foreplay needed tonight.

He ran his hands down the inside of her knees, spread her legs, then hooked them around his hips and slid into her. She didn't want slow. She didn't want gentle. He must have sensed it too, because be began to pound into her with a fast, hard rhythm that sucked the breath from her. From somewhere in the recesses of her mind she remembered Viola's comment about safe sex and the padded headboard.

It had only been a few nights since they'd been together, but she felt like a stack of overdried kindling getting its first whiff of fire. Just when she was on the verge of coming, he stopped. Her eyes flew open to find Steve looking down at her. A trickle of sweat dripped off his forehead onto her cheek.

"What's wrong?" she asked.

"You want to know what I was thinking before? I was thinking that if I knew then what I know now, I would have never screwed up and left you that morning to wake up alone."

Without waiting for her response, he picked up the rhythm. This time he went excruciatingly slow. But instead of losing momentum, they were right back to where they'd been. It was perfect.

After a few strokes, he stopped again. She sighed and opened her eyes. "What?"

"Tell me you're going to go to Hawaii with me," he whispered roughly.

Right now, she'd tell him anything he wanted to hear. And it would all be true. "Okay," she whispered back.

37

Kitty tried for the zillionth time to walk out the door, but her mother wasn't having it. "Mom, there won't be anything for you to do but sit and watch. You'd be bored to tears."

"I can be fun," her mother protested. "I play bridge at the country club. I know how to do girl talk and be hip."

"Did you just use the word 'hip'?"

"You'll never even know I'm there. Besides, I've always wondered what goes on in your Bunco group."

"Sorry, Mom, but the answer is no."

Her mother's eyes watered up. "Please, don't leave me alone in this house again. It's been five days since I've heard from Larry. I can't stand it. And you keep putting me off about the house offer. Has it fallen through and you just don't want to tell me? Please, darling, I need to know."

"Of course it hasn't fallen through," Kitty said. "It's just . . . tricky is all."

"Tricky?" Her mother began to cry. "I knew it. There's no offer, is there?"

"Of course there is! Don't cry, Mom. There's an offer. A good one." There was no sense keeping it from her mother a minute longer. Tomorrow Kitty was going to be outed by the *Whispering Bay Gazette* and the entire town would know. "The offer's from me."

"From you?" Her mother swiped away her tears. "But you keep telling me business has been slow lately. How can you afford to buy the house?"

"I'm going to be making a big commission soon. A huge one actually, and I'm going to use that money as a down payment on the house. So you see, everything is going to be fine."

"How big a commission?" her mother asked suspiciously. "I mean, I know you can turn a nice little profit off a house, but—"

"It's not from a house. It's a large tract of land. Beachfront property, to be exact."

"Oh." Her mother looked impressed.

"There's a developer from south Florida who's going to build condos on the beach. And he selected me to be his broker."

"Katherine, that's wonderful!" Her face clouded over. "But are you sure you want to use the money to buy this house?" She waved a hand through the air. "Darling, I know this place holds some sort of sentimental value for you, but really. It needs a lot of work and this town is so . . . well, so uninspiring."

"I'm positive, Mother. Now, don't you feel better?"

"A little. But I still don't want to stay here alone. Please, Katherine. I'll never ask for anything again."

Kitty's shoulder sagged. Tonight, she'd wanted to laugh and get drunk and pretend everything was all right. Her proverbial Last Supper, so to speak. The last thing she needed was to babysit her mother. But she wasn't heartless enough to look her mother in the eye and say no. Not when her mother was looking at her with puppy-dog eyes.

"All right, you can come. But don't complain if you're bored."

Her mother raised her finger and made an X over her heart. "I promise. I'll just sit in the corner and watch like a good girl."

"This is Shea. At the sound of the beep, leave a message."

"It's me," Kitty said into her cell phone. She was standing in Pilar's kitchen, alone. "Where are you?" For that matter, she wanted to add, where was Pilar? At least Pilar had called to say she was running late to her own Bunco party. Work. Again. But Shea didn't have an excuse. Kitty tried Shea's house next. A sitter by the name of Courtney answered. Shea and Moose had both gone out for the evening but she'd be happy to take a message.

Okay. That was good. Shea must be on her way over.

It was twenty after seven. The rest of the Babes, minus Shea and Pilar, were already here. With Nick's help, Kitty had managed to keep everyone happy with ample servings of tonight's signature drink, mango daiquiris. But the natives were getting restless. She could only hold them off for so long.

Nick brought in an empty pitcher and started in on another batch of the daiquiris. "Sorry about this," he said, filling the blender with a load of crushed ice. "Pilar's job sucks."

"I guess you're used to it, huh?" Kitty asked, opening a bag of potato chips.

"Having an absentee wife? It's harder on Anthony." Nick put in the rest of the daiquiri ingredients. "Has she told you she wants me to get a vasectomy?"

A sour-cream-and-onion chip stuck in her throat. Kitty took a sip of her daiquiri and thought about the best way to answer that. She had promised Pilar's mother she would talk to Pilar about the vasectomy, but so far there hadn't been an opportunity. Which wasn't exactly true, she thought guiltily. She could have talked to Pilar at least half a dozen times if she'd really wanted to. She'd just been too busy with the condo deal and with Steve and her mother and everything else going on in her life.

"You don't have to tell me," Nick said. "I already know. She's told you everything. She always does."

"She's my best friend, Nick."

He stared stonily ahead.

Fuck it. Nick was her friend too. "Okay, she told me about the vasectomy. And that the two of you hadn't . . . well, hadn't had sex in a while."

"A while?" He snorted.

"Look, I'm like a Catholic priest trying to give married people advice here. Not a lot of practical experience to go by, you know? It just seems to me that the two of you can reach a compromise."

"Pilar doesn't want to compromise. It's her way or the highway. You know how she is."

For a second, Kitty was speechless. She'd never imagined things were this bad. Nick and Pilar were the perfect couple. If they couldn't make it, no one could.

"What's the real problem here?" Kitty asked. "You want more kids and Pilar doesn't?"

"The real problem is that her job comes first. Before anything or anyone. Look at you. Holding down the fort at her own fucking Bunco party. Her job comes before her friends, her husband, and even her own kid."

"So you want to make it worse and have more kids?"

"I want her to quit her job, that's what I want. If she gets pregnant again, then maybe she'll have to."

"That's so unfair. Pilar has worked hard to get where she's at. But if her job is interfering with your marriage, then you have to tell her. Don't try to force her into having another baby if she's not ready. Stand up and be a man, Nick. Tell her you don't want a vasectomy. Tell her it's your body and the answer is no. Tell her everything you've just told me."

"Gee, am I interrupting something?"

Kitty and Nick spun around to see Pilar standing in the kitchen doorway.

"Nick and I were just . . . talking," Kitty said, trying not to act guilty.

"Sounds like it," Pilar said tightly.

Shit. What had Pilar heard? "Can we talk about this later? Everyone is waiting on us."

Pilar suddenly looked tired. "Sure."

"I'll go read Anthony a bedtime story," Nick said, ignoring Pilar.

Kitty watched him exit the kitchen. She started to say she was sorry but Pilar cut her off by putting her hand in the air. "You're right. We'll talk about this later. For now let's put up a united front for the Babes."

Nick had set up the Bunco tables in the living room. The

Babes were milling around, drinking their daiquiris and munching on the goodies Kitty had put out earlier.

"What's your mom doing here?" Pilar whispered in Kitty's ear.

Kitty glanced at her mother, who was sitting on the living room couch sipping a daiquiri with a little pink umbrella hanging over the side of the glass. "She insisted on coming."

"Good thing Isabel didn't catch wind of that. Could you imagine? Our mothers at Bunco?"

"I think your mother would be awesome at Bunco."

Pilar rolled her eyes. "Yeah, right." She lowered her voice a notch. "Have you talked to Mrs. Pantini yet? About the senior center?"

"I'm putting it off as long as I can."

"It's not your fault," said Pilar. "Just remember that."

Kitty nodded. It was exactly what Steve had told her last night. Speaking of which, she still hadn't packed for her trip to Hawaii. Or even told anyone about it for that matter. Maybe tonight, after everyone had left and she and Pilar had cleared up their misunderstanding, the three of them could have a long talk. She would confront Shea about her lies, and then she'd confess to the two of them about Steve.

"Where's Shea?" Brenda asked.

"Shea's running late," Mimi said.

"Don't worry, she'll be here," Pilar said. "I talked to her this afternoon."

"We could play with a ghost until she gets here," Brenda said.

Frida made a face. A ghost was an imaginary player, which meant one of the Babes wouldn't have a partner. It sucked playing with a ghost.

"Why doesn't Kitty's mom fill in?" Mimi suggested.

"Good idea," said Lorraine.

"Mom doesn't know how to play," Kitty blurted.

Her mother jumped from the couch. Some of the mango daiquiri splashed onto Pilar's carpet. "I'd love to play!"

"But you don't know how," Kitty protested.

"I play bridge at home. Bunco can't be that difficult."

"It's settled then," said Pilar.

What happened to her mother's promise to sit in the corner and watch like a good girl? Kitty should have known this would happen. She counted to three before responding. "I guess it couldn't hurt to let you play until Shea gets here."

Her mother plucked the pink umbrella from her glass and chugged down the rest of her drink. "I really have to get the recipe for this smoothie."

Kitty frowned. "How many of those have you had?"

Her mother looked offended.

"Okay, Mom, you'll be my partner on this first round. That way I can talk you through the game. We're rolling for ones. The goal is to roll as many ones as possible. If we roll three sixes, that's a Bunco and you try to grab the dice—"

"You're going too fast, dear. Slow down. What's the object of the game again?"

Kitty gritted her teeth. "Never mind. Just roll the dice when I tell you to."

"Can I have another smoothie first?"

The game went by in a blur. Everyone was busy chatting, catching up on post–Fourth of July vacation gossip. Liz's son Dex was going to need braces, but she thought that at nine he was too young, so an entire conversation ensued about the pros and cons of orthodontics at an early age.

Kitty had trouble concentrating. Every few minutes she'd

catch herself looking at the front door. When was Shea going to get here?

"Did you hear the latest about the big condo deal?" Lorraine asked. "There's an article about it in tomorrow's paper. Apparently they're going to tear down the senior center."

"So the Flamingos were right!" exclaimed Tina.

It was Kitty's turn to roll. The dice went flying off the table. "How did you get a copy of tomorrow's paper?"

"I ran by Corbits on my way home from work. They already had tomorrow's edition stocked. I only had a second, so I just skimmed the front page. I don't know any of the details yet."

Great. Corbits couldn't keep their vegetables crisp but they were Johnny-on-the-spot when it came to fresh gossip.

"What do you think?" Lorraine asked Frida. "Do you think the condos will be good for business?"

Frida shrugged. "It could go either way for me. It could help, but if a big chain like Starbucks decides to come in, I'll be done for."

"I adore Starbucks," Kitty's mother said. "I especially love their pumpkin spice latte. But they only serve that in the fall."

"Starbucks is the devil," said Frida.

Her mother looked alarmed. "I never knew that!"

Dear God. How many mango daiquiris had her mother drunk?

"Frida owns a small independent coffeehouse," Pilar explained gently. "It's only natural she'd feel threatened by a big national chain like Starbucks."

"Oh," said her mother. "Well, I'm still very proud of my girl. This condo deal is going to set her up."

Everyone stopped rolling the dice. "Kitty, are you the Realtor in that deal?" Lorraine asked.

Her mother took another sip of her daiquiri and smiled. "Not only that, but Katherine's life is *really* picking up. You should see her hunky new boyfriend."

"Boyfriend?" repeated Frida. "Kitty, I didn't know you had a boyfriend."

Kitty tried to laugh it off. "Mom, you just rolled a one. You get to roll again." She looked over at Pilar to find her staring at her. Kitty made an "isn't my mother crazy?" face. But Pilar didn't smile back.

"I suppose the fact that this Steve what's-his-name has been married and divorced three times doesn't bode well in his favor," continued her mother, "although personally, I don't see multiple marriages as the big failure my daughter does. But if it doesn't work out between them, I think Katherine should consider moving. She's never going to find an eligible man in this town. Don't you girls agree?"

"Steve Pappas?" Frida set her dice on the card table. "I thought you told us there was nothing going on between you two," she said, staring at Kitty.

Kitty swallowed hard.

Her mother nodded. "Steve Pappas, that's his name. Doesn't it sound sexy? And believe me, there was plenty going on," her mother said, chuckling. "Katherine thinks I'm too naïve to know when a man has spent the night. But I wasn't born yesterday."

"We aren't dating. Not really," rushed Kitty. Only they were, but this wasn't how she had planned to break the news to them. "Whose turn is it?" she asked, desperately wishing they'd go back to playing. Why had she ever agreed to let her mother come along?

"If you aren't dating, then what are you doing?" asked Tina.

"Yeah," said Pilar. "What are you doing?"

Maybe if she was vague enough, Pilar would think her mother was talking about the one-night stand.

"*You know,*" Kitty said, purposely catching Pilar's eye. "It was just . . . well, it was sort of like friends with benefits, but without the being-friends part."

"What are the benefits?" asked her mother, looking around the room in confusion.

"Sex," said Pilar flatly.

"Oh," her mother said, nodding. "I already knew they were having sex. I practically caught them at it the morning I came in. I just didn't realize 'benefits' was the new term for it." She laughed. "Benefits, unclogging the toilet. My generation just called it screwing."

Pilar stood and faced Kitty. "I can't believe you're still seeing that loser! You lied to me."

"I didn't. Not exactly." She narrowed her eyes at her mother. "Mom, I think you've had too much to drink."

Her mother stared down at her empty glass. "You mean there's liquor in here?"

"Kit, didn't you sit here at Bunco a couple of weeks ago and tell us you weren't seeing this guy?" asked Tina.

"I guess, maybe, I might have . . ."

"Why didn't you tell us the truth?" Frida asked. "I thought we told each other everything. You know, what happens at Bunco stays at Bunco."

"I—"

"If you didn't want us to know, all you had to do is tell us to mind our own business," Pilar said, having the audacity to look hurt.

Kitty felt a bolt of anger shoot through her. "Yeah, right."

"What's that supposed to mean?" Pilar asked.

"It means that maybe if you were there for me a little bit more instead of always running off to work, then I would have told you." Kitty picked up the dice and rolled. "I just got two ones."

Pilar grabbed the dice off the table. "What do you mean I'm not there for you?"

Kitty placed her palm out. "Hand over those dice!"

"Not until you tell us what's going on."

"What's going on?" she repeated, sounding a little hysterical to her own ears. "I'll tell you what's going on. The past few days have been the shittiest of my life. The senior center is going to be torn down and even though it's not directly my fault, it seems that way. How I am I going to explain that to Mrs. Pantini? And every time I talk to you and Shea about it all you two do is brush me off. And then you walk in on me and Nick talking and you think there's some sort of conspiracy between us."

"I can't believe you're taking Nick's side in this," Pilar said.

"I'm not taking anyone's side," Kitty said.

"Well, you should! I'm your best friend, for fuck's sake!"

"And then there's Shea, off doing who knows what!" Kitty collapsed in her seat. "I think . . . I think Shea's having an affair. With Walt Walters," Kitty managed in a horrified whisper.

Pilar's mouth dropped open.

"No way!" protested Frida.

The room began to buzz.

Kitty placed her head in her hands. How had the evening deteriorated so quickly? "I've seen her Navigator parked in front of Dolphin Isles twice now. And both times she's denied it. But I *know* it was her car. And she admitted to me the other day that she was bored with her love life. If she's not having an affair with Walt Walters, then what's she doing at Dolphin Isles? She despises the place!"

"Shea and Walt Walters?" croaked Brenda. "But she was homecoming queen! She could do a lot better than Walt Walters."

"Maybe Moose is having an affair?" suggested Tina.

Pilar glared at Tina. "Just because you thought Brett was having an affair doesn't mean Moose is," she said referring to Tina's husband.

"But Brett wasn't having an affair. He was off gambling," said Liz.

"Do you think Moose is gambling?" asked Brenda. "Maybe they have to sell their big house to pay off his gambling debts and that's why Shea is hanging out at Dolphin Isles. Maybe they have to downsize."

"Moose and Shea are *not* buying a house at Dolphin Isles!" shouted Pilar. "And Shea is not having an affair with Walt Walters. Or anyone else."

"Then what's she been doing there?" asked Kitty. "Every time I ask her about it, she comes back with some bullshit reason. And where is she now? Don't you think it's strange she's an hour late for Bunco? Shea's *never* late for Bunco."

For a moment, the room went silent.

"You're right," Pilar finally admitted. "Something's wrong."

"I say we find Shea and confront her," said Tina. "The way we confronted Brett about his gambling problem."

Kitty's mother stood, wobbling slightly. "Count me in."

"How many cars are we going to need?" asked Lorraine,

running to retrieve her keys. "If I pull out the car seats, my minivan can seat seven."

"So does mine," said Tina.

"Then we're only going to need two cars," said Mimi.

Liz gulped down the rest of her daiquiri. "Where should we look first?"

Pilar met Kitty's gaze. "I think we should start at Dolphin Isles."

Brenda frowned. "Does this mean we're not playing Bunco tonight?"

No one bothered to answer that. They were all too busy grabbing purses and running for the door.

Frida looked at Kitty and shook her head. "I knew we should have done a book club instead."

38

‖‖‖‖

It was a quarter past eight and still light outside. The model homes at Dolphin Isles were conveniently open till nine. Tina and Lorraine parked their minivans on Seagull Drive, two blocks from the subdivision's main street.

"Why did we park way out here?" asked Kitty.

"So they won't see us coming. This is how we did it when we confronted Brett. Remember?" said Mimi. "It's called 'the element of surprise.'"

Kitty glanced at Pilar, who looked as tense as Kitty felt. Whatever they found out tonight, it wouldn't be the end of the world. Would it? Or maybe it would. At least their world as they knew it.

Brenda swiped her palm over her bottom, brushing off a shower of cookie crumbs. "Gross. You shouldn't let your kids eat in the car, Lorraine."

Lorraine began to protest but Tina cut her off. "We don't have time for this now. Look," she said, pointing to the white Lincoln Navigator parked around the corner. "There's Shea's car."

Kitty's heart sank. It was true. Shea was having an affair with Walt Walters. The visual on that was too much to think about. "We can't just all go barging in there," she said.

"Why not?" asked her mother. "It's how you do an intervention."

"Your mom's right," said Frida. "There's strength in numbers."

"We could circle around the house and each of us could go in from different doors," suggested Tina. "That way if Shea and Walt Walters try to escape, we'd have them cornered."

"I really hope that's a joke," Kitty muttered.

"I say we go into the house, look Shea in the eye, and demand to know what she's doing here instead of playing Bunco where she should be," said Liz.

Eleven pairs of eyes turned to Kitty.

"I say we do it Liz's way," said Kitty.

"Agreed," said Pilar.

They marched up to the model home. It was the Blue Lagoon, although it didn't look any different from the Calypso or, for that matter, any of the other models Kitty had seen.

The Babes and her mother all crammed into the foyer.

Walt Walters was sitting in the living room, looking over paperwork. Kitty felt some of the coiled-up tension ease off. At least they hadn't caught Walt and Shea in the act. She was about to demand to know where Shea was when she caught sight of a man with dark hair sitting across from Walt.

Kitty did a double take.

It was Steve. And sitting next to Steve was Ted's attorney, Teresa.

"What are you doing here? With her?" she asked him, looking at Teresa.

Steve stood, his mouth set in a grim line.

Walt looked delighted at the prospect of a large crowd entering one of his model homes. "Anyone looking for a house, ladies?"

Kitty's mother turned to Steve. "Are you two-timing my daughter with this . . . this hussy?" she asked, pointing a finger at Teresa.

Teresa raised a perfectly tweezed brow. "This is your mother, Katherine? How charming." She gave Kitty's mother a smile that would freeze water in August. "I'm Teresa Hargrove, Steve's wife."

"Ex-wife," Steve said. He eyed the crowd behind Kitty. "Can we talk? In private?"

"I thought your ex's name was Terrie."

"Anything you have to say to Kitty, you can say in front of us," declared Pilar. "She doesn't want to be your fauxship anymore. She's too good for that. Right, girls?"

"Right!" shouted the Babes.

Teresa folded her arms across her chest. "Aren't you going to introduce us to the rest of your posse, Katherine?"

"We're not her posse," declared Liz. "We're the Bunco Babes."

"What's a fauxship?" Kitty's mother asked right before letting out a huge burp.

Kitty winced. "Transition relationship gone bad."

"Transition relationship?" echoed Steve.

Teresa looked amused. "That's the person who helps you get over someone else."

"I know what it is," he said to Teresa over his shoulder. He narrowed his eyes at Kitty. "Is that what you thought you were? Someone to help me get over my ex-wife?"

"I don't know. Maybe."

Teresa shook her head. "First Steve, now Ted." Her eyes with the impossibly long lashes widened. "Are you the woman who almost burned my house to the ground?"

"*Our* house," Steve shot back at Teresa.

"That was *your* house?" Kitty sputtered. She shook her head to clear the fuzz between her ears. "You never answered my question. What are you doing here at Dolphin Isles?"

"Mr. Pappas owns this place," Walt announced. He puffed his chest out proudly. "I told you I knew the bigwigs at TNT."

Kitty took a step back. "*You're* TNT?"

"I can explain. In private," Steve emphasized again.

"Yeah, you keep saying that." It was all happening so fast she couldn't think straight. "You *lied* to me."

"I never lied to you," Steve said.

"You told me you were an out-of-work construction worker. I thought you were poor! I actually felt sorry for you!"

"I said I was in between jobs and that I'd worked construction in the past," Steve said, his voice tight. "Anything else you thought about me, you assumed."

"Katherine's not going anywhere with you," her mother said. "I should have seen it right away. You're just like her father. A no-good philanderer. A male jezebel!"

Kitty whipped around to face her mother. "Mom, don't talk about Daddy like that."

"It's time you knew the truth, Katherine. Your father was an unfaithful SOB who cared more about his own selfish pleasures than he did his family."

Kitty threw her hands in the air. "Talk about the pot calling the kettle black! Mother, you're the most selfish person I know! You're here because you've given your husband an ultimatum between you or his daughter. I mean, *who does that?*"

Her mother flinched.

The room went silent. Everyone was staring at her. The Babes and Walt Walters looked shocked. Teresa looked like the cat who'd swallowed the canary and Steve... well, she couldn't tell what Steve was thinking. His face was eerily blank. Of course he'd have an excellent poker face. It went hand in hand with the liar thing.

Kitty swallowed hard. How could she have said all that to her own mother? And in front of everyone? "Mom, I'm sorry. I didn't mean it."

Walt made a loud harrumphing sound meant to get everyone's attention. "Did I mention that TNT"—he threw an awkward smile Steve's way—"is holding a sale this month? Buy any one of our homes and get a free washer and dryer."

"We didn't come to look at your little houses," Pilar said. "We came to find Shea Masterson. Where is she? We know you're hiding her here somewhere."

Walt sniffed. "The Mastersons are here to buy a home. I'm sorry, but I can't have my customers harassed by a bunch of ... Bunco broads or whatever you call yourselves."

"Bunco Babes," Frida clarified.

"We're not here to harass any *customers*," Kitty said. "We just want to look over the model." She took off down the hallway, fending Walt off before he could get in her way. She was determined to confront Shea. And get away from Steve. At the moment, she wasn't sure which one she wanted more.

She looked into the two bedrooms on the right. In between the bedrooms was a bathroom decorated in an island motif. All three rooms were empty.

"Do you think she ran out the back?" Tina asked.

Kitty turned the corner to find a small hallway leading to what she assumed was the garage. There was a door on her right and one on her left.

Steve came up behind her. "We need to talk."

"*I need* to find Shea," she said, opening the door to her left. It was an empty linen closet.

"Wow," said Liz. "I wish I had a linen closet that big."

"I'd love to show you the Calypso," said Walt. "The linen closet in that model is even bigger. And you should see the pantry!"

"Will you shut up? I already told you, no one wants to buy a house from you," Pilar said, giving Walt what Kitty knew was the evil eye. Pilar swore only low-class Cubans ever went around giving anyone the evil eye. Walt must really be getting on Pilar's nerves if she was stooping to that.

Kitty turned around. Eleven Babes, including herself, her mother, Steve, Teresa, and Walt Walters were all crammed into one narrow hallway like a big conga line. "This is ridiculous. What are we doing here?"

"I thought we were confronting Shea," said Pilar.

"Well, it's obvious she's not here," said Kitty.

There was a muffled sound from behind the door on the right. "What's in there?" Kitty asked Walt.

"The laundry room. Complete with a state-of-the-art washer and dryer," Walt added, trying to catch Liz's eye.

Kitty put her ear to the door. There was a distinct thud-

thud-thud noise coming from the room. She turned to the Babes. "There's something in there," she whispered.

"I hope it's not palmetto bugs," said Brenda. "I can take anything but palmetto bugs."

"There are no bugs in this house," Walt said indignantly. "We spray every Monday."

Kitty threw back the door. The Babes, plus her mother and Walt, all fought one another to jockey for a position next to her in the doorway.

At first, all Kitty could see was a man's back. His pants were bunched around his ankles, exposing his bare ass. Then she spotted Shea sitting on the edge of the dryer. The near-naked man was Moose, and he had Shea's long legs wrapped around his waist. Moose made a jerking motion with his hips and let out a loud groan.

Someone in the crowd must have made a noise because Moose whipped his head around, his expression a mixture of surprise and disbelief.

Shea let out a loud shriek and buried her face in Moose's chest.

"Someone close the door!" Kitty croaked. She tried to do it herself but Walt was blocking the way.

Steve reached around Walt and slammed the laundry room door shut. "Show's over, people."

Oh my God. Had they really just caught Moose and Shea having *sex* in the laundry room of a Dolphin Isles model home?

Walt cleared his throat. His eyes looked a little glazed. "I believe the Calypso model has a lock on the laundry room door," he said to no one in particular.

Steve looked like he was trying not to laugh.

"It's not funny," Kitty said.

Steve shrugged. "I told you she was the hot one."

Kitty suddenly remembered her mother. Hopefully she hadn't passed out from the shock. She searched her out in the crowded hallway. "Mom, are you okay?"

Her mother's eyes were bright and shiny. "Oh, I'm having a wonderful time, sweetie! Why on earth would you ever think I'd find Bunco boring?"

39

The Babes walked to their cars in stunned silence. Pilar avoided eye contact with her. The only person talking was Kitty's mother. Nonstop. She'd seen her mother have an occasional glass of wine, but Kitty had never seen her drunk before.

Steve followed them outside. "Let me give you a ride home," he offered.

"I don't think so."

"We need to talk."

"You keep saying that. By the way, your ex is like . . . ridiculously gorgeous." And whip smart, she wanted to add. But she figured one glowing adjective was enough.

"She's not a nice person, Kit."

That made her feel better. But not much. "So . . . are you like a millionaire or what?"

"That's sort of a relative term—"

She cut him off with a glare.

"Okay, yeah, I guess you could call me a millionaire."

For some reason, that made her angrier. "You want to talk? I have two questions for you: Are you the owner of Dolphin Isles? And was that really your house we nearly burned down?"

He grimaced. "Yes."

For a second, she was speechless. Even though he'd basically admitted it in the house, hearing him say it directly was a shock. "Then we don't have anything else to say to each other."

"I can explain—"

"No, you can't. You lied to me. About everything. I thought . . . I thought I was special." She started to laugh. "God, I thought I was falling in love with you."

"Kit—"

"You know, I was actually worried about you spending all that money on those first-class tickets. I thought you'd blown your savings in some sort of macho meltdown to impress me. What do you do? Go around targeting lonely women to seduce for kicks? Is it some sort of game?" She was shouting again. But she didn't care. "I told myself the reason you were married so many times is because you picked these shit women who didn't understand you. But you're the real shit, aren't you?"

Beneath the streetlamp she could see his face turn red.

"Aren't you?" she demanded. She wanted to hit him. She was afraid she was going to. She blew out a breath. He wasn't worth it. He wasn't the man she thought he was. He was . . . for God's sake, he was TNT!

"You're right," he said quietly. "I'm a shit."

"Yeah? Well, tell me something I don't know." She turned around and never looked back.

By the time they got back to Pilar's house no one was in the mood to continue Bunco. Kitty helped her mother into her BMW convertible and drove home. She felt numb. But maybe that was a good thing. She stopped at Corbits to get an early edition of tomorrow's *Whispering Bay Gazette*. Lorraine was right. It was all there in black and white. How Ferguson and Associates had bought beachfront property from Earl Handy and their master plan to build condos and turn Whispering Bay into one of Florida's premier vacation spots.

Ted was quoted as saying, "*It's a shame really about the senior center. It's a lovely old building, but it's in such disrepair that to keep it standing is a potential hazard. We would hate to be responsible for an injury to any of Whispering Bay's beloved senior citizens.*"

Bleh.

Kitty scanned the article. Vince was quoted and of course, so was Bruce Bailey. "*Ted Ferguson is a visionary. A man ahead of his time.*"

She flipped to the next page to continue reading. Alongside the article was a picture of her (the one from her business card) with the caption, *Kitty Burke, local residential real estate agent, seals the deal.*

Kitty's hands began to shake.

The reporter stated that he had tried to talk to her during the celebration party, but that she had left early. However, "reliable" sources had heard Ms. Burke say, "*Personally, I hate the idea of condos on the beach. I'm only in it for the commission.*"

Oh my God.

She read it again.

And again and again. But each time it was the same. "*I'm only in it for the commission.*"

What would Viola think? And the rest of the Gray Flamingos? And for that matter, the rest of the town?

She dialed Ted's number.

"Ferguson here."

"Are you responsible for that quote in the *Whispering Bay Gazette?*" she demanded.

"Who is this?"

"You know perfectly well who this is."

"I'm not sure who gave the quote. It could be any number of people. Could have been Vince or maybe even Earl. Are you denying you said it?"

"Not like that!"

Ted chuckled maliciously. "Welcome to big business, Ms. Burke. We get misunderstood all the time. Take that little petition going around town. If I didn't know any better, I'd say that's *your* name at the top of the list."

"I'm not denying I signed the petition. I had no idea you were planning to tear down the senior center."

"And take that little incident between us at the party," Ted continued. "I think you thought I was actually making a pass at you."

Kitty nearly squeezed the phone in half. "You *did* make a pass at me, you bastard."

There was a split second of silence.

"Okay, listen up. Those fucking Gray Geezers have gotten the town in an uproar. This 'meeting' they're holding could be a potential PR nightmare. Tomorrow night you're going to dress up in your prettiest little Junior League outfit, plaster a smile on your face, and get your oversized ass to the senior center seven p.m. sharp and do some damage control. Got it?"

Oversized ass? "Are you kidding me? Get yourself another lackey. Get Teresa to do it."

"I never kid about business. And I wouldn't waste Teresa's time on this. Why do you think I hired you? 'Help me help you'?" he mocked. "What a joke. You can't even read a contract right. But for some reason the yokels in this town consider you their resident princess. You even managed to bamboozle a sharp old coot like Earl. So I suggest if you don't want any more 'misquotes' in the local mullet wrapper, you'll do as I say. And another thing, don't sic your boyfriend on me again. Now do you *got it*?"

Kitty's throat tightened up. Boyfriend? What was Ted talking about? Tears misted her eyes. *Do not let him hear you cry!* "I suppose I don't have a choice, do I?"

"Oh, we always have a choice, Katherine. But nine times out of ten, we go with the highest bidder."

40

She felt like one of those gunslingers in an old-time Western. The ones hired by the evil railroad men determined to choke out the God-fearing ranchers. The ranchers would gather at the church while someone like Gary Cooper or Jimmy Stewart played the role of local sheriff. Her part on the other hand was usually played by . . . oh, Lee Marvin or some other old-time baddy.

She rummaged through her closet, looking for the right dress. Fuck Ted Ferguson and his Junior League outfit. She would wear black. Something with an obscenely low neckline and ultrashort skirt. It would suit her role.

She flipped through her clothes. She had to have at least *one* shocking dress in her wardrobe. She tossed outfit after outfit onto her bed. It was a little disconcerting to discover she didn't have anything even slightly resembling shocking.

In the end, she settled on an above-the-knee ratty-looking denim skirt and a Save the Manatees oversized T-shirt she'd bought at a garage sale from Frida last year. A pair of flip-flops completed the outfit. "Take that, Ted Ferguson," she said, sticking her tongue out at her reflection in the mirror. Childish, to be sure, but it made her feel better. At the last minute she decided to add Viola's flamingo pin to her outfit.

She hadn't gone out all day and the phone had only rung once—from a telemarketer wanting to know if she was interested in participating in a survey on SUVs. No phone call from Pilar or Shea.

Or Steve.

Not that she wanted Steve to call. She never wanted to see him again, so there was no use in his calling.

But she had expected a call from Shea. And had hoped for one from Pilar.

Kitty had never felt so alone in her life.

Tonight would suck. Big time. But she would get through it. She would plaster a fake smile on her face (after all, she was used to that, wasn't she?), and she'd do her best. No one could fault her for doing her job. She'd make her six-figure commission, buy Gram's house, and go back to doing what she knew. Selling houses.

Her mother was waiting for her in the living room. Her gaze took in Kitty's outfit. "Interesting choice, dear."

"Are you going somewhere?"

Her mother looked surprised by the question. "With you of course."

Kitty didn't remember telling her mother about the town meeting. "Mom, I'd rather you didn't. It won't be pleasant."

"Nonsense. It's an important night for you." Her voice softened. "I know I haven't always been there for you in the past. Maybe I can make it up to you tonight."

"I'm not sure what I'm going to say."

Her mother gave her a hug. "You'll do fine, darling. Just be yourself."

Be herself? Right now "herself" was the last person on earth she wanted to be.

Kitty had never seen so many people in the senior center. There must have been over two hundred folding chairs set up, but it wasn't enough. A large crowd stood in the back and along the walls. There was a refreshment table with muffins (a lot more than six dozen), cookies, and even a punch bowl. Kitty recognized the cookies. They were the kind Frida baked and sold at the Bistro.

She scanned the room looking for Frida or Ed, but every time she made eye contact with someone their gaze quickly slid away. She'd never had that happen before.

Her mother sat next to Pilar's parents and the other Gray Flamingos. Viola and Mr. Milhouse were seated in the front row, next to Bruce Bailey. Bruce motioned for her to take a seat next to him.

She'd wanted a chance to talk to Viola before the meeting began, but it didn't look like she'd get the opportunity. What had Viola thought about the quote in the paper?

Viola stood and walked to the podium. "Can you hear me?" she asked, tapping the mic with her finger.

"The mic's not working, Vi," a male voice called out. It was Gus.

"Neither is anything else in this place," Mr. Milhouse rumbled loudly.

This caused an affirmative furor from the rest of the crowd.

Kitty turned to see Gus sitting five rows behind her. Steve and Nathan were there too. Kitty's heart began to thud. What was Steve doing here?

"Oh, for Pete's sake," said Bruce Bailey, his cheeks red. "Let me see that thing." He got up and tinkered with the microphone, but he couldn't get it to work.

"Looks like you're just going to have to talk real loud, Vi," shouted Gus.

Bruce slithered back to his seat.

Viola smiled at the crowd. "First, I'd like to thank everyone for coming. It's a Friday night and I know all of you have better things to do than hear a bunch of us retirees whining about losing our center. As most of you know by now, Earl Handy has sold the land this center is located on, and some fancy developer from south Florida is going to build condos over it."

The crowd began to boo.

A trickle of sweat ran down Kitty's spine and her thighs felt glued to the metal chair.

Viola's voice turned serious. "I don't know much about the condo business, but I do know this. This center shouldn't be torn down. When I first retired, I wasn't sure what to do with myself. I was better off than a lot of people my age. I'd saved and had a good pension and my house was paid off, but other than taking a couple of trips a year, what was I going to do? I volunteered at church and did the Meals On Wheels things, but like a lot of senior citizens, I missed the socialization I got by getting out there every day and interacting with people. That's when my good friend Amanda Hanahan stepped in." Viola searched Kitty out and smiled at her.

Kitty felt the blood rush to her head. Viola had smiled at her! Of course, there was always the chance Viola hadn't read the article yet. No, Viola was too sharp. She'd have read the article.

"Amanda and I decided that the senior center needed a face-lift. Now, notice I said the senior center. I for one, have never had plastic surgery."

This prompted a smattering of chuckles.

"Together, we established the Gray Flamingos, and over the last ten years, the Flamingos have raised nearly twenty thousand dollars. That money has been put into improvements and other community projects that have benefited the retired citizens of Whispering Bay. But it's not enough. We've pleaded with the city council to take our cause seriously. We've protested and we've formed petitions but it's been no good. The council doesn't want to hear us and neither does Earl Handy."

Viola's eyes shot to the back of the room. Everyone, including Kitty followed her gaze to see Earl Handy standing near the refreshment table. He was leaning on his cane, with DeeDee at his side.

"Now don't get me wrong. It was perfectly legal and certainly within Earl's rights to sell his own land. So the question is, what's the city going to do to make up for our loss?"

Bruce recognized this as his cue. He reluctantly stepped up to the podium and leaned down to speak into the mic. "Fellow citizens of Whispering Bay," he began.

"The mic isn't working, Bruce!" someone shouted. "Remember?"

The crowd laughed.

Bruce's face turned even redder. "I can understand that a few of you are upset right now . . ." The crowd began to hiss. "But you're looking at this all wrong. The city council merely follows the wishes of our citizenry. And the majority of citizens in Whispering Bay don't want to pour our hard-earned tax dollars into a center for the retired folks. It's as simple as that. People would rather spend money on the school, or improving the roads—something we can all benefit from. Sorry, Viola," Bruce said, looking genuinely unhappy, "but that's the honest-to-God truth."

Mr. Milhouse yelled, "How do you know that's what the people want if you never give them a chance to vote on it? Every time we try to get a referendum going you shoot it down!"

A round of applause supported Mr. Milhouse's outburst.

Bruce took a handkerchief from the back pocket of his pants and wiped his neck.

"Too hot for you, Bruce?" one of the Flamingos yelled. "Well, that's cause the air-conditioning isn't working!"

The crowd laughed.

"If the city council isn't going to help us, then what about this Ted Ferguson fellow? Where's he? What's he got to say about all this?" someone else yelled.

Somewhere from the middle of the room, Kitty recognized Ted's smooth voice. "I'm Ted Ferguson," he said, "and I just want to say that I'm extremely proud to be joining a community that shows so much spirit."

Bruce applauded Ted's "speech." "Excellent point, Mr. Ferguson!" No one in the room joined the clapping. After a few seconds Bruce gave up. "Kitty Burke is representing Ferguson and Associates tonight. Maybe you'd like to get her take on all this? After all, she's a local girl. Her grandmother was the founder of the Gray Flamingos, yet she's wholeheartedly in support of the condo project. If anyone can give us an impartial view of this situation, it would be her."

It felt like a million eyes zoomed in her direction.

This was it.

She unglued herself from the chair and made her way to the podium. She glanced at Viola, who smiled at her, which made Kitty relax. But only for a second. The rest of the room was staring at her expectantly.

She kept her eyes trained to the back wall. "Hello. As most of you know, I'm Kitty Burke." She didn't recognize her own voice. It sounded too deep and her breath came out all huffy like she'd just run a marathon. Her heart felt ready to explode from her chest.

"I'm here because—"

"You're here because of the commission!" someone shouted from the right side of the room.

She squinted to see the direction of the heckler, but the room was so packed she couldn't tell where he was. She averted her gaze to the back wall again.

That's when she noticed the Babes standing together in a group. Shea and Pilar caught her eye and waved. Frida and Lorraine gave her a big thumbs-up and Tina yelled, "Go, Kitty!"

There was a polite round of applause after that.

She took a deep breath and started again. "I can't deny what the *Gazette* wrote. I did say I was in this deal for the commission. And I did say I hated the idea of condos on the beach."

She stole another glance at Viola, who seemed mesmerized by the flamingo pin. Without thinking, Kitty reached up to her collar and touched it. "I gather that a lot of us don't like the idea of condos."

"No, we don't!" someone shouted.

"Then . . . then we all better get used to the idea of Whispering Bay dying."

There was a lull. The crowd leaned forward in their seats. What did they expect her to say? She knew what Ted expected. He wanted her to spin the condos into a positive for the community. To convince them that Ferguson and Associates was the best thing to hit Whispering Bay since sliced bread.

And she knew what Viola expected. But Viola wanted the impossible. Saving the senior center was out of her hands. Her mother had told her to be herself. In the past, that had meant keeping everybody happy. But there was no way in this mess to keep everybody happy. Someone was going to lose. Maybe Steve was right. Maybe the people who really cared about her wouldn't blame her. For once, maybe she should just tell it like it is. No pretty spin. No glossing over the facts. Just Kitty Burke, saying what was *really* on her mind.

"Whispering Bay is dying," she repeated. "The only new blood moving into this community are retirees. And while there's nothing wrong with that, the town needs a mixture of people, old and young, to keep it thriving. As much as I hate the idea, condos will bring in work. New jobs and new opportunities."

So far, no one was throwing rotten fruit at her. She took another breath and went on. "For the past ten years I've sold residential real estate, and I've made a pretty good living, but I've had a couple of bad years in a row now. My friend Frida owns this great coffeehouse on the beach. But she has to depend on tourists from nearby towns to keep afloat."

"Amen!" someone shouted. Kitty looked into the audience. It was Ricky, from the Harbor House. Kitty gave him a shaky smile.

"I don't want to see Whispering Bay shrivel up. I don't want to have to move to Panama City or Destin to make a decent living. If it wasn't Ted Ferguson, then it would have been someone else."

She looked out into the crowd and saw Steve smile at her. He urged her on with a nod. Despite the fact she never planned to speak to him again, she was grateful for the support.

"And if I hadn't been the broker in this deal, then it would have been another broker." She looked directly at Viola. "I wanted the commission so that I could buy Gram's house. I thought that by keeping her house I'd be keeping her memory . . . no"—Kitty cut herself off with a frown—"that's not right. I thought that by keeping her house I'd be keeping things *the same*." She looked at Shea and Pilar and the rest of the Babes. "I moved to Whispering Bay twenty-five years ago and I fell in love with this town and the people here. They made me feel welcome and safe. But if there's one thing we all know, it is that nothing stays the same. Change is inevitable. Like the condos. If we don't keep up with the rest of the coast, then we're going to be swallowed up."

She waited for a reaction, but no one said anything.

"And Viola is right," she continued. "This town needs a center for its retired citizens."

This produced a round of wild clapping from the Gray Flamingos.

Bruce Bailey frowned at her.

"But . . . Bruce is right too. It's not his fault the city doesn't want to put money into something that's only going to benefit a portion of our population."

Bruce nodded vigorously. And that's when it came to her. Maybe there was a way to make everyone happy after all.

Kitty cleared her throat. "What this town needs is a place for our teenagers to play basketball and a community pool for our kids to swim in and tennis courts and an indoor running track. We need a place that the Gray Flamingos can hold their meetings and take art classes and yoga classes and whatever else they get the itch for. What Whispering Bay *needs* is an all-purpose recreation center."

There was a moment of stunned silence, then the Babes let out a loud cheer.

Viola stood and clapped.

Bruce was looking at her with interest, and the rest of the room . . . well, they were clapping now too.

Her mother beamed proudly.

This being-herself thing wasn't too shabby.

She put a hand up in the air to quiet the room. "I'd like to present you all with a challenge. I say that while we embrace new commerce like the condo project, we should never forget that Whispering Bay is *our* town. If we let ourselves be run over, then it's no one's fault but ours. Tonight, I challenge each and every one of you to make a difference." She placed her hands on the sides of the podium to steady herself. "Mr. Handy?" she shouted loud enough so that no one could mistake her. "You own most of the land in this town. Surely you can come up with a couple of acres to donate for the construction of a new recreation center."

All heads swiveled in Earl's direction. For a minute, no one said anything, not even Earl. But Instead of looking mad or shocked, he began to chuckle. "Damn! You're Amanda's granddaughter, all right. Okay, missy, you talked me into it. I'll donate some land." This generated a loud round of clapping. Earl clasped DeeDee's hand and held up his cane to quiet the noise. Even from across the room, Kitty could swear she saw Earl's eyes twinkle. "But I don't think I should be the only one making a sacrifice. What about the rest of you?" he asked. "What are all of you gonna do?"

Viola jumped from her seat to stand next to Kitty. She reached out and squeezed Kitty's hand. It was a like a tonic to her frazzled nerves. And that's when it came to her.

"I'd like to make a donation," Kitty blurted.

Viola smiled at her. "That's lovely. And that's exactly the sort of enthusiasm we need to—"

"Three hundred thousand dollars to be exact," Kitty said, before she could change her mind.

"Three hundred thousand dollars?" Viola asked weakly.

"That's the amount of commission I'm making off this deal," Kitty said to the crowd. "And I'd like to challenge Ferguson and Associates to match it!"

The clapping was now verging on the wild. It took Ted a couple of minutes to stand, but when he did, he had a smile ready for the crowd. "Excellent idea, Ms. Burke," he said, sounding a little resigned. "We at Ferguson and Associates would be happy to match your donation."

Viola clasped her hands together. "That's six hundred thousand dollars!"

"And the Bunco Babes are volunteering to form a committee to raise the rest of the money!" Shea shouted, causing the Babes to let out a whoop.

Kitty started to laugh. But then, that's what she did whenever she was overcome with big emotion. This was so much better than anything she could have ever imagined. The applause eventually died down and Viola looked on the verge of saying something, when Steve stood up.

An electric current filled the air. At least, it did for her. Damn it. She should hate him. But the truth was, she didn't.

"Most of you don't know me, so I'd like to take this opportunity to introduce myself. I'm Steve Pappas and I'm the owner of TNT, the corporation that built Dolphin Isles. Mr. Ferguson and I were actually business partners at one time, but we officially split a few months ago. I came to Whispering Bay with the same intention as Mr. Ferguson—to buy land to build condos on. Unfortunately, I wasn't smart enough to hire the right broker"—he paused and smiled at Kitty—"but I believe everything happens for a reason. Recently it's been brought to my attention that maybe there's a little too much going on too fast. As a result, I've decided to halt further expansion at Dolphin Isles and concentrate on upgrading the existing subdivision. I'm going to go back to doing what I do best, supervising construction from the ground up. I'm starting a new company here in Whispering Bay and I'd like to be considered as a potential builder for the new rec center. Pro bono."

The crowd clapped again, louder this time. Steve nodded his acknowledgment and sat down.

"I don't think I can top that," said Viola, her voice scratchy with emotion. "Now unless someone else wants to jump up and offer a free swimming pool or something?" She scanned the room. "No?" The crowd laughed. "Then there's refreshments along the wall. Nothing fancy. Just some punch and homemade muffins and a delicious platter of cookies donated by Frida Hampton, who owns the Bistro. Y'all don't forget to patronize her establishment," Viola said, putting some southern in her voice.

"Oh! Hold on," she added. "I almost forgot. Bruce Bailey

from the city council wanted to have the final word." Viola stepped aside. "Bruce?"

Bruce gave the crowd an anemic-looking smile. "I just wanted to add that the city council is in full support of the Gray Flamingos and we look forward to working with them side by side on this glorious project."

Half the room was already at the refreshment table before Bruce finished his "speech." The place was filled with wall-to-wall bodies, most of them coming up to congratulate her. Kitty craned her neck trying to spot Steve. He hadn't left already, had he?

Viola gave her a big hug. "I'm so proud of you!"

"Really? I mean, I was part of the problem, you know?"

"You were a bigger part of the solution and that's what's important."

"I wanted to tell you the other day about my role in all of this, but I couldn't."

Viola nodded sympathetically.

"And I had no idea what I was going to say tonight until I stood up there."

Viola smiled. "You followed your heart and you can never go wrong when you do that."

Bruce Bailey slapped Kitty on the back. "Excellent speech, Ms. Burke. Have you ever thought of running for city council?"

Viola winked at Kitty, then linked her arm through Bruce's. "Now, about that support you just promised us," she said, leading him away to the refreshment table.

Kitty looked around the room again, hoping to find Steve. Instead, she found her mother.

"Katherine, are you serious about that donation?"

"I'm sorry, Mom. I know this ruins all your plans, but I think Gram would have wanted me to do this."

Her mother opened her mouth to speak, but just then Kitty spied Steve heading out the side door. "Mom, I have to go."

41

Steve was almost to his truck by the time she reached him. She tapped him on the shoulder. "Were you going to leave without saying good-bye?" Kitty asked.

"You looked pretty busy." He stuck his hands in the pockets of his khaki slacks. "Plus, to be honest, I didn't think you'd want to talk to me."

"I didn't," she admitted. There was a moment or two of awkward silence between them. She crooked her head in the direction of the building. "Was that wild or what?"

He smiled. "You were great in there. I told you you knew how to push the right buttons."

She felt her cheeks go warm.

"So you're really donating your commission?" he asked.

"I love my grandmother's house, but it doesn't seem so important to hold on to it anymore."

"You're going to sell it?"

She nodded.

"I'm sorry."

She shrugged. She had so much to ask him, she wasn't sure where to begin. "Are you really going to start your own company here in town?"

"That's the plan."

She waited for him to elaborate. A tiny wave of frustration bit her like a bug. She should be used to his short, clipped answers by now. Of course, he'd offered to explain everything last night. Maybe she should have stayed and listened. Only she'd been so angry anything he could have said wouldn't have mattered. A thought suddenly occurred to her. "Hey, you didn't talk to Ted about me, did you? He told me not to sic my boyfriend on him again."

"I asked him to reconsider tearing down the senior center." Steve shrugged. "He told me to fuck off and mind my own business."

Kitty shook her head. "I just can't see the two of you as business partners."

"We met through Terrie. She convinced me to break away from my old partner and join the company she and Ted owned."

Kitty blinked. "Don't tell me TNT stands for—*Teresa and Ted*?"

"I need to come up with a new name, don't I?"

Kitty laughed. "Uh, yeah. So what happened?"

"The whole thing got huge. I was on the construction end of things and they handled the finance and selling. We were building condos, strip malls, you name it. Then I got lax and let my site supervisors take over. One day I came home early from a fishing trip and I caught them in bed together."

Kitty caught her breath. But she wasn't surprised by that last part. "I'm sorry. You must really hate him."

"I thought I did, but the truth is he did me a big favor. The marriage was a mistake from day one. But I'd been determined to stick it out. Third time and all," he added with a shrug. He seemed embarrassed.

"So the house in Mexico Beach, the one we almost burned—"

"I built that house myself. Terrie's been in it maybe all of twice. Once when it was built and I guess another time to do that redecorating of hers. It's the last piece of property we own jointly. We decided in the divorce agreement to sell it and split the profits. Only she refuses to lower the price."

"How did you end up with Dolphin Isles?" Kitty asked.

"We divided the company. Since I had connections in town, it seemed logical." He paused. "I'd never been out there until just a few days ago. You were right. About everything." He frowned. "Well, almost everything. I still don't think affordable tract homes are responsible for the decline of America."

"Maybe that was a bit of an exaggeration," she admitted.

"I came to Whispering Bay to one-up Ted on that condo deal. But I'm glad I lost out."

"You are?"

"It's not what I want anymore."

"What do you want?" *Say you want me,* a little voice inside her whispered. It startled her. Is that what she wanted? A relationship with Steve?

"I want to get back to where I started. I want to build solid, affordable houses that people can live in. I want to build a company I can be proud of, one that turns a good profit." He paused. "And I want to be someone Nathan can look up to.

You were right about that too." He shook his head. "I don't get it, but for some reason, the kid thinks he wants to be like me. I'm going to give him a job in my company, teach him everything I know. Which should take the kid about a week. After a year, if he still likes what he's doing, he's going to take that scholarship and major in Building Construction."

"I think that's awesome," she said. And she meant it. "So, what's next?"

"A long-needed vacation."

Her throat went tight. He didn't have to elaborate on that one.

"The offer's still open, you know," he said, gazing at her intently. "I'd like you to come with me to Hawaii." There was an uncomfortable silence. "Look, Kit, I'm really sorry I wasn't truthful with you."

"Yeah, I've been wondering about that."

"I wanted to tell you everything the night I came over to apologize after our fight. But you were so miserable about this senior center thing, and then I thought maybe I'd save it till we were away from here." He shook his head. "I guess I'm still not too smart when it comes to women."

She smiled.

"And you have to admit we started off all wrong," he said.

"I guess accusing you of stealing my underwear didn't inspire a lot of confidence in me as a sane person."

"It's a story to tell the grandkids, that's for sure."

Grandkids? What was that supposed to mean?

"Nobody's perfect, Kit. Not me. Not even you. Although"—his voice turned husky—"I think you're as close to perfect as anyone can be."

Her breath hitched.

"Kitty!" She heard her name shouted from off in the parking lot. She spun around. Pilar was waving to her. "C'mon, we're meeting at the Bistro!" The rest of the Babes and her mother were getting in their cars. She'd almost forgotten about them. She had about a million questions. Like how they found out about the meeting and what they were doing here. And what the hell Shea and Moose were doing having sex at Dolphin Isles and if Pilar was still mad at her for talking to Nick.

"I . . . I have to go."

He nodded, but she could tell he didn't want her to leave. "How's your mom doing? She looked pretty plastered last night."

"She's okay."

"She was fantastic."

"Fantastic?"

"I don't think I've ever been called a male jezebel before," he said dryly.

Despite her mood, she had to smile. "Yeah, that's definitely a Dana original."

"She was only protecting her cub. Like any good mother."

Kitty's smile faded. She'd never thought of her mother as "good" before, but she'd never thought of her as bad either. She was just . . . her mother.

"I don't think Hawaii is a good idea for me right now," she blurted. The minute she said it, she wanted to take it back. But so much had happened in the past twenty-four hours. The last thing she needed to do was run off with Steve. Not when her feelings were so jumbled about everything.

He nodded, like he had been expecting it. "Maybe when I get back we can do coffee sometime," he offered.

"I don't even know how you take it," she said ruefully.

"Actually, I don't drink coffee," he said. "I kind of meant it as an expression. I drink tea."

He drank tea? Good thing Shea and her metrosexual theory weren't around to hear that.

"Well, there you go. I'm a coffee and Mets kind of girl, and you're a tea and Braves kind of guy."

He laughed and got in his truck. But Kitty could have sworn she saw a look of remorse in his eyes.

Or maybe it was just wishful thinking on her part.

42

IIIIII

"It's called house humping," said Shea. She bit the edge of her thumbnail and looked around the table set for thirteen. "Moose read about it in *GQ*. Supposedly, it's all the rage."

"I knew it!" said Kitty. Shea blinked at her in surprise. "I mean, I suspected Moose was getting *GQ*, but I figured it was just for the pictures. He's been dressing so well lately."

"Leave it to Moose to read the articles too," said Pilar.

They'd all gone to the Bistro. Frida had banished a curious Ed to the upstairs apartment while she'd made cafe lattes and Kitty and Pilar had scrambled eggs on the big industrial stovetop.

"How many times have you done it?" Tina asked.

Lorraine leaned forward in her seat. "Have you ever been caught? I mean, before us?"

Shea flushed. "Almost. We've only done it a few times."

"I can't believe I thought you were having an affair with Walt Walters," Kitty said.

"Or that you wanted to buy a house in Dolphin Isles," added Pilar.

Shea's eyes rolled to the back of her head. "*Please.*"

"How did it start?" Pilar asked.

"A couple of weeks ago Moose had to drop some papers off at Dolphin Isles for Walt Walters. He's a client," she clarified. "They were talking money, and I got bored and started wandering around the model. It's hideous, you know," she said, with a serious look on her face. "So I started thinking about how I would have done the décor, the colors I would have used, that sort of thing. Moose found me in the bathroom, and we could hear Walt talking to another couple out in the living room. One thing led to another and before I knew it, Moose was ripping off my panties and we were having sex."

Moose had ripped off her panties? A vision of Steve doing the exact same thing on the patio at Mexico Beach flashed in her head. She cleared her throat.

Shea took a sip of her coffee. "It was really exciting," she continued. "We're each other's first, and with the girls and all, we don't get much opportunity for spontaneity. After we realized we'd gotten away with it, it became a game. So we kept going back on the pretense of buying a house."

"Wow," said Mimi.

"Why didn't you tell us?" asked Pilar.

Shea looked down at her coffee. "I was mortified. I mean, how many couples do you know who run off to open houses to have sex?"

Kitty laughed. "At least you didn't have sex in one of *my* open houses." She instantly sobered. "Shit. I wonder if anyone's ever done it while I've been doing an open house?"

"I'm sorry I lied to you, Kit," said Shea. "I felt horrible. I made Moose promise last night was it."

"How horrible do you feel?" asked Kitty.

Shea stilled. "What do you mean?"

"Horrible enough to give me your secret frozen margarita recipe?"

"Not that horrible."

"Do you think you and Moose will really stop house humping?" asked Pilar.

"We've been banned from Dolphin Isles. Walt was furious when he found out Moose was stringing him along about buying a house."

"Poor Walt," said Kitty, unable to keep from smirking.

"Poor Moose," said Pilar. "I thought he was going to die of embarrassment. Do you think he'll ever be able to face us again?"

"Who cares about his face? I never knew Moose had such a great ass," said Mimi.

The Babes laughed.

Pilar caught Kitty's eye. "I'm sorry about last night," she said. She grabbed Kitty's hand and squeezed it. "Nick and I got into a huge fight when I got home."

"Oh no," Shea said.

Kitty shook her head. "I had no right to get in the middle of you and Nick and this vasectomy thing."

"No. You did. I've just been under a lot of pressure at work lately. I wanted this partner thing so badly. At least, I thought I did. Taking time off to have Anthony put me on the slow track. If I have another baby, I can kiss a partnership at Hillaman, Soloman, and Kaufman good-bye."

"Those assholes," Shea muttered. "We should have known

this would happen. I mean, the whole law firm ends in 'man.' What you need is a law firm with only women."

"What you need is to quit that job," said Kitty.

Pilar took a sip of her coffee. "That's exactly what I'm thinking of doing."

"Quitting your job?" Shea asked.

"The fight turned out to be just what Nick and I needed." Pilar's face went a little red.

Kitty grinned. "I take it the two-month abstinence streak is over?"

"Let's just say Shea wasn't the only one getting a little nooky last night."

"Now there's a word from my generation!" her mother piped up. Kitty glanced down the table, where her mother sat eating eggs and listening in on their chatter. No one seemed to mind she was there.

"I promised Nick that I would cut down on my hours. And if that doesn't work out, then I'll find a less stressful job. We're going to put off talking about a baby for now, but maybe next year . . ." she said, smiling.

"I have a confession to make," Kitty said. "Well, it's not really a confession, since almost everyone knows." *Thanks to my mother,* she wanted to add. "I lied to everyone about my relationship with Steve. We've sort of been seeing each other for the past few weeks."

Shea came to attention. "Why didn't you tell us?"

"The truth?" Kitty thought about it a minute. "I knew you guys didn't like him—"

"We never said we didn't like him," Pilar said. "We don't even know him."

"Exactly. You don't know him, but you guys had already

labeled him a loser. You made that pretty clear the night of my Bunco birthday bash. But here's the thing. He's not a loser. I liked him. I mean, I *really* liked him. And I didn't want to hear the two of you trash-talk him."

Shea looked stunned. "We wouldn't have trash-talked him!"

Pilar was quiet for a few seconds. "Yeah, we would have," she admitted. "He's not good enough for you, Kit. Look how he lied to you about the whole Dolphin Isles thing."

"Is anyone good enough for me, Pilar?"

Pilar clamped her mouth shut.

"So he's been married and divorced three times. But he's also a decent guy. And he's smart and sexy and he makes me laugh and . . ."

Shea gasped. "Oh God, Kit, he's your Crash!"

"No, he can't be. I mean—"

"Are you in love with him?" Pilar asked softly.

Two days ago, she would have answered yes. "I've only known him a few weeks."

"I knew I was in love with Brett the minute I met him," said Tina. "It can happen."

Frida and Lorraine nodded in agreement.

"How does he feel about you?" Pilar asked.

"He wants me to go to Hawaii with him. He . . . said he was crazy about me—"

"Kit!" Pilar said, grabbing her arm. "That means he loves you!"

"It does?"

"Everyone knows when a guy says he's crazy about you that he really means he loves you," said Shea.

The Babes nodded.

Kitty frowned. Was there some secret relationship manual out there she'd never heard about?

"It's actually the precursor to 'I love you,'" clarified Pilar. "But it's the next step."

"I'm not so sure about that. He told me he wasn't in the market for a fourth mistake."

"Why does he think your relationship is going to be a mistake?" Mimi asked.

Her mother looked up from her scrambled eggs. "Because he doesn't trust his instincts."

Kitty couldn't help but feel a tiny surge of anger. "Is that the reason you're going to divorce Larry? Because your 'instincts' tell you it's over?"

"I'm not going to divorce Larry," her mother announced.

"Since when? I thought you were through with him!" Kitty suddenly remembered about her lost commission. "Mom, is this because now I can't buy the house? We'll find another buyer, I promise. I'll list it first thing in the morning."

"I'm not putting the house on the market. I talked to Larry this afternoon. I'm driving back to St. Augustine in the morning." Her mother smiled regretfully. "You were right. I should never have made him choose between Pam and me. It wasn't fair."

Did her mother just admit she was right?

"I really do love Larry, you know. I just . . ." Her mother shook her head. "I get a little crazy sometimes. But that's me. I'm impulsive. I talk before I think."

"It's not too late, Mom. People change."

"That's the thing, hon. I don't want to change that about me. Sure, being impulsive has gotten me in trouble, but it's made me happy too."

Kitty must have looked skeptical, because her mother went on. "Being impulsive isn't the worst thing. If I hadn't followed my heart and taken a chance with Larry, I'd probably still be here in Whispering Bay. Lonely and divorced from Jim."

"Mom—"

"Don't look at me like that. I know you think I broke up Larry's marriage, but the truth is, he *was* separated when I met him. I love him, Katherine. He's probably the only man who's really understood me. Not that I didn't love your father or Jim. But I think in the grand scheme of things they were just the warm-ups before I met the real love of my life. I love Larry enough to crawl back and suck up to Pam. And if that's what I have to do to win him again, then that's what I'm going to do."

Her mother was going to follow her heart? Kitty had never heard her talk like this before. "Are you and Viola in some sort of conspiracy against me?"

"Not everything is about you, hon."

Huh? "I'm sorry for yelling at you in front of everyone," Kitty said. "I didn't mean it. About being selfish and all."

"Yes, you did," her mother said.

Kitty thought about it a second. "Okay, I guess I did."

Her mother smiled.

Kitty glanced at the faces around the table. It was weird, talking to her mother like this in front of the Babes, but then, for the past ten years, they'd been there for all the big events in her life. It seemed only natural that they'd be here for this conversation too.

Her mother pulled a piece of paper from her purse. "This is the deed to the house. I want you to have it."

"Mom, I told you. I can't afford to buy it now."

"I didn't say I was going to sell it to you. You'll have to pay the insurance and the taxes, of course. But the house is yours, free and clear. You said you think your grandmother would have wanted you to donate that commission money. Well, I think she would have wanted you to have this house too."

"But what about your inheritance?"

"The house might be my inheritance, but you're my legacy." She smiled. "Anyway, who needs an inheritance when you have love?"

The Babes all began to clap. Shea wiped away a tear. "That's the most beautiful speech I've ever heard."

"I wish my mom would talk like that," said Pilar.

Kitty's mother smiled, obviously pleased with herself. "See, hon, I can do girl talk. I can be—"

"Mom, please don't say hip."

"So what are you going to do now, Kit?" asked Pilar.

"About what?"

Shea and Pilar gave each other *the* look.

Kitty slapped her napkin on the table. "Okay, can I just say that I really, really, really hate it when you two do that?"

"Maybe we wouldn't do it if you'd stop being so obtuse," said Shea.

"If you're talking about Steve, there's nothing to do. He's going to Hawaii on vacation and when he comes back we'll be friends. He's even invited me to coffee already." She figured she'd leave the tea part out. For now.

"That sounds awesome!" Pilar gushed in a fake voice. "The guy of your dreams is flying off into the sunset, but you'll just wait here till he comes back so you can have coffee together."

"What do you want me to do?" Kitty asked, exasperated. "Chase him down? Tell him that . . . that maybe I love him? That maybe he's my Crash?"

"That's exactly what we want you to do," Shea said.

"Have we ever steered you wrong before?" Pilar asked.

Kitty raised her brows.

"Okay, in the last five minutes have we ever steered you wrong?" Shea clarified.

In the past (with the exception of the last few weeks) she'd always taken their advice. She realized now it had kept her safe. But what Shea and Pilar were advocating wasn't safe. What if Steve had changed his mind about wanting to take her to Hawaii? What if he rejected her?

What if Susan Sarandon had slammed the door in Kevin Costner's face in Bull Durham?

But she didn't, did she?

She opened the door and he walked in and they made wild and passionate love and then they lived happily ever after. Well, after a couple more hurdles. But the point was, they did get their happy ending.

"Just do it, Kitty!" yelled Tina and Liz in unison, followed by the rest of the Babes. The chant seemed to go on forever. Kitty shook her head and laughed. It was a Nike moment if ever there was one.

Maybe you should listen to your gut more, instead of your friends.

Only this time, her gut *was* telling her to listen to her friends.

"Hey! I have a question," she said. "How did you all know to go to the meeting tonight?"

"Your mom called us," said Frida. "She said you needed us."

Kitty went over to her mother and gave her a kiss.

"What's that for?" her mother asked.

"For being my mom," Kitty said.

"I'm afraid I can't take all the credit," her mother said. "It was Steve who told me about the meeting. He asked me to call your friends. Your real friends. He said you would be needing them."

Her throat suddenly felt tight. She turned and blew a gigantic air kiss to the rest of the Babes. "And that's for being . . . well, you. All of you. I love you guys!"

"We love you too!" they shouted.

43

||||||

She pulled her BMW convertible in front of Gus's house. Suddenly it seemed silly to come barging over in the middle of the night. Maybe she should come back tomorrow when everyone was awake. She hadn't really thought about what she'd actually say to Steve.

Before she lost her nerve, she pulled out her cell phone and hit his name on her search list. At least this way, she wouldn't wake up Gus and Nathan by knocking on the door.

Steve answered on the fifth ring. "Yeah?" He sounded groggy.

"Oh, I woke you up. I'm sorry, I'll just come back tomorrow," she babbled. The cell phone nearly slipped from her hand, her palm was so sweaty.

She heard the rustling of sheets. "Where are you?"

"Here. Outside of Gus's."

There was a moment of silence. "Don't go anywhere."

Her phone went dead. A couple of seconds later, the front door to the house opened. Steve wore a pair of shorts and was slipping a T-shirt over his head. He was barefoot and his hair was sticking on its ends. He looked so utterly sexy, she wanted to cry.

He rubbed his hand over his face. "What's wrong?"

"Nothing. I . . ."

He didn't let her finish. Instead, he grabbed her hand and led her to the beach. They walked for a bit without saying anything, but he didn't let go of her hand.

That was good, wasn't it?

"Here's the thing," she began. Good Lord. There went her heart again. Thumping like it was going to jump through her rib cage. After tonight, she was going to have to go the ER and get an EKG just to make sure everything was all right. "You said I was a good Realtor because I was . . . attractive and smart and not too aggressive, but mostly because I knew how to push the right buttons."

He nodded slowly. "I remember."

"So I came here tonight to seal the deal."

"The deal?"

"Between us. I think I finally figured out how to push the right buttons. Your buttons."

"Oh yeah?" It was too dark to see his eyes clearly, but she just *knew* he was gazing at her with that smoky look he got.

"You told me before that I should listen to my gut. And you were right. But you're not taking your own advice."

"I'm not?"

"Let me finish. I know you said you're not looking for a long-term relationship, and that you're not willing to make mistake number four, but I also know something else. Something I really believe deep down inside me." She took a deep breath. "I'm *not* a mistake. I'm the best thing that ever happened to you. You said I was the nice one. Well, I'm nice. But I'm also sharp. And it just so happens that a lot of guys find me hot."

The corners of his mouth twitched.

"So if you still want me to go to Hawaii with you, I'm ready. Only this isn't some quickie romance going on here. Remember that first night we hooked up? I said I wasn't going to fall in love with you and you said you weren't going to fall in love with me either. Well, we were both wrong."

Silence.

Oh God. It was coming. He was going to slam the proverbial door in her face. He was going to—

"Did I say you were a good Realtor?"

She nodded, too frozen to speak.

"You're not good; you're fucking brilliant."

"I am?" she whispered hoarsely.

"I was going to make you the same exact speech this morning. Only I was going to wait till a decent hour."

"What were you going to say?"

"I didn't have it rehearsed or anything. But it went something like this: I don't want to go to Hawaii unless you go with me. I know I've made mistakes in the past and I'm no prize, but if you give me a chance, I want another shot."

"That was it?"

He nodded.

"My speech was better."

"You're damn right it was." He bent his head to kiss her. It was a long, slow, sweet kiss. After a couple of minutes, he broke it off and stared at her incredulously. "I'm hearing music now too."

She smiled. "It's 'Free Bird.' "

"Oh." He stuck his hand in his shorts pocket and flipped his phone open. "Yeah?" He listened for a second and then handed her the phone. "It's for you."

"For me?" Kitty took the phone. It was the Babes. All of them. "We tried your cell but it went to voice mail," Pilar said, sounding way too giddy to only be drinking cafe lattes.

"I must have left my cell in the car," Kitty said. "Why are you calling? And how did you get this number?"

"We got the number from Gus!" shouted Shea.

"Are you on speakerphone? And did you just say you woke up Gus?"

"We have to know, Kit!" said Shea. "Did you find him? Is he your Crash?"

Kitty glanced over at Steve. He was smiling patiently, looking at her like . . . well, like he had that first night they'd met. Only it was different. That night there'd been humor and lust and an unnamed connection she'd felt immediately. Tonight there was something extra in the mixture. She might not know he preferred tea over coffee, but all the really important stuff about him, somewhere deep down inside, she already knew.

She laughed. "Yes! To both questions!"

"She said yes!" Shea shouted. She could hear the Babes cheering in the background. She snapped the phone shut and handed it back to him.

"Have I ever told you that I love it when you laugh?"

"Not in so many words," she said.

"I was thinking," Steve said. "Now that I'm going to be moving here permanently, I'll need to get a place. And with your mother's house back on the market—"

"I almost forgot! My mother's giving me the house."

"That's great," he said, looking genuinely happy for her.

She wondered what he'd been about to say before she'd interrupted him. *Listen to your gut, Kit.* "And it just so happens I'm looking for a roommate. It's a pretty big place for just one person. So, if you know anyone who's interested—"

"I'm interested."

"Yeah?"

"Definitely."

She smiled at the vehemence in his voice. "Maybe you could do some of that remodeling we talked about. Like tearing down the wall in the den to let in the light?"

"Sounds good." He pulled her into his arms and started nibbling on her neck.

"I have to warn you," Kitty said, moving her head to the side so he could get better access. "I'm a horrible cook."

"I'm not."

"And we'll want to keep our finances separate. I'm terrible with money."

"I could help you with that."

"And you owe me one toenail-painting session. Tied up."

"It's at the top of my agenda," he said, placing a kiss below her ear.

"And here's the most important part." She pushed against his chest so he'd be forced to look her in the eye. "I play Bunco on Thursdays. Every Thursday. *No* exceptions. It's sort of like my religion."

He smiled. "I know. I get it now."

How to Play Bunco

Want to know how to start a Bunco group of your own? It's simple! Here's how Kitty, Shea, and Pilar formed the Bunco Babes of Whispering Bay.

Step one: Find twelve fun women. Twelve is an essential number. Bunco is played in groups of four and you need at least three groups for a lively game. If you can't find twelve fun women, then find as many fun women as you can, and fill in the rest with women who have the potential to be fun. Don't worry. After a few games, you won't be able to tell the difference between the two groups.

Step two: You'll need the following:

Three card tables, each with four chairs. Number the tables one, two, and three. Table number one is the head table.
Nine dice (three for each table).
Cowbell or other noisemaker to signal the end of a game.
Score cards—the Babes like to make homemade name tags/ score cards that they wear around their necks. That way,

each player can easily visualize everyone's score (something Brenda and every other Bunco Nazi appreciates). The name tag should have two columns with a space to record wins and Buncos. At the end of the night, the hostess collects the name tags and places them in the Bunco Box. The Bunco Box is a large cardboard box or container that contains the dice, hole punchers, and cowbell. It gets passed from hostess to hostess and at the end of the year, the Babes go through the name tags for fun. Shea keeps vowing to make a huge scrapbook with all the name tags. As soon as she finds a nanny and has the time, she plans on doing just that.

Hole puncher for each table.

Boobie hat—the more humiliating, the better.

Prizes—some Bunco groups play for money, but the Babes love prizes. The hostess provides four gifts of her choosing. The Babes chip in ten dollars apiece to help the hostess offset the cost of the prizes and refreshments. Here's how the Babes do their prize breakdown:

Winner of **most games**—$30 prize

Winner of **most buncos**—$20 prize

Person with the **least wins**—$20 prize (because even losers get rewarded in Bunco!)

Person who rolled the **last Boobie**—$10 prize

Rules of the Game

Rules vary from group to group. But here's how the Babes like to roll the dice:

The object of the game is to roll as many points as possible. You start by rolling for ones, then twos, threes, etc.

Once you get through six games, you start back at ones again.

Start out by choosing a table. The person sitting opposite you is your partner for that game and that game alone (unless you are the winners from table one, which will be explained below).

Roll all three dice at once. If you get a one, then you go again. You keep rolling until you don't roll a one, then you pass the dice to the person to your left. If during your turn you rolled four ones, then you and your partner's score is now four. Whatever points your partner gets, you add to your score. Once a team at table one (and only table one) gets twenty-one points, they ring the cowbell and the game ends for everyone.

The teams at tables two and three with the most points win (even if they didn't reach twenty-one yet), and they move up a table. For example, if you were at table three and won, you move to table two. If you were at table two and won, you move to table one. If you are at table one and are on the winning team, you stay at table one with your partner. This is the only time you keep your partner—when you are winning at table one.

The losers from table one go to table three and the losers from tables two and three stay at their tables, but everyone switches partners.

Rolling Buncos: Any time during the game, regardless of what number you're rolling for, if you roll three sixes that's called a Bunco and you and your partner get three points. But the Babes play this with a little twist. If someone from the other team scoops up the dice after you roll a Bunco, then that team gets three points too. If they are able to scoop up one of the dice, then they get one point. If they scoop up two dice, then they get two points. If you roll a Bunco and you or your partner can grab the dice off the table, then you get six points total. This can make for some aggressive play and is how you learn who the really serious players are!

Rolling a Boobie: Anytime you roll three ones (the only exception being when you are trying to roll for ones) it's called a Boobie and it wipes out your and your partner's score. To make the humiliation complete, you are required to wear a special hat that the Babes call the Boobie hat. It can be any hat of the hostess's choice. You continue to wear the Boobie hat until another player rolls a Boobie and then you pass the hat to them. At the end of the night, the player wearing the hat gets a "Boobie" prize.

Every time you win a game or roll a Bunco, you punch a hole under the column on your scorecard.

The Babes like to play two rounds or twelve games.

At the end of the night, they tally who won most games and most Buncos, and who the big loser of the night is, and hand out the prizes. Then they pack up the Bunco Box, give it to the hostess for the next week, and leave for home, counting down the days until they play again.

Refreshments

Before the Babes sit down to play, they spend anywhere from a half hour to an hour socializing, and of course, eating and drinking. Here are some of the Babes' favorite recipes. And don't forget to have some munchies to eat at the tables—peanuts and/or M&M's are always appreciated.

Kahlua Dip

1 8 oz. cream cheese (softened)
¾ cup light brown sugar
8 oz. sour cream
8 oz. Cool Whip
⅓ cup Kahlua
⅓ cup chopped pecans

Mix ingredients and chill. Serve with strawberries or other fresh fruit.

Piña Colada Cake

1 box yellow cake mix (and ingredients required on box)
1 can piña colada mix
1 can sweetened condensed milk
1 large container Cool Whip
1 package frozen shredded coconut

Bake cake according to the package's directions in sheet pan. Punch holes in cake after cooked while still hot. Combine piña colada mix and condensed milk and pour over cake. Let cake cool off completely, then top with Cool Whip and coconut.

Parmesan Bread Sticks

(Kitty was given this recipe by her friend Jan, who plays with the Bunco Broads of Tallahassee)

1 package of bacon
1 box thin bread sticks
Parmesan cheese

Cut each slice of bacon in half lengthwise. Take a single bacon strip and spiral it around a bread stick, covering the bread stick from end to end. Roll bacon-covered bread stick in Parmesan cheese until coated. Place on baking sheet. Repeat until all bread sticks are wrapped and rolled.

Place baking sheet in very low (250 degrees) oven and bake for about one hour. Serve hot.

Champagne Cocktails

Small bottle of Angostura bitters
Sugar cubes
Chilled champagne

Place a few drops (or more to taste) of bitters over each sugar cube and let soak a few minutes. Drop soaked sugar cube to the bottom of your flute and then pour chilled champagne over it. Simple, but tasty!

RB&V

(This is one of Pilar's favorite drinks because it's so simple and doesn't require any special prep. She started drinking these when she visited another sister Bunco group—the Tallahassee Bunco Babes)

Red Bull
Vodka

Red Bull and vodka to taste (preferred vodkas are Skyy Melon and Grey Goose). A nice RB&V from time to time keeps the dice rolling!

Shea's Secret Frozen Margaritas

If Shea won't give Kitty or Pilar her recipe, then do you really think she's going to give it to you?

Keep reading for a preview
of the next Bunco Babes novel
by Maria Geraci

Bunco Babes Gone Wild

Coming November 2009 from Berkley Books!

It is a truth universally acknowledged that when a woman gets a boob job, she must show it off to her closest friends.

If Georgia Meyer were a man (or a lesbian), she'd have died and gone to heaven. But she wasn't either of those, so staring at a complete stranger's breasts while standing behind the counter at her sister's coffee shop, no matter how "firm and uplifted" the breasts in question now were, was making her a little uncomfortable. The fact that the breasts belonged to one of her sister's best friends and that the coffee shop was closed should have put her at ease. But it didn't. For one thing, her sister Frida seemed to have a lot of "best friends," and secondly, the Bistro by the Beach had these large plate glass windows that any passerby could easily look into.

She mentally shrugged. Maybe they did things differently here in Whispering Bay, Florida. After all, it *was* a beach town.

"They're so perky!" Frida crooned, nudging Georgia on

with a roll of her eyes. This must be Georgia's cue to say something.

"Yeah, totally awesome," Georgia replied, hoping she sounded more enthusiastic than she felt. Since she'd never seen the boobs in question before the "firming and uplifting," she really couldn't make a fair comparison, but the petite, dark haired owner of the now fabulous tatas seemed pleased with her response. So did the two other "best friends" standing by her side.

"Thanks!" Pilar Diaz-Rothman gushed, carefully covering up the prized twins with a sturdy sports bra.

"Are they sore?" Frida asked.

"A little. But it was totally worth it. I finally have boobs that point north again."

"What does Nick think?" Frida asked.

"He's crazy about them, of course," interjected Shea Masterson, a tall, stunning redhead who appeared to have been the recipient of her own upper-body surgery.

Pilar grinned. "He was a little freaked at first that I went through with it. But he's totally on board now."

"Nick is Pilar's husband," Kitty Burke, the last of the Charlie's Angels trio, explained. Kitty was tall, like Shea, and while she lacked Shea's Heidi Klum–like model looks or Pilar's more compact exoticness, she made up for it with a wholesome prettiness and a warm smile. Definitely the Drew Barrymore of the group.

"So, Georgia," Shea said, "you're coming to Bunco tonight. Right? Great outfit, by the way. Is that Alexander McQueen?"

Georgia blinked, not quite sure which question to respond to first.

"Don't mind Shea," Pilar said. "She has two little girls under the age of five so she's experienced at bi-processing."

"That's multi-tasking, but in your brain," explained Kitty, sensing Georgia's confusion. "Pilar likes to make up words to fit the occasion."

Boy, things sure were different down here in Whispering Bay. Maybe it was all that sodium floating in the air.

"You must really know your designers," Georgia said, pleased that Frida's friends had noticed her Alexander McQueen high-waisted navy silk trousers and matching top. Georgia took pride in her appearance. It was one of the things Spencer loved about her. She fought back a frown. She wasn't going to think about Spencer. Not now. Not for the entire weekend. Maybe not ever. Although that would be impractical, considering he was her boss. "And I'm afraid I'm not sure about the Bunco thing."

Shea turned to Frida. "You didn't invite your sister to Bunco?"

"I didn't know my sister was coming to visit until she walked through the door ten minutes before you three did."

"I wanted to surprise you," Georgia said, trying not to squirm beneath her older sister's level gaze.

"Where are you from, Georgia?" asked Kitty.

Georgia hesitated. It was one of those generic questions people always asked one another. Despite years of practicing a pat answer, it sometimes took her off guard.

"You know, Georgia and I are from everywhere," Frida said, saving Georgia from responding.

"That's right!" Pilar said. "You guys were raised by hippies. That is sooo cool."

Groupies, not hippies, Georgia wanted to clarify. Although in her mother's case, there probably wasn't much difference between the two. Instead, she said, "I've lived in Birmingham for the past five years."

"Georgia's the Chief Financial Officer for a major electronics company," Frida said proudly. "She graduated from Stanford."

"Impressive," said Pilar, giving Georgia a thumbs up.

Georgia felt herself blush. "It's a small company and I'm really a glorified bean counter." Although a damn good one, she had to admit, even if it was just to herself.

"Moody Electronics is the Southeast's fastest growing company. Georgia was selected one of Birmingham's top ten businesswomen last year," said Frida. "Which explains why she never comes to visit me. She's too busy working."

Georgia ignored the dig.

Pilar sighed. "I know how that goes. I'm an ambulance chaser," she confided to Georgia. "Only I really don't chase ambulances. I read contracts all day. But for the past few years, my life has revolved around billable hours."

"Not anymore," said Kitty. "You're cutting back at work, remember?"

"That's right," said Pilar, looking chastised. "I keep forgetting."

Kitty smiled at Georgia. "Are you on vacation?"

Frida gazed at her expectantly.

"Sort of," Georgia said, hoping she wouldn't have to elaborate. "I'm here for a long weekend. All work and no play . . ." she added with a shrug.

"How's Spencer?" Frida asked. "Is he coming too?"

"He wanted to," Georgia said quickly, "but he couldn't get away."

"Spencer is Georgia's boss," explained Frida. "He's also her fiancé."

"Congratulations!" said Shea. "When's the wedding?"

Georgia wondered the exact same thing. "Actually, we're not officially engaged yet."

Frida's brows scrunched together. "But I thought—"

"The timing's not right." Georgia gave Frida's friends what she knew was a shaky smile. But she couldn't help it. She'd always sucked at subterfuge. "Spencer has children from his previous marriage, and they're both at a very fragile age. We need to make sure they're in the right place first."

Her sister's friends went quiet.

"He's a wonderful father," Georgia rushed. "I wouldn't want it any other way."

"Well, you have to come to Bunco," Shea said. "It just so happens one of our regular members isn't going to make it, which means we need a substitute. Naturally, being Frida's sister, you get first dibs."

Kitty frowned. "What about Christy? Christy Pappas is number one on the sub list," she explained to Georgia. "Not that I don't want you to come, it's just that—"

"What Christy doesn't know won't hurt her. Besides, the three of us make the rules, and I say family goes before the sub list," said Shea.

Pilar nodded. "Shea's right. Family comes first. You're just sensitive since you live with Christy's cousin-in-law," she said to Kitty.

"Kitty has a new boyfriend. A really *hot* new boyfriend," Frida supplied.

"Please, don't worry about it. I don't even know what Bunco is," said Georgia.

The Charlie's Angels trio looked flabbergasted.

Pilar was the first one to find her voice. "It's a dice game. A *really* fun dice game. We play every Thursday night. We're the Bunco Babes," she said, as if that explained everything.

"Actually, we're only part of the Babes," Shea said. "There's twelve of us all together. You have to have twelve to play Bunco. But the three of us are the founders. We make up the rules and we insist you come."

Maybe Frida had mentioned this Bunco thing a few times, but Georgia hadn't been paying attention. She'd hoped to spend some alone time with Frida tonight. Socializing with a bunch of giggly women wasn't Georgia's idea of a good time, but there was no graceful way out of it. And it would make Frida happy. "Sure, I'll come. Thanks."

"Great!" said Shea. "My house. Seven p.m. sharp."

"Shea makes these awesome frozen margaritas," said Kitty. "You'll love them!"

She watched as Frida said good-bye to her friends and locked the door to the Bistro behind them. Frida took off her work apron and tossed it into a laundry bin beneath the counter. It had been six months since Georgia had seen her sister, but Frida never seemed to change. She wore almost no makeup and let her curly auburn hair go natural. No blow dryers or flat irons for her.

"What's really up?" Frida asked. "You look terrible."

"Gee, thanks."

"You know what I mean. Something's not right."

"How's business?" Georgia glanced around the small café. The walls were gold with hand-painted murals of seascapes and mermaids. The wooden tables and chairs were scarred and each table had a vase with fresh-cut flowers from the outside garden. There was a smallish kitchen area behind the counter where the customers placed their orders. Frida served coffee, homemade bagels, muffins, and pastries. She opened at the crack of dawn and closed by eleven a.m. But Georgia knew that Frida's day started at four and didn't end until well after two p.m. when she finished cleaning and organizing her kitchen. Frida's insinuation that Georgia was a workaholic was like the pot calling the kettle black. Running a small-town cafe was a hard business, and from what Georgia could see, the payoff wasn't anything to brag about. But Frida seemed content.

"Business is business," said Frida. "Slow one week, crazy busy the next. It all depends on the weather and the tourists. Now answer my question. Why are you here?"

"I thought you'd be happy to see me."

"You know I am. And Ed's going to be thrilled."

Ed Hampton was Frida's husband. He was an artist (as-yet-undiscovered), a fact Georgia found ridiculously ironic considering her and Frida's upbringing. Ed helped out in the coffee shop during the morning and painted the rest of the day. He and Frida lived in a small apartment above the Bistro. Despite his lack of ambition, Georgia was fond of Ed. Although she couldn't help but think that Frida could have done better. They'd been married for twelve years and had no children. Georgia had never asked her sister about that. She'd always assumed it was by choice. "Speaking of Ed, where is he?"

"He went to see a potential client," Frida said, her voice turning enthusiastic. "There's a local restaurant that wants to feature Ed's paintings. This could be a terrific opportunity for him." She glanced at her watch and frowned. "I'm supposed to meet him so we can have an early dinner with the manager."

"Go on then. I know my way around upstairs. I'll just take a quick shower and unpack. I hope I'm not going to put you out," Georgia added. "I know your place isn't big."

"Of course you're not putting me out. You're my sister. You're always welcome. You know that."

"Thanks."

Frida studied Georgia's face. "You're sure there's nothing wrong?"

For a brief moment, Georgia thought about telling Frida everything. It had been a long time since they'd talked. About anything important, that is. But if she did, Frida would cancel her dinner with Ed, and Georgia didn't want that. She put on a bright smile. "You're always bragging about how great Whispering Bay is. I thought I'd take you up on a few days of sun and fun."

"Okay, I'll buy that." Frida narrowed her eyes at her. "For now."